Voices in Echo Alley: Whispers Between Worlds – Daybridge Chronicles: Tales from the Nexus

INTRODUCTION:

Dear Readers,

The story you are about to experience represents a unique branch in the Daybridge Paranormal Investigations timeline. While featuring our familiar paranormal detective Alice Chen, "Voices in Echo Alley: Whispers Between Worlds" exists in what we might call a parallel dimensional thread of the Daybridge universe—which seems particularly fitting, given the story's subject matter.

Those familiar with Alice Chen's previous cases in "Shadows Between Thoughts" and "The Quantum Detective: The Alice Chen Files" may notice certain divergences in this narrative. Consider this tale as occurring in an adjacent reality where certain events unfolded differently, particularly regarding Alice's background, abilities, and her relationship with the scientific community of Daybridge.

As anyone who has spent time investigating the paranormal phenomena of Daybridge knows, the city exists at the intersection of multiple realities. It should come as no surprise that stories from Daybridge might occasionally bleed across dimensional boundaries—indeed, such boundary-bleeding forms the very core of this particular case.

Whether you view this as an alternate timeline, a parallel universe, or simply another facet of the complex and ever-expanding Daybridge mythology is entirely up to you. After all, in a city where a detective specializing in paranormal phenomena investigates rifts between realities, the question of which timeline is the "correct" one becomes particularly poignant.

Enjoy your journey through this particular version of Daybridge's warehouse district. And as always, if you hear an echo that knows too much, perhaps it's best to listen carefully.

CHAPTER ONE: THE UNCONVENTIONAL DETECTIVE

The call came at 3:17 AM, because that's when they always came. Alice Chen rolled over in bed, squinting at her phone's harsh glow in the darkness. Unknown number. Of course.

"Chen," she answered, voice clear despite the hour. Sleep had always been optional in her line of work.

"We've got another one for you." Detective Rivera's voice carried the familiar blend of reluctance and resignation. "Warehouse district. Multiple reports of... voices."

Alice sat up, already reaching for the notepad she kept on her nightstand. "Just voices? Or something more?"

"Workers claim they're having conversations with people who aren't there. Security footage shows them talking to empty air." A pause. "Look, the captain wanted to file this under 'mass hysteria' or 'warehouse workers finding creative ways to day-drink,' but there's something else."

Alice waited, pen poised.

"The voices are telling them things they couldn't know. Specific details about shipments that haven't arrived yet. Personal information about coworkers who've never met. And all of it's happening in this one dead-end alley between buildings."

"Address?"

Rivera provided it, then added, "This is unofficial, Chen. Just like always."

"Just like always," she echoed, a small smile forming. "I'll bill the department my usual rate."

"The captain said—"

"The captain will approve it when I solve his problem," Alice finished. "He always does."

After disconnecting, Alice moved with practiced efficiency through her apartment. The space was small but meticulously organized—half living quarters, half paranormal investigation headquarters. One wall was covered with a map of Daybridge marked with colored pins indicating past cases, active investigations, and unexplained phenomena. Another held shelves of equipment: modified EMF detectors, thermographic cameras, custom recording devices designed to capture frequencies beyond normal human hearing.

She dressed quickly in dark jeans, boots, and a charcoal blazer over a simple black shirt. Professional enough for official interactions, practical enough for crawling through abandoned spaces if needed. As she gathered her equipment, her fingers lingered on the smooth stone pendant hanging from a leather cord around her neck—a gift from her grandmother, who'd been the first to recognize Alice's sensitivity to the spaces between worlds.

The pendant warmed slightly beneath her touch, as it always did when she prepared to cross paths with something beyond ordinary explanation.

Outside, Daybridge was transformed in the pre-dawn hours. Streetlights cast pools of amber glow on empty sidewalks. The city felt liminal, caught between states of being. Alice had always done her best work in these threshold hours.

Her car, a ten-year-old Subaru plastered with parking permits from various municipal lots, started reluctantly. The dashboard was cluttered with coffee receipts and hastily scribbled notes from previous cases. A small digital recorder sat in the cupholder, ready to capture thoughts as they came.

"Case file: Warehouse District Voices," Alice spoke toward the recorder as she drove. "October 10th, 4:03 AM. Multiple witnesses reporting interactive auditory phenomena concentrated in a specific location."

She navigated through Daybridge's gradually shifting landscapes—from the renovated Victorian homes of her neighborhood to the gleaming downtown district, finally entering the industrial sprawl of the warehouse zone. Buildings loomed like sleeping giants, their loading docks empty at this hour.

Alice parked near the address Rivera had provided. The security guard at the main gate recognized her—or rather, recognized her type.

"Another spook hunter?" he asked, eyebrow raised as he checked her ID.

"Detective consultant," Alice corrected mildly. "Daybridge PD sent me."

The guard snorted but waved her through. "Good luck with the haunted alley. Hope you brought a voice recorder."

"Several," Alice replied with a thin smile.

She followed his directions through a maze of warehouses until she reached a narrow passage between two buildings. The alley ended at a brick wall, creating a dead end roughly thirty feet deep. Nothing remarkable distinguished it from any other service alley—dumpsters, utility meters, emergency exits from both adjoining buildings. Yet something about the space made the hair on Alice's arms rise.

Alice set her equipment bag down and removed her primary recorder, an expensive model she'd modified with expanded frequency sensitivity. She placed it carefully on a ledge near the mouth of the alley, then took out a small notebook.

"Preliminary observations," she murmured as she wrote. "Temperature 48 degrees Fahrenheit. Time 4:32 AM. No visible unusual characteristics. Minor temperature drop at alley entrance—approximately two degrees cooler than surrounding area." She frowned, making another note. "Acoustic properties feel... contained."

Alice had learned to trust her instincts. Ten years of investigating paranormal phenomena had honed her sensitivity to spaces where reality thinned. This alley felt like those places—like the abandoned hospital where whispers carried through walls that no longer existed, or the lighthouse where time occasionally ran backward for precisely 17 minutes.

She moved deeper into the alley, her footsteps echoing crisply against the brick walls. The sound bounced back with unusual clarity, almost like—

"Hello?" she called experimentally.

"Hello," came the perfect echo, rebounding from the dead end.

Alice nodded, making another note. Perfect acoustic reflection. Not unusual for this configuration of space.

She tried again, this time with more words. "My name is Alice Chen."

"My name is Alice Chen," the echo returned, perfectly mimicking her inflection.

She took a few more steps forward, reaching the halfway point of the alley. "I'm investigating reports of voices at this location."

The echo began normally: "I'm investigating reports of—" but then shifted subtly, "—you finally arriving, Alice."

Alice froze, pen poised above her notebook. She'd encountered many paranormal phenomena in her career—apparitions, psychokinetic events, time slips, even a few legitimate hauntings among countless frauds. But this was new. An echo that altered itself, that responded rather than merely repeated.

"Who am I speaking with?" she asked, keeping her voice calm and professional.

The echo rippled back. "Someone who's been waiting for you specifically."

Alice felt the familiar rush of discovery—part excitement, part apprehension—that had drawn her to this work from the beginning. She pulled a small device from her pocket, a custom-built electromagnetic field detector. The needle jumped erratically, confirming that something beyond normal environmental conditions was occurring.

"How do you know who I am?" she asked.

A pause longer than an echo should take. Then: "In some versions of reality, we've already met."

Alice's heart quickened, but she maintained her composure. In her experience, paranormal entities often spoke in riddles or made grandiose claims. Verification was essential.

"Prove it," she challenged. "Tell me something specific that demonstrates you know me."

The alley fell silent for several seconds. Alice waited, the recording device capturing the unnatural stillness. Then the voice returned, not as an echo but seeming to originate from the surrounding air.

"The scar on your right palm came from breaking a mirror when you were eight. You told everyone you cut yourself washing dishes, because you didn't want them to know you smashed it after seeing something move in the reflection that shouldn't have been there."

Alice's breath caught. She instinctively turned her palm upward, tracing the thin white line that crossed from thumb to wrist. She had never told anyone the true story—not her parents, not her colleagues, not even the therapist she'd briefly seen after the Holloway House case left her with nightmares.

"What are you?" she whispered.

"Not a what," the voice replied. "Many whos. This place—this alley—sits at a junction point between timelines. A weak spot in the fabric between realities. We can communicate through it, but only here, only under certain conditions."

Alice's analytical mind raced to categorize this phenomenon within her extensive knowledge of paranormal manifestations. Not a haunting in the traditional sense. Not psychokinetic projection. Something closer to the theoretical quantum breach she'd read about in Dr. Okafor's controversial papers.

"You're claiming to be... people from alternate timelines?" Alice asked, carefully documenting the conversation in her notebook.

"Yes, versions of Daybridge residents from realities adjacent to yours. Sometimes very similar, sometimes dramatically different."

Alice took a moment to process this. If true, this wasn't merely another paranormal case—it was potentially revolutionary. Evidence of parallel timelines that mainstream science acknowledged only as theoretical.

"Why are warehouse workers hearing you?" she asked. "Why now?"

"The breach is widening," the voice explained, now seeming to come from the brick wall at the alley's end. "What was once a pinprick allowing minimal communication has grown. More of us can speak through now, but with less control over who hears us. We need your help, Detective Chen."

"My help with what?"

"Finding out why the breach is expanding. And stopping whoever is deliberately making it worse."

Alice felt a chill that had nothing to do with the pre-dawn air. "Someone is intentionally widening this... reality breach?"

"Yes. In multiple timelines. Including yours." The voice lowered, becoming more urgent. "There are people who know about this place, Alice. They've known for decades. And they want to use it."

Before Alice could ask more questions, the sound of a door slamming echoed from one of the adjoining warehouses. Footsteps approached—real ones this time. The voice in the alley fell silent.

A security guard rounded the corner, flashlight beam cutting through the dimness. "Hey! This area is restricted. How'd you get past the front gate?"

Alice smoothly produced her consultant badge. "Alice Chen, investigating for Daybridge PD. Your front gate security cleared me."

The guard lowered his flashlight, looking embarrassed. "Oh. Sorry, ma'am. Didn't know they were sending someone so early. You here about the weird voices?"

"Yes, have you experienced them personally?"

He shifted uncomfortably. "Once. Last week during my rounds. Thought I was losing my mind when the alley started talking back to me. Told me to watch out for a shipment coming in on Tuesday—said there'd be contraband hidden in it." He lowered his voice. "There was too. Management found unmanifested electronics tucked inside furniture from overseas. Would've cost the company thousands in legal issues if they'd missed it."

"And no one else could have known about this shipment beforehand?"

"That's just it—the manifest only came in hours after I heard the voice. Impossible for anyone to know."

Alice nodded, making notes. "Thank you. I'd like to continue my investigation, if that's alright."

"Sure thing. Just check in before you leave." The guard retreated, glancing nervously at the alley before disappearing around the corner.

When his footsteps faded, Alice turned back to the dead end. "Are you still there?" she called.

Silence greeted her. The moment—or the conditions allowing communication—had passed. Alice spent another hour taking readings, documenting the alley's dimensions, and attempting to reestablish contact without success. As dawn brightened the sky, she packed her equipment and headed back to her car.

Driving home, Alice's mind buzzed with questions. If this were truly a breach between timelines rather than a conventional paranormal phenomenon, it represented something far beyond her usual cases. Something potentially dangerous on a scale she'd never encountered.

She needed more information, more evidence before taking this to Rivera. The department already viewed her work with skepticism—coming to them with claims of parallel realities would only damage her credibility further.

Her apartment was bathed in morning light when she returned. Alice transferred her notes to her case board, creating a new section labeled "Echo Alley." She pinned up her preliminary findings and connected them with red string to three previous cases involving reported doppelgängers and time anomalies in Daybridge.

A pattern was emerging—one that suggested the warehouse district might be just one of several thin spots in reality throughout the city.

Alice stared at the board, exhaustion finally catching up with her. But sleep would have to wait. She reached for her phone and pulled up a contact she'd saved but never called: Dr. Maya Okafor, theoretical physicist.

If anyone could help her understand what was happening in that alley, it would be the woman whose academic career had been nearly destroyed for suggesting exactly what Alice had just experienced—that parallel timelines might sometimes bleed into one another, and that these bleeding points could be detected, measured, and perhaps even manipulated.

Her finger hovered over the call button. Involving someone else meant a commitment to this case, meant acknowledging that she might be dealing with something far beyond ghosts and local hauntings.

The stone pendant at her throat grew warm again. Alice made the call.

As the phone rang, she glanced back at her case board, at the web of string connecting seemingly unrelated incidents throughout Daybridge. If the voice in the alley was right, these weren't isolated paranormal events but symptoms of a larger pattern—one that someone was deliberately accelerating.

The question was: why would anyone want to tear open the barriers between realities? And what might come through if they succeeded?

CHAPTER TWO: FIRST CONTACT

Alice Chen arrived at Echo Alley shortly after sunset, exactly seventeen hours after her first visit. The warehouses stood like sentinels against the darkening sky, their daytime bustle replaced by cavernous silence. She'd chosen this time carefully—paranormal phenomena often intensified during threshold hours, and she needed clearer communication than her dawn encounter had provided.

This time, she came prepared. Her shoulder bag contained an array of custom equipment developed over years of investigating Daybridge's unexplained corners: a modified digital recorder with expanded frequency capture, an electromagnetic field detector calibrated to register subtle fluctuations, a thermal imaging camera, and her newest acquisition—a quantum field variance monitor borrowed from Dr. Maya Okafor.

Their morning phone call had been brief but productive. The physicist had listened to Alice's account without the skepticism she'd expected, instead asking precise, technical questions about the alley's dimensions and the exact phrasing of the voices. They'd agreed to meet tomorrow, but not before Dr. Okafor had couriered over the monitoring device with strict instructions for its use.

"Remember, detective," she'd said, "if what you're describing is real, we're not dealing with supernatural phenomena but with a quantum reality intersection. The distinction matters."

Alice approached the alley cautiously, setting up her equipment with practiced efficiency. The security guard—a different one from the morning shift—had been expecting her, waving her through with a mix of curiosity and relief.

"Glad someone's checking it out," he'd said. "Place gives me the creeps. I take the long way around on my rounds."

The air felt different tonight—denser somehow, as if the narrow space between buildings existed slightly out of sync with its surroundings. Alice noted the temperature—52 degrees, seven degrees cooler than the surrounding area. A significant differential that couldn't be explained by normal environmental factors.

She positioned her primary recording device on a small tripod at the alley's entrance, then advanced slowly toward the dead end, carrying a secondary recorder. The brick wall loomed before her, unremarkable in appearance yet somehow expectant.

"This is Detective Alice Chen," she spoke clearly, her voice bouncing crisply against the bricks. "I've returned to continue our conversation from this morning."

The echo formed normally, repeating her words with perfect fidelity. Alice waited, counting seconds in her head. One... two... three...

"We've been waiting for you to return, Detective." The voice emerged not as an echo but as a distinct response, originating from the center of the alley rather than reflecting from the walls.

Alice felt the familiar rush of adrenaline—the confirmation that she stood in the presence of something genuine. In a career filled with frauds, misidentified natural phenomena, and occasional true encounters, she'd learned to savor these moments of authentic contact.

"I have questions," she said, activating her secondary recorder. "Many questions."

"As do we." The voice sounded masculine, with a slight accent Alice couldn't place. "Though time moves differently across the breach. We must be efficient."

Alice nodded, making quick notes. "Who am I speaking with?"

"Thomas Webb. In my timeline, I was—am—a physicist at Daybridge University, specializing in quantum field theory and multiverse hypothesis."

Alice consulted her phone quickly. "There's no Thomas Webb in the university's physics department here."

A soft laugh echoed through the alley. "In your timeline, I never completed my doctorate. I died in a car accident in 1998. At least, that's what the record shows."

The implications sent a chill through Alice. "Are you claiming to be dead in my timeline but alive in another?"

"Precisely. Though 'dead' may not be the right term. In your timeline, Thomas Webb's identity was erased when he discovered something dangerous—the existence of these breach points between realities."

Alice made rapid notes, her mind racing. "How many of these breach points exist?"

"We've identified seven in Daybridge alone. This alley is the most stable and the most accessible. The others fluctuate, appearing and disappearing based on quantum variables we don't fully understand."

"We?" Alice pressed. "Who else is involved?"

A moment of silence stretched, then: "Others who exist across multiple timelines. Some you know in your reality, some you don't." The voice shifted location, now seeming to come from near the alley entrance. "Including you, Alice."

Alice's pen paused above her notebook. "Me?"

"Versions of you exist in multiple adjacent timelines. In some, you're a detective, as you are here. In others, you followed different paths. In my timeline, Alice Chen is a quantum physicist who helped develop the theoretical framework for understanding these breaches."

The quantum variance monitor in Alice's bag emitted a soft beep, its display showing fluctuations beyond baseline parameters. Whatever was happening in this alley, it was registering on instruments designed to detect reality distortions.

"How is this communication possible?" Alice asked, forcing herself to maintain professional detachment despite the staggering implications.

"Think of reality as a book with many pages," Thomas's voice explained. "Normally, these pages remain separate, but occasionally—at certain points in space-time—the pages touch. Information can bleed through, sometimes even physical properties. This alley exists at such a junction point."

Alice circled the alley slowly, noting how the voice seemed to follow her movement. "The warehouse workers who reported voices—they heard different people, not just you."

"Yes. As the breach widens, more of us can communicate through it. Some intentionally, others accidentally. People in your timeline who enter this space can hear echoes from corresponding points in adjacent timelines."

Alice stopped walking. "You said the breach is widening. Why?"

The temperature in the alley dropped suddenly, causing Alice's breath to fog in the air. The quantum variance monitor's beeping intensified.

"Someone is deliberately destabilizing the barriers between timelines," Thomas's voice became urgent. "An organization that exists across multiple realities is attempting to create permanent passages. They've been working toward this for decades."

"What organization?" Alice pressed. "Why would anyone—"

"Consider the implications, Detective," Thomas interrupted. "Access to technology from more advanced timelines. Intelligence about future events. The ability to acquire resources that don't exist in your reality. The strategic advantage would be incalculable."

Alice thought of the security guard's story—the voice that warned about contraband in an upcoming shipment. "They're using the breaches for information gathering."

"Currently, yes. But their ambitions extend far beyond passive observation."

Alice was formulating her next question when she felt it—a sudden pressure change, as if the air in the alley had compressed. The hairs on her arms stood up, and her pendant grew uncomfortably warm against her skin.

Then came the whisper, directly in her ear though no one stood beside her: "They're watching you now, Alice."

She spun around instinctively, reaching for the weapon she didn't carry. The alley remained empty, but the quality of emptiness had changed—as if the space itself had become aware of her presence.

"Who's watching?" She demanded, fighting to keep her voice steady.

"Department of Temporal Security," Thomas replied, his voice now seeming to come from multiple directions simultaneously. "They monitor breach points. They'll have detected our communication."

The name meant nothing to Alice, but the urgency in Thomas's voice was unmistakable. She glanced toward the alley entrance, suddenly conscious of her vulnerable position.

"I need to know more," she insisted. "How do I contact you again? How do I verify any of this?"

"The breach is strongest at threshold times—dawn, dusk, midnight. Return during these hours." Thomas's voice began to fade. "And Alice—look up Project Resonance in your timeline. The original experiments. 1956."

The quantum variance monitor flatlined suddenly, its readings returning to baseline. The temperature in the alley normalized, and the pressure sensation dissipated. Whatever window that had allowed their communication had closed.

Alice quickly gathered her equipment, a prickling sensation between her shoulder blades making her movements hurried. The feeling of being watched remained, though she could see no one in the vicinity when she exited the alley.

Back in her car, she immediately connected her recording devices to her laptop, anxious to confirm she had documentation of the encounter. The primary recorder had captured everything—her questions, the responses, the temperature fluctuations registered by its built-in thermometer.

But when she played back the secondary recorder—the one she'd carried deeper into the alley—she found only static, punctuated by fragments of Thomas's voice. The critical portions about the Department of Temporal Security and Project Resonance were completely obscured by electronic interference.

Alice frowned, running the audio through filtering software. Nothing improved the quality. Either the proximity to the breach point had corrupted the recording, or...

Or something had deliberately interfered with it.

She started her car, checking her mirrors before pulling away from the warehouse district. The streets were nearly empty at this hour, but Alice couldn't shake the sensation of being followed. Three blocks from the warehouse, she took a sudden turn, then another, employing counter-surveillance techniques she'd learned years ago.

No headlights followed her unorthodox route. Still, she drove for twenty additional minutes before heading home, taking a circuitous path through Daybridge's quieter neighborhoods.

Her apartment welcomed her with familiar silence. Alice immediately transferred her recordings and data to her secure server, then made backup copies on encrypted drives. If Thomas was correct about being watched, her evidence needed protection.

At her investigation board, she added new notes beneath the "Echo Alley" heading: "Thomas Webb—physicist in alternate timeline, deceased/erased in this one? Claims deliberate widening of reality breaches by 'Department of Temporal Security.' Reference to 'Project Resonance—1956.'

She stepped back, studying the connections forming between this case and previous unexplained phenomena she'd investigated in Daybridge. If what Thomas suggested was true—if multiple reality breach points existed throughout the city—it could explain dozens of previously unsolved cases: the doppelgänger sightings in Westlake Park, the time slips reported near the old clock tower, the building that appeared and disappeared on Morrison Street.

Alice rubbed her eyes, fatigue finally catching up with her. She needed sleep, but her mind continued racing with implications. If she were being watched by some covert government agency, her usual investigative approaches might put her at risk. She needed allies, resources, information.

She needed to verify Thomas Webb's existence in her timeline.

Moving to her computer, Alice began searching public records. If Thomas had been "erased" as he claimed, finding evidence would be difficult—but Alice had spent years developing contacts and access methods for exactly this kind of investigation.

After an hour of searching, she found it—a single reference in Daybridge University's archived faculty newsletter from 1997: "Doctoral candidate Thomas Webb awarded prestigious Kellerman Fellowship for groundbreaking work in quantum field theory."

The next mention came six months later in a brief obituary: "Thomas Webb, 28, died in an automobile accident on Route 16. The physics department has established a small memorial scholarship in his name."

Alice leaned back in her chair, a chill running through her that had nothing to do with the temperature in her apartment. The timeline matched exactly what the voice in the alley had told her.

Her phone chirped with a text message. Dr. Maya Okafor: "My equipment detecting unusual readings. Need to meet sooner. Breakfast, 7 AM, Blackbird Café?"

Alice sent a quick confirmation, then turned back to her research. One more search term to investigate before she could allow herself to rest: "Project Resonance 1956."

The search returned nothing in public databases. Alice switched to more specialized resources, using access credentials from past investigations. Still nothing.

She was about to give up when she remembered a contact—an archivist at Daybridge's Historical Society who specialized in classified government projects from the Cold War era. Alice sent a carefully worded email request and then finally allowed herself to prepare for bed.

As she was changing, her pendant—the smooth stone given to her by her grandmother—slipped from around her neck, the leather cord having frayed without her noticing. The stone hit the hardwood floor with a sharp crack and split perfectly in half.

Alice knelt to examine it, surprised to find something embedded within the stone's interior—a small microchip, certainly nothing her grandmother could have placed there when giving her the pendant thirty years ago.

She stared at the discovery, a new possibility forming in her mind. If Thomas was right about multiple versions of herself existing across timelines... had some version of Alice Chen been trying to communicate with her all along?

The pendant had always warmed when she approached paranormal phenomena. She'd attributed it to family superstition, to her grandmother's belief in protective talismans. But what if it had been technology disguised as tradition—a quantum receiver of some kind, connecting her to other versions of herself?

Alice carefully placed the broken pendant and its embedded chip into a small evidence bag, adding another note to her investigation board: "Potential cross-timeline technology already in my possession?"

Sleep would be even more elusive now, but Alice forced herself to lie down. Tomorrow's meeting with Dr. Okafor would require clarity, and the investigation was only beginning.

As she drifted toward uneasy sleep, Alice couldn't shake one thought: if she was correct about what was happening in Echo Alley, she wasn't just investigating another paranormal case. She was standing at the edge of a discovery that could reshape humanity's understanding of reality itself.

And someone—some organization powerful enough to erase people from existence—didn't want that discovery made.

The last thing Alice remembered before sleep claimed her was Thomas's warning, echoing in her mind: "They're watching you now, Alice."

She would need to be very, very careful about what steps she took next.

CHAPTER THREE: THE CASE FILES

Dawn filtered through the blinds of Alice Chen's apartment, painting stripes across the hardwood floor as she nursed her third cup of coffee. She hadn't slept more than two fitful hours. The broken pendant lay on her desk beside the evidence bag containing its mysterious microchip, a constant reminder of how quickly certainties could fracture.

Her meeting with Dr. Okafor was still two hours away, providing a narrow window to organize her thoughts and evidence. Alice moved to the eastern wall of her living room—what she called her "office" despite its lack of conventional furnishings. Instead of a desk and filing cabinets, the space featured an elaborate organizational system of her own design: floor-to-ceiling bookshelves filled with labeled archive boxes, color-coded folders arranged chronologically, and walls covered with maps, photographs, and connection threads.

To an outsider, it might have appeared chaotic. To Alice, it was a meticulously crafted external memory system, holding ten years of investigations into Daybridge's paranormal undercurrents.

She pulled out her oldest case files first—the foundation cases that had established her reputation among those who believed and her notoriety among those who didn't. The Holloway House haunting. The Westlake Park apparitions. The temporal anomalies at St. Christopher's Hospital.

Alice spread the files across her coffee table, extracting key photographs and witness statements. If Echo Alley represented a breach between timelines, as Thomas Webb claimed, similar phenomena might have manifested at other thin points throughout Daybridge's history.

She was looking for patterns, connections that might have eluded her when she'd investigated each case in isolation.

The Holloway House file came first—her second professional case, five years ago. The century-old Victorian in Daybridge's historic district had become briefly infamous when its owners reported encountering themselves inside the home—doppelgängers that vanished when directly addressed. Alice had classified it as a time-slip haunting, theorizing that traumatic events had somehow imprinted themselves on the location's temporal fabric.

Now she re-examined the case with fresh eyes. The original homeowners' statement leaped out at her: "It wasn't like seeing a ghost. It was like seeing ourselves in a mirror, except we were doing things we hadn't done. When my duplicate saw me, she looked shocked—like she was seeing a ghost."

Alice pinned the statement to her investigation board under a new heading: "Potential Timeline Bleeds." If Echo Alley represented a breach point between realities, perhaps the Holloway House did as well—a place where residents occasionally glimpsed their alternate selves going about different lives.

She moved to the Westlake Park case next. Three years ago, over a six-week period, twelve separate witnesses had reported encountering people who vanished when approached. Unlike typical apparition reports, these figures appeared solid, engaged in ordinary activities, and were often recognized as living Daybridge residents—yet when confronted, the actual people had alibis placing them elsewhere.

Alice had never satisfactorily resolved the case. Her official report cited mass hysteria amplified by media coverage, though she'd never fully believed that explanation herself.

She extracted the map from the file, noting the concentration of sightings around the park's central fountain. Another potential breach point? She added it to her board, connecting it with red string to Echo Alley and the Holloway House.

The St. Christopher's Hospital case was more complex. Staff and patients on the fourth floor had reported time discrepancies—clocks running at different speeds, shifts that seemed to last hours longer than scheduled, patients whose conditions progressed too rapidly or too slowly. Alice had documented the phenomenon extensively but found no conventional explanation. The hospital administration had eventually closed the entire floor for "renovations," and when it reopened, the temporal anomalies had ceased.

Alice frowned, pulling out the hospital's original architectural plans from her files. She'd obtained them during her investigation but had focused primarily on the fourth floor. Now she examined the building's location within Daybridge, plotting it on her city map alongside the other potential breach points.

A pattern emerged—one she hadn't seen before. All three locations formed a rough triangular configuration around the warehouse district. If she added Echo Alley to the map...

"It's the center," she whispered, marking the point. The warehouse district didn't just contain a breach point—it appeared to be the nexus from which other anomalies radiated.

Alice quickly pulled additional files, focusing on cases she'd previously categorized as low-priority or inconclusive. A restaurant where patrons occasionally received food they hadn't ordered but insisted they had. A street corner where pedestrians reported brief disorientation and memory discrepancies. A public garden where visitors sometimes encountered plant species that didn't exist in any botanical reference.

She plotted each location on her map, watching as the pattern expanded—concentric circles of anomalies radiating outward from the warehouse district, decreasing in frequency and intensity with distance.

Alice stepped back from the board, her heart racing. This wasn't just about one alley with unusual acoustic properties. The evidence suggested that Daybridge itself sat atop some kind of reality distortion field, with the warehouse district as its epicenter.

But why there? What made that location special?

She pulled out her laptop, searching historical records of the warehouse district. Before the current buildings were constructed in the 1970s, the area had housed a research facility operated by Quantum Dynamics, Inc.—a defense contractor active during the Cold War. The facility had closed in 1959 following what official records described as a "containment incident."

Alice's eyes narrowed. "Project Resonance," she murmured, remembering Thomas Webb's parting words. The timeline matched.

Her phone rang, interrupting her thoughts. The caller ID showed her contact at the Historical Society.

"Elena," Alice answered, "thank you for calling back so quickly."

"I got your email about Project Resonance," Elena replied, her voice lowered despite the early hour. "Alice, where did you hear that name?"

"It came up during an investigation. I'm trying to verify—"

"Not over the phone," Elena interrupted. "Those files are still under restricted access. Official restrictions expired twenty years ago, but someone keeps renewing the classification through back channels. Nobody's supposed to know they exist."

Alice's grip tightened on her phone. "But they do exist?"

A pause. "Meet me in the Archives basement at noon. Alone. I can give you thirty minutes with what I have." Elena disconnected before Alice could respond.

Alice set down her phone, turning back to her investigation board. Elena's reaction confirmed at least part of Thomas Webb's story—Project Resonance had been real, and someone still considered it sensitive enough to maintain classification decades later.

She had an hour before meeting Dr. Okafor. Alice used it to dig deeper into three specific case files that now seemed critically connected.

The first came from fifteen years ago, before her time as an investigator: a warehouse worker had claimed to witness the entire district "shift" for approximately seventeen seconds, during which the buildings appeared newer, the signs different, the very air "tinted blue." The man had been dismissed as suffering from carbon monoxide poisoning, though medical tests showed no evidence of this.

The second case, from eight years ago, involved a security guard who reported having a thirty-minute conversation with a woman who identified herself as Dr. Eliza Kaufmann—a quantum physicist who claimed to be "temporarily visiting from elsewhere." The guard had been convinced of the encounter's reality, but no Dr. Kaufmann existed at any research institution in the country. Alice had filed it as a possible stress-induced hallucination.

The third case had occurred just fourteen months ago. A delivery driver reported that while making a routine stop in the warehouse district, his truck's GPS had suddenly shown him in a different part of Daybridge entirely. When he looked up from the device, he saw unfamiliar buildings around him for approximately twenty seconds before everything "snapped back" to normal.

Alice created a timeline, arranging these and two dozen similar incidents chronologically. The pattern was unmistakable: reports of reality distortions in and around the warehouse district had been increasing in both frequency and duration. Whatever was happening at Echo Alley wasn't new—it was escalating.

She photographed her updated investigation board, uploaded the images to her secure server, then carefully removed the most sensitive materials—including her notes about Thomas Webb and the Department of Temporal Security—and locked them in her hidden wall safe. If someone were monitoring her investigation, she wouldn't make it easy for them.

The broken pendant and its microchip she placed in a small lead-lined box—originally purchased to transport sensitive electromagnetic equipment—hoping it might block any signals the device could be transmitting or receiving.

Before leaving to meet Dr. Okafor, Alice made one final connection on her board—a thin blue thread linking Echo Alley to a small photograph in the corner, showing a young Alice with her grandmother. The woman who had given her a pendant containing impossible technology, who had told her stories about "thin places" where worlds touched, who had looked at seven-year-old Alice with tears in her eyes and whispered, "In another life, I think I knew you differently."

Alice had always assumed it was poetic sentiment from an elderly woman. Now she wasn't so sure.

She locked her apartment carefully, taking a circuitous route to the Blackbird Café. The familiar weight of the pendant was absent from around her neck, leaving her feeling strangely vulnerable as she navigated the morning crowds of downtown Daybridge.

The café was busy with the breakfast rush when Alice arrived, but she spotted Dr. Maya Okafor immediately—a woman in her early forties with close-cropped silver-streaked hair, intense eyes behind rectangular glasses, and the distinct air of someone who had long ago stopped caring what others thought of her theories.

Alice approached the corner table where the physicist sat surrounded by papers and a laptop displaying complex equations.

"Dr. Okafor," she said, extending her hand. "Thank you for meeting me."

Maya Okafor looked up, studying Alice with scientific precision before shaking her hand. "Detective Chen. Your quantum variance readings kept me awake all night." She gestured to the chair opposite her. "Please sit. We have a great deal to discuss what you've encountered in Echo Alley."

"You believe me, then?" Alice asked as she took the seat, surprised by the physicist's immediate acceptance.

Dr. Okafor's expression remained serious. "Detective, I've spent fifteen years being ridiculed by my colleagues for theorizing exactly what your readings confirmed. The question isn't whether I believe you." She lowered her voice, leaning forward. "The question is whether you're prepared to accept what these readings actually mean for our understanding of reality—and why someone might kill to keep that understanding suppressed."

Alice felt a chill at the physicist's words, recalling Thomas Webb's fate in her timeline. "That's precisely what I want to discuss with you. But first—" she glanced around the crowded café, "—is this location secure for such a conversation?"

Dr. Okafor's slight smile held no humor. "No place in Daybridge is truly secure for this discussion. But the ambient noise provides reasonable cover, and I've taken certain precautions." She gestured to a small device on the table that resembled a wireless charger. "Signal disruptor. Limited range, but effective for our immediate vicinity."

Alice nodded, relieved by the physicist's caution. "Then let me tell you exactly what I encountered in Echo Alley, and what I've pieced together from my case files this morning."

As Alice began her account, the morning light through the café windows strengthened, illuminating dust motes that danced between them like particles caught between worlds—insignificant individually, but together forming patterns that connected everything.

CHAPTER FOUR: THE PHYSICIST'S ECHO

Alice Chen stood at the mouth of Echo Alley as sunset painted Daybridge's warehouse district in amber and shadow. The meeting with Dr. Maya Okafor had lasted three hours, extending well beyond breakfast into a strategic planning session that left Alice's mind buzzing with theoretical physics concepts she'd never encountered before.

"What you're describing isn't paranormal at all," Maya had explained, sketching quantum field equations on café napkins. "It's a localized breakdown in quantum coherence between adjacent probability fields—what laypersons might call parallel universes."

Maya had modified Alice's equipment, recalibrating the quantum variance monitor and adding several new sensors designed to measure subatomic particle behavior. The device now hummed softly in Alice's hand, already registering readings above baseline as she approached the alley.

"Remember," Maya's parting words echoed in her memory, "if you encounter Thomas Webb again, ask about the Resonance Cascade Theory. In academic circles, it was his most controversial work—proposing that quantum reality barriers could be artificially thinned through concentrated energy application. The paper was widely discredited, then mysteriously withdrawn from all journals."

Alice had spent the afternoon at the Historical Society archives with Elena, reviewing the limited declassified documents on Project Resonance. The records confirmed that in 1956, Quantum Dynamics had conducted experiments involving "non-standard particle acceleration" and "dimensional barrier testing" at the facility beneath what was now the warehouse district. The project had been terminated after an unspecified "containment failure" that required evacuation of a three-block radius.

Most disturbing were the personnel records—specifically, the name of the project's lead theoretical physicist: Dr. Margaret Chen, Alice's grandmother.

The discovery had left Alice reeling, forcing her to reevaluate her entire understanding of her family history. Her grandmother had never mentioned working for Quantum Dynamics or any defense contractor. She'd described herself as a mathematics teacher who later focused on raising her family. Yet the records clearly showed she'd been integral to Project Resonance—until she'd abruptly resigned following the containment incident.

Now, standing at the threshold of Echo Alley with equipment humming and the last light of day fading, Alice felt the weight of connected mysteries pressing on her. The pendant's microchip. Her grandmother's secret past. The increasing reality disturbances throughout Daybridge. And somewhere in the center of it all, a physicist named Thomas Webb who existed across timelines but had been erased from her own.

Alice checked her watch: 7:42 PM. Sunset. A threshold hour.

She activated her recording equipment and stepped into the alley, moving purposefully toward the dead end. The temperature dropped immediately—a ten-degree differential that registered clearly on her instruments. The quantum variance monitor's display shifted from yellow to orange, indicating significant reality fluctuations.

"Thomas Webb," Alice called clearly, her voice echoing against the brick walls. "I've returned as you suggested. I need to speak with you about Project Resonance."

The echo rebounded normally, then faded. Alice waited, counting silently. One... two... three...

"Alice Chen." The voice materialized not as an echo but as if someone stood directly behind her. "You've been busy since our last conversation."

Alice turned slowly, finding only empty air, yet the voice had been so clear she could have sworn someone stood within arm's reach. "I've been researching," she confirmed, activating additional sensors. "I know about Project Resonance now. I know my grandmother was involved."

A pause. When Thomas spoke again, his voice had shifted location, now seeming to emanate from the brick wall at the alley's end.

"Margaret Chen," he said, the name carrying weight even across realities. "In my timeline, she's revered as the pioneer of quantum barrier theory. Her work laid the foundation for everything we now understand about multiverse communication."

"In my timeline, she was a mathematics teacher who gave her granddaughter a pendant containing technology that shouldn't have existed." Alice removed the small lead box from her pocket, opening it to reveal the broken stone and its embedded microchip. "What is this, Thomas? Why would she give it to me?"

The quantum variance monitor spiked suddenly, its display flashing red. The temperature in the alley dropped another five degrees.

"She was protecting you," Thomas's voice shifted again, now seeming to come from directly overhead. "Or rather, connecting you to protection. That device is a quantum resonator—a receiver that allows your consciousness to maintain stability during reality fluctuations."

Alice frowned, studying the tiny chip. "I don't understand."

"Those who regularly experience reality breaches without protection can suffer psychological fragmentation—their consciousness bleeding across timelines, memories becoming confused, identity destabilizing. The resonator acts as an anchor, keeping you tethered to your native reality while still allowing you to perceive the breaches."

Alice recalled the pendant's consistent warming when she approached paranormal sites—sites she now understood might be reality breach points. "But why me? Why would my grandmother think I needed protection?"

The air in the alley shimmered slightly, like heat waves rising from asphalt, though the temperature continued to drop. For a moment, Alice thought she glimpsed a figure against the brick wall—the transparent outline of a man in his late twenties with wire-rimmed glasses and an intense expression.

"Because in most timelines, Alice Chen discovers the breaches," Thomas's voice strengthened as his image flickered. "Different paths, different careers, but the same ultimate discovery. Your grandmother understood this—she'd seen it during Project Resonance. The project didn't just detect other timelines; it observed patterns across them."

Alice's heart raced as implications cascaded through her mind. "Are you saying my grandmother saw my alternate selves during those experiments? That she knew I would eventually investigate the breaches regardless of my career path?"

"Precisely." Thomas's image stabilized momentarily—a tall, thin man in a rumpled button-down shirt and khakis, looking exactly like the faculty photo Alice had found in the university archives. "Project Resonance documented thousands of timeline variations, but certain events remained consistent across most of them. One was that Margaret Chen's granddaughter eventually discovered the truth about reality breaches—usually around this point in her life."

Alice struggled to process the revelation. "In your timeline, you said I'm a physicist?"

Thomas nodded, his image flickering like a poorly tuned television channel. "Dr. Alice Chen, quantum theorist. We worked together at Daybridge University until—" His image distorted, face contorting with sudden pain.

"Until what?" Alice pressed, stepping closer despite the plummeting temperature.

Thomas's form stabilized with visible effort. "Until the Department shut us down. They came for our research first, then for us. Alice—my timeline's Alice—managed to escape. I wasn't so fortunate."

"The Department of Temporal Security," Alice said. "Who are they? Government?"

"Yes and no." Thomas's voice lowered, though they were alone in the alley. "They exist across multiple timelines, operating quasi-independently from any single government. Their original mandate was to prevent catastrophic reality collapses by monitoring breach points and neutralizing threats."

"Original mandate?" Alice noted the distinction.

"Over time, their mission evolved. They discovered that information from alternate timelines provided strategic advantages—technological innovation, investment opportunities, political intelligence. What began as protection became exploitation."

Alice thought of the warehouse worker who'd received advance knowledge of contraband shipments. "They're using the breaches to gather intelligence."

"Initially. Now they're actively working to widen them for greater access." Thomas's image distorted again, rippling like a reflection in disturbed water. "The breach in this alley has expanded 217% in the past year alone. Similar expansions are occurring at other thin points throughout Daybridge."

Alice consulted her quantum variance monitor, noting the elevated readings. "Is the expansion dangerous?"

"Catastrophically so." Thomas's expression was grave. "Reality barriers exist for a reason, Alice. When they break down beyond a certain threshold, adjacent timelines begin to bleed into each other uncontrollably. Imagine multiple films projected onto the same screen simultaneously—coherence breaks down. If the process continues unchecked, both timelines can collapse entirely."

"How do we stop it?" Alice asked, the investigator in her immediately focusing on solutions.

Thomas's image stabilized, becoming almost solid for a moment. "The Department believes they can control the expansion—create stable passages between realities. They're wrong. My calculations—our calculations, in my timeline—proved that artificial breaches will always destabilize exponentially once they exceed certain parameters."

"The Resonance Cascade Theory," Alice said, recalling Maya's suggestion.

Thomas's expression shifted to surprise. "You know about that?"

"Only the name. Dr. Okafor mentioned it."

"Maya Okafor." Thomas's image flickered with what might have been a smile. "In my timeline, she's Alice's closest collaborator. Brilliant mind." His expression darkened. "The Department came for her first. Her disappearance was what warned us they were onto our research."

Alice felt a chill that had nothing to do with the alley's dropping temperature. "I met with her this morning."

"Be careful," Thomas warned. "The Department monitors quantum physicists whose work approaches breach theory. If you're openly collaborating with her, they'll notice."

"Too late to worry about that now," Alice said. "I need her expertise to understand what's happening."

"Then you need to protect her." Thomas's voice became urgent. "And yourself. The Department's standard procedure is to eliminate researchers who discover too much, then erase evidence they ever existed."

Alice recalled the university records showing Thomas Webb had died in a car accident shortly after receiving a prestigious fellowship. "Like they did with you in my timeline."

"Yes." Thomas's image began to fragment, breaking apart into pixelated sections that flickered independently. "Our connection is destabilizing. I don't have much time left in this session."

"Tell me how to stop the expansion," Alice pressed, stepping closer despite the now-painful cold. "How do we repair the breaches?"

"The Department is using quantum resonance amplifiers to widen the breaches. The technology was developed from Project Resonance's original work. Locate and neutralize these devices." Thomas's voice began to break up, words coming in disjointed fragments. "Start with... warehouse sublevel... original facility... still accessible through..."

His image collapsed entirely, dissolving into particles of light that briefly illuminated the alley before vanishing. The temperature began to normalize immediately.

"Thomas?" Alice called, her voice echoing normally against the brick walls. No response came.

The quantum variance monitor showed readings returning to baseline. Whatever window had allowed their communication had closed—though the data had been captured. Alice quickly checked her recording equipment, confirming she had documentation of the entire exchange.

As she packed up her equipment, Alice's mind raced with implications. If Thomas was correct, the Department of Temporal Security was actively destabilizing reality throughout Daybridge, putting countless lives at risk for strategic advantage. And based on Thomas's fate in her timeline, they wouldn't hesitate to eliminate anyone who interfered.

Alice had investigated dangerous situations before—angry spirits, psychokinetic events that turned violent, even a few human criminals exploiting belief in the paranormal. But she'd never faced an adversary with government resources and the ability to erase people from existence.

She needed allies. Maya Okafor, certainly. Perhaps Detective Rivera, though bringing him into this would put his career—and possibly his life—at risk. She needed access to the sublevels beneath the warehouse district, where Thomas indicated the resonance amplifiers might be located.

Most importantly, she needed to understand her grandmother's role in all this. Margaret Chen had helped create Project Resonance, then left it abruptly. She'd given Alice a quantum resonator disguised as a family heirloom. She'd known her granddaughter would eventually discover the breaches.

What else had she known? What else had she done to prepare Alice for this moment?

As Alice exited the alley, she noticed a black sedan parked across the street that hadn't been there when she arrived. Its windows were tinted, its license plate partially obscured by mud—or deliberately dirtied. As she watched peripherally while packing her car, a figure in the driver's seat appeared to speak into a communication device.

Alice drove away from the warehouse district taking a deliberately complex route, employing every counter-surveillance technique she knew. After thirty minutes of random turns, doubling back, and brief stops, she was reasonably confident she'd lost any tail.

Instead of returning to her apartment, she drove to an all-night diner on Daybridge's outskirts. From a booth in the back, she sent carefully worded texts to both Maya Okafor and Detective Rivera, arranging separate meetings for the following day.

Then she opened her laptop and began composing a detailed case file documenting everything she'd learned so far. If the Department was monitoring her, they already knew she'd discovered the breach. Her only protection now was ensuring the information spread beyond her alone.

As Alice typed, she couldn't shake the image of Thomas Webb's face as it had briefly stabilized in the alley—the expression of someone who had seen the consequences of failure firsthand. She thought of her grandmother, a brilliant physicist who had hidden her true work behind the persona of a mathematics teacher yet had carefully ensured her granddaughter would have protection when she inevitably encountered the truth.

And she thought of her other selves—the physicist who had worked with Thomas, the federal agent who had warned her about the Department, and how many other Alice Chens existing across timelines, all somehow converging on this same discovery.

The waitress refilled her coffee cup, breaking her concentration momentarily.

"Working late, honey?" the older woman asked kindly.

Alice managed a smile. "Important case."

"Must be, to keep you looking so serious. World-ending stuff, is it?"

Alice's smile faded slightly. "Something like that."

After the waitress moved on, Alice returned to her work with renewed determination. She had encountered many inexplicable phenomena in her career as a paranormal investigator, but never before had she faced something with such far-reaching implications. If Thomas was right, the very fabric of reality was unraveling beneath Daybridge—and someone was deliberately pulling the threads.

She needed to find those quantum resonance amplifiers, and soon. Before the Department of Temporal Security found her.

CHAPTER FIVE:
INTERDIMENSIONAL COLD CASE

The archives room at Daybridge University smelled of dust and forgotten knowledge. Alice Chen sat surrounded by stacks of academic journals, personnel files, and scientific papers—a paper trail stretching back nearly thirty years. Morning light filtered through high windows, illuminating dancing dust motes that swirled when she turned each brittle page.

"Thomas Webb," she murmured, scanning a faculty photograph from 1997. A group of physics department members posed stiffly before an outdated particle accelerator. In the back row stood a tall, lanky man with wire-rimmed glasses and an intense expression—exactly matching the flickering apparition she'd seen in Echo Alley.

Alice had begun her day at 5 AM, using her consultant credentials to gain early access to the university archives. Her meeting with Detective Rivera wasn't until noon, and Maya Okafor was busy recalibrating equipment for their next investigation of the alley. That gave Alice precious hours to pursue the investigation approach she knew best: thorough background research.

If Thomas Webb had been "erased" as he claimed, there would be inconsistencies in the official record—gaps, contradictions, and altered narratives that wouldn't quite align. She'd seen similar patterns in paranormal cover-ups: official explanations that satisfied casual scrutiny but fell apart under methodical investigation.

The university's records showed Thomas Webb had been a promising doctoral candidate specializing in quantum field theory. His dissertation adviser, Dr. Elijah Northwood, had praised his "revolutionary approach to quantum barrier dynamics" and "unusual intuitive grasp of multidimensional mathematics." Webb had published three papers in prestigious journals between 1996 and early 1998, then abruptly died in a car accident on Route 16 just months before completing his doctorate.

Alice carefully photographed each document with her phone, creating a digital record beyond anyone's easy reach. She'd learned that lesson years ago—evidence had a way of disappearing when powerful interests were involved.

The official accident report was suspiciously thin. Single-vehicle collision. No witnesses. Mechanical failure cited as the probable cause. Body cremated quickly due to extensive damage. No photographs in the file.

"Convenient," Alice noted, jotting observations in her notebook. The timing aligned perfectly with Thomas's claim that the Department had "eliminated" him after he discovered too much about reality breaches.

She turned next to Webb's published academic work. His final paper, "Quantum Coherence in Multi-Dimensional Probability Fields," had been published in the Journal of Theoretical Physics just two months before his death. Alice skimmed the dense mathematical formulas and technical jargon, recognizing concepts that aligned with what Thomas and Maya had described about reality breaches.

Most interestingly, the paper included a citation of a 1957 study by M. Chen titled "Temporal Displacement in Quantum Field Irregularities"—her grandmother's work. Alice noted the reference carefully. That paper wasn't included in the university's archives.

When the archives opened to regular staff at 8 AM, Alice approached the head archivist, a rail-thin man named Dr. Winters who'd overseen the university's historical records for decades.

"I'm looking for information about Dr. Thomas Webb's final research project," she explained, displaying her consultant badge. "There are references to a classified study he was conducting for the Department of Energy in 1998."

Dr. Winters's expression shifted subtly—a tightening around the eyes, a slight compression of his lips. "I'm afraid we have limited information about Dr. Webb. He was only a doctoral candidate, not a full professor, and his time here was cut short by his tragic accident."

"But he was working on a classified project," Alice pressed. "There should be documentation of the security clearance process, funding allocations, equipment requisitions."

"As I said," Winters repeated with practiced smoothness, "we have very limited records concerning Dr. Webb."

Alice recognized the response for what it was—not merely bureaucratic obstruction but practiced deflection. She changed tactics.

"I'm also interested in Dr. Elijah Northwood's work from that period. As Webb's adviser, he would have overseen the project."

Winters's expression flickered again. "Dr. Northwood retired quite suddenly in late 1998. Health issues, I believe. I'm not sure we have comprehensive records of his final projects either."

Both Webb and his adviser disappearing within months of each other. The pattern was becoming clearer.

"Is there anyone still at the university who worked directly with Webb? A colleague, research assistant, even administrative staff?"

Winters appeared to consider this, perhaps calculating the least problematic response. "You might speak with Dr. Cassandra Liu in the Physics Department. She was a graduate student when Webb was here. I believe they shared lab space briefly."

Alice thanked him and left, sensing his relief at her departure. Outside the archives, she checked her watch—9:15 AM. Plenty of time to visit the Physics Department before meeting Rivera.

The Grayson Science Building stood at the northern edge of campus; a brutalist concrete structure built during the Cold War era when government funding for physics research had flowed freely. Alice navigated its labyrinthine hallways until she found the office marked "Dr. Cassandra Liu, Associate Professor, Quantum Mechanics."

The woman who answered her knock was in her early fifties with silver-streaked black hair pulled into a practical bun. She regarded Alice with immediate suspicion.

"Dr. Liu? I'm Alice Chen, consulting for Daybridge PD." She displayed her badge. "I was hoping to ask you about a former colleague—Thomas Webb."

The physicist's expression changed instantly—a flash of recognition, quickly replaced by careful neutrality. "Thomas Webb died nearly thirty years ago. What could possibly be relevant to a police investigation after all this time?"

"May I come in?" Alice asked instead of answering directly.

After a moment's hesitation, Dr. Liu stepped aside, closing the door firmly behind Alice once she entered. The office was cluttered with books, papers, and equipment—the organized chaos of an active researcher.

"Why are you asking about Thomas?" Liu repeated, remaining standing.

Alice made a calculated decision to be direct. "Because I have reason to believe his death was falsified to cover up his discovery of quantum reality breaches."

Liu's face drained of color. She moved to her desk chair, sinking into it slowly. "Who sent you?"

"No one sent me," Alice said truthfully. "I'm investigating unusual phenomena in the warehouse district that appears connected to Webb's research."

Liu glanced at her office door, then reached for a small device on her desk—similar to the signal disruptor Maya had used at the café. She activated it before speaking again.

"Thomas wasn't killed in any car accident," she said quietly. "That was the official story we were told to accept. What really happened was..." She paused, struggling visibly. "He was conducting an experiment in the subbasement lab. Something about quantum field oscillation. I wasn't directly involved, but I helped with some of the preliminary calculations."

Alice leaned forward. "What happened?"

"One day, men in suits came to the lab. They showed credentials—Department of Energy, they claimed. They confiscated all of Thomas's equipment, his notes, his computer. When I asked what was happening, they said his project had been classified and was being relocated to a secure facility." Liu's hands twisted in her lap. "Thomas was furious. He argued with them, said they couldn't take his work, that they didn't understand the implications."

"And then?" Alice prompted when Liu fell silent.

"They took him too. He left with them that day. Three days later, the department chair called an emergency meeting to inform us that Thomas had died in a car accident on Route 16." Liu met Alice's eyes directly. "There was no body at the funeral. Closed casket, immediate cremation afterward. Dr. Northwood gave the eulogy. He looked... afraid."

"Did you believe it? The accident story?"

Liu's laugh held no humor. "None of us did. But Dr. Northwood made it very clear that asking questions would be detrimental to our careers. A month later, he took early retirement. Moved to Arizona, I think. We never heard from him again."

Alice made notes as Liu spoke. "What was Webb working on? Do you remember the details?"

"Something he called 'quantum reality interfaces.' He believed that what we experience as reality is just one probability field among infinite variations, and that these fields occasionally overlap at thin points." Liu shook her head. "It sounded like science fiction to most of us. But Thomas was brilliant—unorthodox, but brilliant. And he had data that couldn't be explained by conventional theories."

"Data from where?" Alice asked, sensing they were approaching something crucial.

"He never said explicitly. But he mentioned a facility in the warehouse district—some old research site that had been abandoned decades earlier. He'd gained access somehow and set up measurement equipment." Liu frowned. "Now that I think about it, he became especially excited after discovering old research from the 1950s. Said it confirmed his theories about reality breaches."

"Project Resonance," Alice suggested.

Liu's eyes widened. "Yes, that was it. He mentioned that name a few times. Said it was the key to understanding what was happening in Daybridge." She leaned forward suddenly. "Listen, why are you really investigating this? Thomas has been gone for thirty years. What's happening now?"

Alice considered her response carefully. Liu might be a potential ally, but involving her further could put her at risk.

"The phenomena Thomas was studying appear to be intensifying," she said finally. "I'm trying to understand why, and whether it poses any danger to Daybridge."

"And does it?" Liu pressed. "Pose a danger?"

"I believe it might," Alice admitted. "One last question, Dr. Liu. Did Thomas ever mention an organization called the Department of Temporal Security?"

Liu's reaction was immediate and physical—a sharp intake of breath, pupils dilating with what appeared to be genuine fear. "Where did you hear that name?"

"It's come up in my investigation."

"They're not Department of Energy," Liu said, voice barely above a whisper. "Thomas figured that out right before they came for him. He sent me an email that morning—said he'd discovered who was really monitoring his work. That email disappeared from my account the same day he was taken. I've never told anyone about it until now."

Alice felt a chill despite the office's warmth. "Thank you for your honesty, Dr. Liu. You've been extremely helpful."

Liu caught Alice's arm as she stood to leave. "Be careful, Ms. Chen. If you're right about the phenomena intensifying, and if the same people are still monitoring it..." She left the implication unspoken.

"I'll be discreet," Alice promised.

Liu shook her head. "That won't be enough. Thomas was discreet too."

Alice left the Science Building with her notebook full and her mind racing. She checked her watch—10:30 AM. She still had time before meeting Rivera. On impulse, she headed toward the university library, seeking one more piece of the puzzle.

The newspaper archives were stored on microfilm in the library's basement. Alice requested the Daybridge Herald editions from May 1998—the month of Thomas Webb's reported death. She scanned through them quickly until she found what she was looking for: a small article on page 7 about a fatal car accident on Route 16.

The piece was brief, just three paragraphs noting that "promising physicist Thomas Webb, 28" had died when his car apparently suffered brake failure on a curved section of highway. No photographs accompanied the article. No follow-up stories appeared in subsequent editions.

Alice switched to the microfilm for the same period from the Daybridge Examiner, the Herald's now-defunct competitor. There she found something interesting—a slightly longer article that included a quote from a witness: "The car was already on fire before it hit the guardrail. Never seen anything like it."

She noted the witness's name—Harold Mercer—and the fact that he was identified as a truck driver who had been "first on the scene." This contradicted the official accident report that had stated there were no witnesses.

A quick internet search on her phone revealed that Harold Mercer had died three months after the accident—another single-vehicle collision on Route 16.

"Convenient," Alice murmured again, adding this detail to her notes. The pattern was unmistakable now—a systematic erasure of Thomas Webb and anyone connected to his work or its aftermath.

Alice left the library and walked to her car, maintaining casual awareness of her surroundings. Nothing obvious suggested surveillance, but the morning's discoveries had heightened her caution to new levels.

Instead of driving directly to meet Rivera, she took a circuitous route through Daybridge, eventually parking at a shopping center where she entered through one store and exited through another, emerging near a café two blocks from the police station.

Detective Rivera was already waiting at an outdoor table, nursing a coffee and looking uncomfortable in civilian clothes—jeans and a Daybridge Tigers sweatshirt that suggested a day off duty.

"This better be important, Chen," he said as she sat down. "Meeting you in public is already pushing boundaries."

"I need access to old case files," Alice said without preamble. "Specifically, accident reports from Route 16, May 1998, and any investigations involving Quantum Dynamics between 1955 and 1959."

Rivera's eyebrows rose. "That's oddly specific for a paranormal investigator. What exactly are you working on?"

Alice had prepared for this question. Rivera was pragmatic—he needed enough information to justify helping her, but not so much that he'd dismiss her as delusional.

"I believe several cold cases in Daybridge may be connected to classified research conducted in the warehouse district during the Cold War," she explained. "The voices in Echo Alley appear to be a side effect of experiments that never properly concluded."

It wasn't the full truth, but it contained enough truth to be believable coming from her.

Rivera studied her face. They'd worked together for three years—never friends but developing a grudging professional respect.

He'd seen enough of her successful investigations to know she wasn't prone to wild theories.

"These cold cases," he said finally. "You think they're murders disguised as accidents?"

Alice nodded. "I've found a pattern of researchers connected to certain quantum physics projects dying in suspicious circumstances, followed by unusual efforts to limit investigation."

Rivera sighed. "You know how this sounds, right? Secret government conspiracies to silence scientists? Black ops teams staging car accidents?"

"I know exactly how it sounds," Alice acknowledged. "That's why I need official records to confirm or disprove my theory. If I'm wrong, the files will show that."

Rivera considered this, then pulled out his phone, checking something briefly. "The accident reports might be accessible. Cold cases get digitized eventually. But anything involving Quantum Dynamics from the '50s? That's likely still in deep storage if it exists at all."

"Can you check?" Alice pressed. "Just see what's available?"

After a moment's hesitation, Rivera nodded. "I can run a search, see what comes up. But Chen—" he leaned forward, lowering his voice, "—if you're right about any of this, you're poking a very dangerous bear. You need to be certain it's worth it."

"It is," Alice said with quiet conviction. "Lives may depend on understanding what's happening in that alley."

Rivera held her gaze for a long moment, then nodded. "I'll see what I can find. Give me until tomorrow." He stood to leave, then paused. "Be careful, Chen. You look like someone who knows they're being watched."

"Aren't we all?" Alice replied with a thin smile.

After Rivera departed, Alice remained at the café, ordering lunch while she organized her morning's findings. The pieces were fitting together into a coherent narrative: Thomas Webb had discovered reality breaches in Daybridge, connected them to Project Resonance, and been eliminated by a covert organization that had continued monitoring and manipulating the breaches for decades since.

Her phone vibrated with a text from Maya Okafor: "Equipment calibrated. Meeting with a colleague who may have relevant expertise. Echo Alley at sunset?"

Alice confirmed the meeting, then sent a separate encrypted message to the email address Maya had provided, summarizing her discoveries about Thomas Webb and asking Maya to research any connections between Project Resonance and current Department of Energy quantum research.

Her final task before leaving the café was to create a secure backup of everything she'd learned. Alice compressed her photos, notes, and audio recordings into an encrypted file, uploading it to a cloud server accessible only through multiple authentication steps. If anything happened to her, Maya would know how to access the information.

As she walked back to her car, Alice felt the weight of Thomas Webb's cold case settling across her shoulders. What had begun as an investigation into strange voices in an alley had expanded into something far more complex—a conspiracy spanning decades and possibly multiple realities.

Her grandmother had been at the center of it all, developing the very technologies that had created the breaches. And somehow, she had known Alice would eventually follow the same path—would need protection from the same forces that had silenced Thomas Webb.

The quantum resonator microchip from her pendant now rested in a faraday-lined pouch in Alice's pocket. She touched it through the fabric, wondering what other precautions her grandmother might have taken, what other breadcrumbs she might have left for Alice to follow.

As she drove toward her apartment to prepare for the sunset meeting at Echo Alley, Alice formulated her next investigative steps. She needed to locate the entrance to the sublevels beneath the warehouse district that Thomas had mentioned. She needed to identify the quantum resonance amplifiers supposedly widening the breaches. And most importantly, she needed to determine exactly who within the government had the authority and motivation to maintain this decades-long cover-up.

What had begun as a paranormal investigation had transformed into something Alice had never anticipated—an interdimensional cold case where the victim existed across multiple realities, and where the crime scene was the fabric of reality itself.

As she waited at a traffic light, Alice noticed a black sedan three cars behind her—similar to the one she'd seen near Echo Alley. Its windows were tinted, its license plate partially obscured.

When the light changed, Alice made a sudden right turn instead of continuing straight. The sedan followed.

"So it begins," she murmured, accelerating slightly as she formulated a counter-surveillance route. The Department of Temporal Security—or whatever they called themselves in this reality—had noticed her investigation.

The game of interdimensional cat and mouse had officially begun.

CHAPTER SIX: THE RELUCTANT ACADEMIC

"This is either the most elaborate hoax in scientific history or the most significant discovery of our lifetime," Dr. Maya Okafor said, removing her headphones. The sun had set an hour ago, casting Echo Alley into deep shadow relieved only by the soft blue glow of monitoring equipment. "And I'm not sure which possibility terrifies me more."

Alice Chen watched the physicist's expression transition from skepticism to awe as the implications settled in. Maya had listened to Alice's recording from the previous day—Thomas Webb's voice describing quantum resonance principles that perfectly aligned with Maya's own unpublished research. Research she had shared with no one.

"It's not a hoax," Alice said quietly. "And I think you already know that."

Maya nodded slowly, her fingers tracing the edge of her laptop where complex equations filled the screen—equations that Thomas Webb had somehow known the solutions to despite having died decades before Maya formulated them.

Their meeting at Echo Alley had begun tensely. Despite providing Alice with equipment, Maya had maintained a professional distance—the caution of an academic approached by someone investigating the paranormal. That reserve had crumbled as the evidence mounted, culminating in the recording that now had Maya reconsidering everything she thought she understood about quantum reality.

"Three years ago, when I first reached out to you," Maya said, "you dismissed my theories about quantum explanations for paranormal phenomena."

Alice smiled faintly at the memory. "I believe my exact words were 'interesting but speculative.' I was focused on documenting paranormal events, not explaining them theoretically."

"And now?"

"Now I need your theoretical framework to understand what we're facing," Alice admitted. "This isn't a standard haunting or psychokinetic event. This is something foundational to reality itself."

Maya turned back to her equipment, checking readings from the various sensors positioned throughout the alley. "The quantum variance patterns are unlike anything I've ever recorded. The subatomic particles in this location exist in a state of what I can only describe as 'reality uncertainty'—simultaneously conforming to the physical laws of multiple probability fields."

Alice nodded. "Thomas called it a breach between timelines."

"That's... actually an elegant description." Maya adjusted one of the sensors. "Though I'd prefer the term 'adjacent quantum reality configurations.' Less science fiction, more peer-reviewable."

Alice suppressed a smile. Even facing evidence that shattered conventional understanding, the physicist clung to academic terminology. It was oddly reassuring.

"The readings are strongest near the dead end," Maya continued, gesturing toward the brick wall at the alley's terminus. "If I had to visualize it, I'd say reality is thinnest there—almost permeable."

Alice approached the wall, running her hand along the cold brick surface. "Thomas mentioned accessing the original facility beneath the warehouse district. Could there be a physical entrance here?"

Maya joined her, examining the wall more carefully. "These bricks don't match the rest of the alley. Newer, different composition." She pressed against various sections, checking for inconsistencies.

Alice pulled out a small UV light from her equipment bag, shining it slowly across the brick surface. Near the bottom right corner, faint symbols became visible—markings that appeared to have been painted with some luminescent material decades earlier, now barely detectable.

"Look at this," she said, directing Maya's attention to the geometric shapes that formed a distinct pattern.

Maya crouched for a closer look. "These are quantum field equations—primitive versions, but recognizable." Her fingers traced the faded symbols. "This is remarkably similar to work published by..." Her voice trailed off as she made the connection.

"My grandmother," Alice finished. "Margaret Chen."

Maya looked up at her, eyes wide. "Your grandmother was Margaret Chen? The Margaret Chen?"

"You've heard of her?"

"Every serious quantum theorist has. Her 1957 paper on temporal displacement was decades ahead of its time. Most of her contemporaries dismissed it as science fiction, but modern quantum mechanics has validated many of her core hypotheses." Maya stood, regarding Alice with new understanding. "She disappeared from academic circles quite suddenly. The official story was that she left to raise a family, but there were always rumors..."

"That she was recruited for classified research," Alice supplied. "Project Resonance."

Maya nodded. "The scientific community suspected something like that, though the project name was never known publicly." She gestured to the symbols. "This confirms it. These equations relate directly to quantum barrier theory—the mathematical foundation for understanding how distinct reality configurations might interact."

Alice photographed the symbols, then continued examining the wall. Near the ground, partially hidden by decades of dirt accumulation, she found a small metallic plate. Brushing away the grime revealed what appeared to be a scanner of some kind—technology that seemed out of place in a simple alley.

"This isn't just graffiti," Alice realized. "It's a marker. Maybe even an access point."

Maya crouched beside her, examining the device. "Biometric scanner, but not a design I'm familiar with. Older technology but sophisticated for its era."

Alice's mind flashed to the microchip from her grandmother's pendant. On impulse, she removed it from its protective pouch and held it near the scanner.

The response was immediate—a soft hum emanated from the wall, and the scanner emitted a faint blue light that pulsed three times before going dark again. Nothing else happened, but the interaction confirmed Alice's suspicion that the two technologies were related.

"Your grandmother left you breadcrumbs," Maya said softly. "She knew you'd eventually find this place."

"But she didn't leave complete instructions," Alice replied, frustration edging her voice. "The pendant activated something, but not enough to gain entry."

Maya returned to her equipment, typing rapidly. "These readings are fascinating. When you placed the microchip near the scanner, there was a momentary spike in quantum variance—as if the barriers between realities thinned even further."

A thought occurred to Alice. "What time is it?"

Maya checked her watch. "11:47 PM."

"Almost midnight," Alice noted. "A threshold hour. Thomas said the breach is strongest at threshold times."

They exchanged a look of understanding. If they were going to attempt communication again, the timing was optimal.

Alice positioned herself near the wall, activating her recording equipment. "Thomas Webb," she called clearly. "We've found your marker. We need to know how to access the facility beneath the warehouse district."

The echo rebounded normally from the brick surfaces. Alice waited, counting silently as she had before. Maya watched intently, sensors recording every quantum fluctuation in the alley.

One... two... three...

Nothing happened. The alley remained silent apart from distant city sounds.

Alice tried again. "Thomas Webb, we need your help. How do we access the sublevel facility?"

Again, only normal echoes answered her. Alice frowned, glancing at Maya, who shook her head—the quantum readings showed no significant fluctuations.

"Something's different," Alice murmured. "The conditions have changed."

Maya checked her instruments. "The quantum variance is actually lower than yesterday, despite the threshold hour. It's as if..."

"As if something is suppressing the breach," Alice finished, a chill running through her that had nothing to do with the alley's temperature.

A soft electronic beep drew their attention to Maya's laptop. A warning indicator flashed on the screen—an unauthorized connection attempt detected by her security protocols.

"Someone's trying to access my system," Maya said, fingers flying across the keyboard as she strengthened her firewalls. "Sophisticated intrusion attempt—not standard hackers."

Alice immediately began gathering their equipment. "We need to leave. Now."

They packed quickly, efficiently, both women understanding the implications without need for discussion. If the Department of Temporal Security was monitoring the alley, they had likely detected Maya's specialized equipment and recognized its purpose.

As they hurried toward the alley entrance, Alice noticed something that stopped her cold—a small black device attached to the brick wall near the mouth of the alley. It hadn't been there when they arrived.

"Don't look directly at it," she warned Maya quietly. "But someone placed monitoring equipment while we've been working."

Maya nodded almost imperceptibly, continuing toward the exit with deliberate casualness. They loaded their equipment into Maya's car rather than Alice's—a precaution they had agreed upon earlier, suspecting Alice's vehicle might be tracked.

Neither spoke until they were several blocks from the warehouse district, Maya driving while Alice scanned for potential surveillance.

"They're actively suppressing the breach," Maya said finally, breaking the tense silence. "That's why we couldn't establish contact. They must have installed quantum dampening technology after detecting your previous communications."

Alice nodded, processing this new complication. "They know we're investigating. They know we've made contact with Thomas."

"Which means we're now targets," Maya said matter-of-factly, her scientific detachment extending to their precarious situation. "Just as Thomas warned."

Instead of returning to Maya's university office or Alice's apartment, they drove to a location they had selected earlier—a 24-hour diner on Daybridge's outskirts, chosen for its open layout, multiple exits, and lack of security cameras.

At a corner booth far from other late-night patrons, they spread out Maya's data, keeping their voices low.

"The quantum variance readings from previous visits confirm Thomas's claim," Maya said, showing Alice a graph on her laptop. "The breach has been expanding at an accelerating rate. What's particularly concerning is this pattern." She indicated oscillations in the data. "These aren't natural fluctuations. They're deliberate manipulations—someone periodically widening the breach, then allowing it to partially stabilize before widening it again."

"The Department testing the limits," Alice suggested.

"Precisely. Like stretching a rubber band repeatedly to determine its breaking point." Maya's expression darkened. "Except in this case, the breaking point could have catastrophic consequences for both connected realities."

Alice added this information to her growing case file. "We need to locate the quantum resonance amplifiers Thomas mentioned. If the Department is using them to widen the breaches, removing them might allow reality to stabilize."

"Finding them won't be easy," Maya cautioned. "Based on the readings, I'd estimate they're using multiple devices positioned throughout Daybridge, likely at other thin points in the reality barrier."

Alice thought of her map showing paranormal hotspots throughout the city. "I may already have a starting point for locating them."

Their conversation paused as the waitress brought coffee. When she departed, Maya leaned forward, her scientific reserve giving way to more personal concerns.

"Alice, I need to know exactly what I'm involving myself in," she said quietly. "My entire career has been spent pursuing theoretical questions about quantum reality. I've faced ridicule, funding denials, and professional isolation because of my insistence that quantum physics could explain so-called paranormal phenomena."

"And now you've been vindicated," Alice noted.

"At what cost?" Maya countered. "If Thomas Webb is to be believed, pursuing this knowledge got him killed in your reality. In his reality, his Alice Chen had to flee. What happens to us if we continue?"

It was a fair question—one Alice had been grappling with since her first contact with Thomas. The responsible approach would be to back away, to alert authorities, to let someone else handle the potentially world-ending implications of reality breaches.

But there was no "someone else." Conventional authorities would dismiss their evidence as elaborate hoaxes or delusions. And the Department of Temporal Security—the only organization that would understand the true significance—was actively causing the problem.

"I can't tell you it's safe," Alice said honestly. "But I can tell you it's necessary. If Thomas is right about the consequences of uncontrolled breach expansion, we may be the only people positioned to prevent a catastrophe."

Maya studied her coffee cup, considering. "When I contacted you three years ago about my quantum theories of paranormal phenomena, you were politely dismissive. What changed? Why are you so certain now?"

Alice hesitated, then reached into her pocket and removed the broken pendant with its embedded microchip. "My grandmother knew. Somehow, she knew I would eventually discover the breaches, and she prepared for it. She left me protection, markers, breadcrumbs to follow."

"Margaret Chen was a brilliant physicist," Maya acknowledged. "If she believed this was important enough to create a decades-long contingency plan..."

"Then it's important enough for us to see through," Alice finished.

Maya fell silent, the weight of the decision evident in her expression. After a long moment, she straightened her shoulders, resolution replacing uncertainty.

"I've spent my career being the academic laughingstock for suggesting exactly what we're now witnessing," she said with quiet determination. "I'm not backing away when I finally have proof."

Relief washed through Alice. Having Maya's expertise would be crucial for understanding the quantum aspects of the breaches—aspects that extended far beyond Alice's paranormal investigation experience.

"Thank you," she said simply.

Maya nodded, then turned back to her data. "We should focus on understanding the access mechanisms for the original facility. If your grandmother left the pendant as a key, there must be more to the access sequence than what we tried."

"The symbols on the wall," Alice suggested. "They might be part of it."

"Yes, but there's something we're missing." Maya frowned in concentration. "The quantum equations represent barrier theory, but they're incomplete. It's as if..."

"As if they're waiting for the other half," Alice finished, a realization dawning. "Maya, when my grandmother gave me the pendant, she said something I never fully understood. She said it was 'half the key to understanding.'"

Maya's eyes widened. "The pendant is only half the access mechanism. There must be another component."

Their theorizing was interrupted by Alice's phone vibrating. A text from Detective Rivera: "Found files you requested. Strange flags on them. Meet tomorrow, usual place, 10 AM."

Alice showed Maya the message. "Rivera's found the old case files on Project Resonance."

"That's potentially valuable, but also concerning," Maya noted. "If these files have 'strange flags,' someone is monitoring access to them. Rivera's request may have triggered alerts."

"We'll need to be careful how we proceed," Alice agreed. "The Department likely has surveillance capabilities within standard government systems."

As they continued strategizing, Alice noticed a black sedan pull into the diner's parking lot. Its headlights extinguished, but no one emerged from the vehicle. A prickle of awareness traveled up her spine—the same sensation she'd felt in Echo Alley when Thomas warned her she was being watched.

"We should leave," she said quietly, gathering her notes. "Separately. I'll take the back exit through the kitchen. You wait five minutes, then leave through the front."

Maya glanced subtly toward the windows, understanding immediately. "Where do we regroup?"

Alice wrote an address on a napkin and slid it across the table. "Go there instead of your home or office. It's a safe location." She didn't elaborate that the address belonged to a property she maintained under a different name—a precaution established years ago after a particularly dangerous investigation had brought unwanted attention.

As Alice prepared to leave, Maya caught her wrist briefly. "Alice, there's something I haven't told you. Something about Thomas Webb's Resonance Cascade Theory."

Alice paused, noting the grave concern in Maya's expression.

"The equations in his final paper—the one published just before his death—contain a warning disguised in the mathematics," Maya continued quietly. "It took me years to recognize it, but it's there if you understand the implications. According to his calculations, once reality breaches exceed a certain threshold, collapse isn't just possible—it's inevitable. And based on the readings we've collected..."

"How close are we to that threshold?" Alice asked, dreading the answer.

Maya met her gaze steadily. "If the expansion continues at current rates, we have less than seventy-two hours before the breach becomes irreversible."

The implications settled over Alice like a physical weight. Three days to locate the resonance amplifiers, neutralize them, and prevent reality collapse—all while evading an organization with seemingly unlimited resources and the willingness to eliminate anyone who interfered.

"I'll see you at the safe house," Alice said, new urgency in her voice. "And Maya—be careful. Really careful."

The physicist nodded, her academic demeanor now replaced by the solemnity of someone who understood exactly what was at stake.

Alice slipped through the diner's kitchen, ignoring the startled looks from late-night staff, and exited into the alley behind the building. She paused in the shadows, scanning for surveillance, then moved quickly toward the adjacent street where she could summon a rideshare vehicle instead of risking her own car.

As she waited in the shadows, Alice reviewed everything they had learned. The Department was actively suppressing the breach at Echo Alley, likely because they had detected her communications with Thomas. They were monitoring both Alice and Maya. And according to Maya's analysis, they had less than three days before reality reached a point of no return.

Alice touched the pocket containing her grandmother's broken pendant. Margaret Chen had known this moment would come. She had prepared for it across decades, leaving a trail for Alice to follow. There had to be more—more breadcrumbs, more keys to understanding what was happening and how to stop it.

The most pressing question remained unanswered: if the pendant was half the key, where was the other half? And what would it unlock when they found it?

CHAPTER SEVEN: DEPARTMENT INTERFERENCE

Alice Chen arrived at Westlake Park fifteen minutes early for her meeting with Detective Rivera, using the time to secure the perimeter—an old habit that had served her well through years of paranormal investigation. The park was busier than ideal, populated with morning joggers, parents with strollers, and office workers taking shortcuts to the business district. Witnesses provided safety, but also complicated surveillance detection.

She chose a bench with clear sightlines to all park entrances, positioning herself to appear casual while maintaining optimal awareness of her surroundings. The broken pendant with its quantum resonator chip rested in her pocket, its absence from around her neck still disconcerting after decades of wearing it.

Detective Rivera appeared precisely at 10 AM, wearing his standard-issue police jacket despite the mild weather—a deliberate choice, Alice suspected, to establish official presence. He carried no visible files, only a paper coffee cup that he gripped too tightly.

"Walk with me," he said instead of greeting her, continuing past her bench without slowing.

Alice fell into step beside him, immediately noting his tension—jaw clenched, gaze constantly shifting, posture rigid. This wasn't the usual irritation Rivera displayed when dealing with her paranormal cases. This was something more profound.

"Problems?" she asked quietly as they followed a winding path away from the main thoroughfare.

"You could say that." Rivera kept his voice low. "Twelve minutes after I accessed those files you requested, I had visitors. Two agents, credentials identifying them as Department of Energy security division. Asked very specific questions about why a homicide detective was pulling decades-old files about Quantum Dynamics."

Alice maintained a neutral expression despite the alarm bells ringing in her mind. "What did you tell them?"

"That I was reviewing cold cases with potential connections to current investigations. Standard procedure." Rivera glanced at her. "They didn't believe me. Made that clear without saying it directly."

"Did they mention me?"

"Not by name. But they asked if I was working with any 'external consultants' on the warehouse district case." Rivera stopped walking, turning to face her directly. "Chen, what exactly have you stumbled into? These weren't regular feds. There was something... off about them."

Alice considered how much to reveal. Rivera had always maintained professional skepticism about her work, acknowledging her results while maintaining distance from her methods. Bringing him deeper into this could put him at risk—but he was already involved.

"I believe Quantum Dynamics conducted experiments in the 1950s that had unexpected long-term effects on the warehouse district," she said carefully. "Effects that are intensifying and potentially dangerous. The voices in Echo Alley appear to be related to these experiments."

Rivera studied her face, clearly recognizing the careful editing in her explanation. "These agents weren't just following up on a records request. They had my complete access history, knew about cases we've worked together, mentioned the warehouse district by name even though I never specified it in my file request."

"They were already monitoring you," Alice concluded. "Because of your association with me."

"Exactly." Rivera's expression hardened. "Which means you've been under surveillance for some time. Whatever you're investigating has serious attention from people with high-level access."

He reached into his jacket pocket and withdrew a small USB drive, passing it to her with a subtle movement that would appear casual to distant observers.

"I copied what I could before they arrived," he said. "Not complete files—many sections were already redacted—but enough to establish that Project Resonance was real, and that it involved your grandmother."

Alice pocketed the drive, a mixture of gratitude and concern washing through her. "Thank you. This was a significant risk."

"That's not all." Rivera hesitated, internal conflict evident in his expression. "After they left, I ran background checks on the credentials they presented. The division they claimed to represent doesn't officially exist. And the agents themselves? No record in any federal database I have access to."

A chill ran through Alice despite the morning sun. "Ghost agents from a shadow department."

"Sounds like one of your paranormal theories," Rivera said with a grim smile. "Except I saw them with my own eyes." He checked his watch. "I need to get back to the station. They're probably monitoring this meeting, but I doubt they can hear us at this distance."

"What will you tell them if they ask?"

"That you're pursuing a theory about toxic chemical exposure causing auditory hallucinations in the warehouse district. That I think you're wasting your time but following up as procedure requires." Rivera met her gaze directly. "Chen, whatever you've found, these people are serious about keeping it contained. Watch yourself."

"You too, Detective. Your involvement won't go unnoticed."

Rivera nodded. "One more thing. After our meeting yesterday, I had the feeling I was being followed. Took countermeasures, thought I'd lost them. This morning, I found this under my personal vehicle."

He showed her a phone screen displaying a small black device—a tracking unit attached to the undercarriage of a car.

"Professional grade," Alice noted. "Not standard FBI or local surveillance."

"Exactly my assessment." Rivera pocketed his phone. "I left it in place. Better to know I'm being tracked than to alert them that I've found it."

"Smart move."

Rivera hesitated, then added, "Chen, I've worked with you on enough strange cases to know when something is beyond standard explanation. Whatever is happening in that alley... be careful. And if you need backup—official or unofficial—you have my number."

The offer surprised Alice. Rivera had always maintained a professional distance, accepting her results while avoiding direct involvement in her methods. This was the closest he'd come to acknowledging the legitimacy of her work.

"Thank you, James," she said, using his first name for perhaps the first time in their professional relationship.

He nodded once, then turned and walked away, resuming the purposeful stride of a detective with too many cases and too little time.

Alice remained in the park for another twenty minutes, using various techniques to detect surveillance—changing directions suddenly, doubling back on paths, observing reflective surfaces for consistent faces or figures. Nothing obvious presented itself, but the sensation of being watched persisted.

Rather than returning to her apartment directly, she took a circuitous route through Daybridge, using public transportation and commercial buildings with multiple exits to create a path difficult to follow. If the Department had resources to place tracking devices on police vehicles, they almost certainly had similar surveillance on her car—which was why she'd left it parked at a long-term garage across town.

When she finally approached her apartment building two hours later, a sense of wrongness immediately prickled at the base of her skull. Nothing visibly amiss—the street looked normal, her building undisturbed—but Alice had learned to trust her instincts about subtle environmental shifts.

Instead of entering through the main door, she circled to the service entrance, accessing the building through the laundry room. She climbed the back stairs rather than using the elevator, moving silently down the hallway toward her unit.

The confirmation of her suspicions came as she approached her door—a nearly imperceptible strip of light visible at the floor edge, indicating the door wasn't fully closed. Alice had left it locked with additional security measures that wouldn't have allowed such a gap.

Someone had entered her apartment.

Alice considered her options. The logical choice was retreat—contact authorities, report a break-in, avoid potential confrontation. But if the intruders were from the Department, official response would be worthless at best, dangerous at worst.

She needed to know what they'd taken, what they knew about her investigation.

Silently, Alice approached her door, listening for movement inside. Hearing nothing, she carefully pushed the door open with her elbow, keeping her body to the side in case of immediate threat.

The apartment beyond was still, but visibly disturbed. Not ransacked with obvious violence—this had been a methodical search by professionals. Books removed from shelves and replaced slightly out of alignment. Furniture shifted minimally from original positions. Computer equipment superficially undisturbed but likely compromised.

Most tellingly, her investigation board had been carefully dismantled—photographs removed, notes confiscated, connection threads cut and discarded. The entire Echo Alley case had been systematically erased from her workspace.

Alice moved through the apartment quickly, cataloging the damage. Her hidden wall safe remained secure—the Department's agents either hadn't found it or hadn't managed to breach its protections. Her backup hard drives, concealed in a hollowed-out section of flooring beneath her bed, also appeared untouched.

But her active case files—particularly those related to the warehouse district and other potential reality breach locations—had been taken. Years of paranormal investigation notes, carefully organized and cross-referenced, gone.

In the kitchen, a final confirmation awaited. The police scanner she maintained had been modified—subtle changes to its casing indicating the installation of surveillance equipment. They hadn't removed it, wanting her to continue using it while they monitored her communications.

Alice resisted the urge to immediately contact Maya. If her apartment had been compromised, her communications were likely monitored as well. Instead, she gathered essential supplies—cash, identification, clothing, and emergency equipment—into a small backpack. She retrieved her backup drives from their hiding place and the contents of her wall safe, adding them to the pack.

As she prepared to leave, Alice noticed one final detail—a small envelope placed in the center of her kitchen table. She approached it cautiously, examining it without touching. No visible name or address, just a plain white business envelope.

Using a pen, she carefully opened the flap, revealing a single sheet of paper inside. The message was brief, typed in standard font without signature:

"Curiosity has consequences. Final warning."

The threat was clear, but its delivery method told Alice something important—the Department wanted to intimidate her into backing down rather than simply eliminating her as they had Thomas Webb. Perhaps her public profile as a paranormal investigator provided some protection; her disappearance would raise questions among clients, witnesses, and contacts like Rivera.

Alice photographed the note, then left it in place. She exited her apartment through the window, descending the fire escape to the alley below. From there, she navigated Daybridge's back streets toward the safe house where Maya was waiting.

The property—a small cottage on the city's eastern edge—was registered to Elena Martinez, a name Alice had created years earlier as a security measure. She had purchased it through a complex series of legal structures that would be difficult to trace back to her. Few people knew of its existence, and she had used it only during her most sensitive investigations.

Maya answered the door immediately when Alice knocked, relief evident in her expression. "I was getting worried. You're three hours late."

"Had to take precautions," Alice explained, stepping inside and securing the door behind her. "My apartment's been compromised. The Department searched it, took my case files on the warehouse district."

Maya's expression darkened. "They moved faster than I expected. Have you been followed?"

"I don't think so, but we should assume they have resources we can't easily detect." Alice set down her backpack, surveying the cottage's main room. Maya had already established a makeshift research station—laptop connected to portable instruments, printouts of data arranged in neat stacks, a whiteboard covered with equations.

"I've been analyzing the readings from Echo Alley," Maya explained, leading Alice to her workstation. "The quantum fluctuations follow a distinct pattern that corresponds to what Thomas described—deliberate widening followed by partial stabilization. But there's something else."

She pointed to a graph showing energy measurements over time. "See these spikes? They occur at precisely scheduled intervals—3:17

AM, 12:42 PM, and 8:05 PM daily. Too precise to be natural phenomena."

"Activation times for the resonance amplifiers," Alice suggested.

"That would be my hypothesis," Maya agreed. "And here's where it gets concerning." She indicated another data set. "Each activation results in a larger quantum variance than the previous one. The expansions are accelerating."

Alice studied the projections. "If this continues..."

"Reality breach reaches critical threshold in approximately sixty-four hours," Maya confirmed grimly. "Slightly sooner than my initial estimate."

"Then we have just over two and a half days to locate the amplifiers and neutralize them." Alice moved to the whiteboard, studying Maya's equations. "Any progress on accessing the original facility?"

"Some theoretical progress," Maya said. "I've been analyzing the symbols we found on the wall in Echo Alley. They form part of a quantum access equation—essentially a mathematical key. But as you suggested, it's incomplete."

"Half the key," Alice murmured, removing the broken pendant from her pocket. "My grandmother said this was half the key to understanding."

Maya nodded. "I believe the quantum resonator chip contains encoded mathematical parameters that complete the equation on the wall. Together, they would form the full access sequence."

"But how do we access the data in the chip? It's not a standard storage device."

"No, it's far more sophisticated." Maya led Alice to a makeshift laboratory setup in the cottage's small dining area. "I've been examining its structure with the equipment I brought. The resonator operates on quantum entanglement principles—it's designed to interact with very specific quantum frequencies."

"Like those in Echo Alley," Alice concluded.

"Exactly. The wall scanner we found is likely calibrated to read both the physical key—the pendant—and the quantum signature of its authorized user." Maya looked at Alice significantly. "Your quantum signature."

Alice processed this. "You're saying my grandmother designed a system that would only work for me specifically? How is that possible?"

"Quantum genetics," Maya explained. "Our quantum signatures are partially inherited—passed down through familial lines like genetic code. Margaret Chen could have calibrated the system to recognize her own quantum signature and those of her direct descendants."

The implications were staggering. Her grandmother hadn't just left breadcrumbs—she had created an entire security system designed specifically for Alice to access decades later.

"We need to return to Echo Alley," Alice said.

"Not possible at the moment," Maya countered. "After you left for your meeting with Rivera, I deployed remote monitoring devices near the alley—small, passive sensors that wouldn't attract attention. The Department has established a permanent presence there. Two agents disguised as security personnel, advanced scanning equipment, and what appears to be a quantum dampening field to prevent further communications through the breach."

Alice frowned. "They're locking down the most accessible breach point."

"Which suggests they know exactly what it is and how it functions," Maya noted. "These aren't people stumbling onto strange phenomena—they've been monitoring and manipulating these breaches for decades."

Alice considered their options. "If we can't access Echo Alley directly, we need another approach. The original Project Resonance facility must have multiple access points—emergency exits, ventilation systems, utility connections."

"Agreed. I've been researching the original building plans for the warehouse district." Maya brought up architectural schematics on her laptop. "Before the current structures were built in the 1970s, the Quantum Dynamics facility occupied approximately three city blocks. Most of it was above ground, but there were extensive sublevels—designated areas for equipment too sensitive to risk exposure."

Alice studied the plans. "These sublevels—do they extend beyond the current warehouse footprint?"

"That's what's interesting," Maya said, highlighting sections of the schematics. "According to these plans, certain sublevel corridors extend well beyond the main facility—connecting to what are labeled as 'auxiliary monitoring stations' throughout this section of Daybridge."

"The other breach points," Alice realized. "The facility was built to monitor and study multiple reality thin spots."

"And those connections might still exist beneath the city, even after the above-ground structures were demolished and replaced." Maya switched to a modern map of Daybridge, overlaying the historical schematics. "If we can locate one of these auxiliary stations away from the warehouse district, we might find an alternative entrance to the facility."

Alice pulled out her own maps of paranormal hotspots throughout Daybridge—locations where she'd documented unexplained phenomena over the years. She compared them to Maya's overlay.

"Here," she said, pointing to a location approximately a mile from the warehouse district. "The Westlake Park apparitions I investigated three years ago. The sightings concentrated around the central fountain. According to these schematics, that area aligns with one of the auxiliary monitoring stations."

"The park would provide good cover for investigation," Maya noted. "Public space, multiple access points, difficult to monitor completely."

"We should move quickly," Alice said. "The Department is consolidating control over Echo Alley, but they may not yet have secured all the auxiliary stations."

Maya began gathering essential equipment. "We'll need the quantum variance monitor, the resonator chip, and..." She hesitated, looking at Alice. "We'll need protection. If the Department is actively removing evidence and threatening you, our next steps carry significant risk."

Alice nodded, retrieving her phone and scrolling through contacts. "I have resources—people who've witnessed paranormal phenomena firsthand, who understand that conventional authorities aren't always reliable in these situations."

"Your network of paranormal witnesses and informants," Maya said with a hint of surprise. "I hadn't considered that aspect of your work."

"People who've experienced the unexplained tend to maintain a connection with others who believe them," Alice explained. "Over the years, I've built relationships with dozens of Daybridge residents who've encountered phenomena beyond conventional explanation. Many of them owe me for validating experiences others dismissed."

She sent a series of carefully worded text messages to key contacts, using prearranged code phrases that would communicate urgency without explicitly stating their situation.

"We'll need transportation, surveillance, possibly temporary shelter," Alice explained as she worked. "People who can move around Daybridge without attracting attention."

"Civilians against a government agency," Maya said doubtfully. "Is that wise?"

"The Department operates in shadows," Alice replied. "Their power comes from official denial and public ignorance. They're not equipped to handle a distributed network of ordinary people who understand what's at stake."

Within twenty minutes, responses began arriving—offers of assistance, transportation, safe houses. The network Alice had cultivated through years of paranormal investigation was activating, creating a web of support throughout Daybridge.

"We move at dusk," Alice decided, checking her watch. "That gives us approximately four hours to prepare. We'll approach Westlake Park separately, from different directions, and meet at the fountain."

Maya nodded, returning to her equipment preparation. "I'll configure the sensors to detect quantum variance patterns similar to those in Echo Alley. If there's an access point near the fountain, it should register on our instruments."

As they prepared for the evening operation, Alice reviewed the USB drive Rivera had provided. The files were fragmentary—many sections redacted even before Rivera's copying—but they confirmed the essential facts about Project Resonance.

The project had begun in 1955 as a Department of Energy initiative to study "non-standard quantum phenomena" observed in specific locations throughout Daybridge. Margaret Chen had joined as a theoretical physicist in 1956, quickly becoming central to the research team's understanding of what they were observing—what one document described as "apparent breaches in conventional reality parameters."

The most significant document was a partially redacted memo from Margaret Chen to project leadership, dated two weeks before the "containment incident" that had shut down the facility:

"... the breaches appear to be naturally occurring quantum phenomena, but our attempts to widen them for observation are creating instability across multiple [REDACTED]. Continued expansion of Breach Point Alpha will probably result in [REDACTED] beyond our capacity to contain. I strongly recommend immediate cessation of all amplification protocols and implementation of the barrier stabilization methods outlined in my previous report."

The memo had apparently been ignored or overruled. The containment incident occurred exactly 16 days later, resulting in project termination and facility evacuation.

Alice shared the findings with Maya, who studied the documents with growing concern.

"Your grandmother saw this coming," she said. "She recognized the dangers of artificial breach expansion decades ago."

"And now the Department is ignoring the same warnings," Alice noted grimly. "History repeating itself, but potentially with far worse consequences."

As dusk approached, they finalized their plans. Maya would approach the park from the north, carrying the scientific equipment disguised in ordinary bags. Alice would come from the south, maintaining surveillance for Department agents.

They packed their essential materials and prepared to leave the safe house, knowing they might not be able to return if the Department had somehow tracked them.

"Sixty-one hours," Maya said quietly, checking her calculations one final time. "That's our remaining window before the breach expansion becomes irreversible."

Alice nodded, the weight of responsibility settling across her shoulders. "Then we'd better not waste a minute."

As they prepared to separate, Alice's phone chimed with an incoming text. The message was from an unknown number, but its content froze her blood:

"Department agents at Westlake Park. Fountain under surveillance. ABORT."

CHAPTER EIGHT: THE OTHER DETECTIVE

"They're watching all the known breach points," said Eliza Weiss, sliding a hand-drawn map across the table. "Westlake Park, St. Christopher's Hospital, the Holloway House—anywhere with documented paranormal activity."

Alice studied the map in the dim light of the basement storage room. Eliza—a former client who now managed inventory for Daybridge Medical Center—had responded immediately to Alice's emergency message, offering both transportation and temporary shelter among the hospital's labyrinthine underground storage facilities.

"How did you get this information?" Maya asked, examining the detailed surveillance notations.

"My brother works security for Hammond Properties," Eliza explained. "They own half the commercial buildings in Daybridge. He noticed men in suits setting up 'maintenance equipment' at specific locations yesterday. No work orders, no prior notification—just federal credentials and terse explanations about infrastructure inspections."

Alice recognized the pattern from the equipment she'd seen in Echo Alley. "They're establishing a perimeter. Securing all potential access points to the sublevel facility."

"Which means they know exactly what we're looking for," Maya added grimly.

The warning text about Westlake Park had forced a rapid change in plans. Instead of approaching the fountain, Alice and Maya had separated and gone dark, using predetermined emergency protocols to reconnect through Alice's network of contacts. They'd spent six hours being shuttled between safe locations before Eliza had arranged their current refuge—a forgotten storage room beneath Daybridge Medical Center's east wing.

"We need to find an access point they've overlooked," Alice said, studying the map. "Somewhere connected to the original facility but not associated with documented paranormal phenomena."

Maya adjusted her glasses, examining the architectural overlays she'd compiled. "The challenge is that the breach points and access points are inherently connected. The facility was built specifically to monitor natural thin spots in reality."

"Not necessarily all of them," Alice countered. "My case files showed paranormal reports predating Project Resonance. The facility studied existing breaches, but they might not have documented every minor anomaly."

She pulled out her own map of Daybridge's paranormal hotspots—reconstructed from memory after the Department's confiscation of her original files. "There are locations with subtle phenomena that never generated enough activity to warrant full investigation. Places I noted but classified as low priority."

Alice indicated several points scattered throughout Daybridge—a stretch of riverside where joggers occasionally reported time discrepancies, an intersection where electronic devices temporarily malfunctioned, a small church where parishioners sometimes heard hymns when the building was empty.

"Minor reality fluctuations," Maya said, understanding immediately. "Potentially connected to the major breach points but too subtle to attract significant attention."

"And potentially overlooked in the Department's surveillance setup," Alice concluded.

They compared the minor anomaly locations with Maya's architectural overlays of the original facility. Most showed no meaningful correlation, but one point aligned with what appeared to be a maintenance tunnel extending from the main sublevel structure.

"Colfax Tunnel," Alice said, identifying the location. "An old pedestrian underpass near the river. It was closed to public access in the 1980s after repeated flooding, but it's still structurally intact."

"And it shows alignment with an auxiliary service tunnel from the original facility," Maya noted, tracing the connection on the overlaid maps. "This could be our access point."

Eliza checked her watch. "It's nearly midnight. Security shifts change at 12:30—that's your best window to move through the hospital undetected."

Alice nodded. "We'll need transportation to Colfax Tunnel. Something untraceable."

"My cousin drives for MetroCab," Eliza offered. "He can pick you up at the service entrance. No digital record, cash payment only."

As Eliza left to make arrangements, Maya continued calibrating her equipment for their expedition. The quantum variance monitor had been modified to detect the subtle fluctuations that might indicate a reality breach, while remaining inconspicuous enough to avoid immediate recognition as specialized scientific equipment.

"If we find an access point," Maya said quietly, "what exactly is our plan? The Department has resources, personnel, and apparently decades of experience with these breaches. We're two people with limited equipment and a theoretical understanding of quantum reality interfaces."

It was a fair question—one Alice had been grappling with since their escape from Echo Alley. The scale of what they faced was daunting: a covert government organization, potentially catastrophic reality destabilization, and less than sixty hours remaining before breach expansion became irreversible.

"We need more information," Alice acknowledged. "Specifically, we need to understand how the resonance amplifiers work and where they're positioned. Once inside the facility, we focus on gathering intelligence, not direct confrontation."

Maya nodded, accepting the pragmatic approach. "And if we encounter Department personnel?"

"We avoid detection at all costs," Alice said firmly. "This is reconnaissance only."

Their preparations continued in focused silence until Eliza returned with confirmation of transportation arrangements. The cab would meet them at 12:35 AM, providing exactly enough time to navigate through the hospital's service corridors to the pickup point.

As they gathered their equipment, Alice felt the familiar weight of investigation settling across her shoulders—the responsibility of pursuing truth regardless of personal risk. But this case had escalated beyond anything in her experience, with consequences extending far beyond Daybridge if they failed.

"Ready?" she asked Maya, who nodded with the determined expression of a scientist venturing beyond theoretical understanding into practical application.

They followed Eliza through the dimly lit corridors of the hospital's basement level, passing storage rooms filled with obsolete equipment and archived records. The facility's night sounds created an eerie backdrop—distant mechanical systems, occasional voices echoing through ventilation ducts, the persistent hum of fluorescent lighting.

At precisely 12:35 AM, they emerged from a service door into the cool night air. A taxi waited with headlights dimmed, its driver offering only a silent nod as they entered the back seat. No words were exchanged as the vehicle pulled away from the hospital, following a circuitous route through Daybridge's quieter neighborhoods.

Twenty minutes later, they were dropped at a public park two blocks from Colfax Tunnel. The driver accepted cash payment and departed without comment, leaving Alice and Maya to approach their destination on foot.

The tunnel entrance was partially concealed by overgrown vegetation and municipal neglect—a curved archway of aged concrete descending below street level, sealed with a chain-link gate bearing faded "No Trespassing" signs. Alice made quick work of the padlock using skills developed during years of accessing abandoned properties for paranormal investigation.

"Stay close," she whispered to Maya as they descended the crumbling concrete steps into darkness. Their flashlights revealed a curved passage extending approximately thirty meters before ending in a collapse of concrete and earth—the reason for the tunnel's closure decades earlier.

Maya activated her equipment, scanning for quantum fluctuations as they moved deeper into the passage. The initial readings showed nothing unusual—just the standard background variance present in any location.

"Either there's no breach point here, or it's too subtle for surface detection," Maya murmured, adjusting her instruments.

Alice examined the tunnel walls carefully, looking for any indication of hidden access or unusual features. The concrete was stained with mineral deposits from years of water seepage, creating patterns that obscured potential markings or modifications.

"Wait," Alice said suddenly, her flashlight illuminating a section of wall near the tunnel's midpoint. "This concrete is different."

Maya joined her, examining the variation in material. A rectangular section approximately two meters high by one meter wide showed subtle differences in texture and color from the surrounding wall—differences only noticeable under direct examination.

"Newer material," Maya confirmed. "Possibly installed decades after the original construction."

Alice ran her hands across the surface, feeling for inconsistencies. Near the bottom edge, her fingers detected a small depression—a circular indentation approximately three centimeters in diameter, almost completely concealed by mineral buildup.

"This could be a scanner similar to the one in Echo Alley," she said, carefully cleaning the depression with a small brush from her equipment bag.

Once cleared, the indentation revealed a metallic surface within—definitely not standard infrastructure for a pedestrian tunnel. Alice removed the quantum resonator chip from her pocket, examining it thoughtfully.

"If this is half the key," she said, "we still need the other half to complete the access sequence."

Maya's equipment suddenly emitted a soft alert, drawing their attention. "Quantum variance increasing," she reported, checking the readings. "Very subtle, but definitely above baseline. There's a breach point nearby."

Alice focused on the modified section of wall, considering options. "My grandmother said the pendant was half the key to understanding. The wall in Echo Alley had mathematical symbols—equations related to quantum barrier theory."

"Which we theorized might be the other half of the access sequence," Maya completed the thought. "But we don't have those equations here."

"Maybe we don't need the specific symbols," Alice suggested. "If the quantum resonator is designed to interact with my specific genetic signature, perhaps that's the primary authentication. The mathematical component might be secondary—a conceptual key rather than a literal one."

Maya considered this. "It's possible. Quantum authentication systems often use multiple factors—something you have, something you are, and something you know. The resonator is what you have, your quantum genetic signature is what you are..."

"And understanding the nature of reality breaches is what I know," Alice finished. "My grandmother wasn't being poetic when she called it a key to understanding. The understanding itself is part of the key."

It was a theoretical leap but aligned with everything they'd learned about Margaret Chen's methodical preparation across decades. She hadn't just left tools for Alice to find—she'd ensured Alice would develop the necessary conceptual framework to use them properly.

Alice placed the quantum resonator chip against the metallic depression, simultaneously focusing her thoughts on what she'd learned about reality breaches—their nature, their behavior, the mathematical principles Maya had explained governing quantum interfaces between adjacent realities.

For several seconds, nothing happened. Then a faint vibration emanated from the wall, accompanied by a low-frequency hum at the edge of audible perception. The quantum variance monitor's readings spiked dramatically.

"Something's happening," Maya whispered, eyes fixed on her instruments.

The rectangular section of wall began to shift—not swinging open like a conventional door, but seeming to phase partially out of alignment with surrounding reality. The concrete surface remained visibly intact while simultaneously allowing passage through it, creating a portal that defied standard physical principles.

"Phase-shifted matter," Maya breathed, scientific awe overriding caution momentarily. "Theoretical quantum tunneling applied to macroscopic objects. This technology shouldn't have been possible in the 1950s."

"I don't think it was," Alice replied quietly. "I think they discovered it rather than invented it."

Beyond the phase-shifted portal, a narrow corridor extended into darkness—clearly not part of the original tunnel infrastructure. The passage was lined with conduits and cabling that appeared both antiquated and eerily advanced, as if technologies from different eras had been integrated into a single system.

Alice stepped forward cautiously, passing through the portal with a momentary sensation of pins-and-needles across her entire body. Maya followed, her equipment continuing to register elevated quantum variance readings.

The corridor extended approximately twenty meters before intersecting with a larger passage. Unlike the rough concrete of the access tunnel, these walls featured smooth, almost pearlescent surfaces embedded with what appeared to be circuit pathways—technology unlike anything Alice had seen before.

"This doesn't match the architectural plans," Maya noted, examining their surroundings with scientific precision. "The materials, the design—none of this aligns with 1950s construction capabilities."

"Because it wasn't built by Project Resonance," Alice said, realization dawning as she studied the alien aesthetics of the passage. "They discovered it. The facility wasn't built to study reality breaches—it was built around them."

They continued cautiously, following the main passage as it curved gradually downward. Environmental systems hummed softly in the background—air circulation, power distribution, other functions less easily identified. Despite being abandoned for decades, the facility appeared to maintain basic operational status.

After approximately five minutes of careful progress, they reached a junction where the passage split into three separate corridors. Each branch featured distinct illumination—subtle variations in the pearlescent glow emanating from the walls themselves.

"Which way?" Maya whispered, consulting her instruments. "I'm detecting quantum variance fluctuations from all three directions."

Alice studied the junction carefully, noting subtle differences in the circuit-like patterns embedded in each corridor's walls. The left passage contained predominantly linear patterns, the center featured more circular configurations, while the right displayed complex geometric shapes reminiscent of the symbols from Echo Alley.

"Right," Alice decided, recognizing the similarity to her grandmother's quantum equations. "This passage seems connected to the mathematics of reality breaches."

They proceeded down the right corridor, which maintained its gentle downward slope while gradually widening. The quantum variance readings continued to increase, suggesting they were approaching a significant breach point.

After another hundred meters, the passage opened into a circular chamber approximately fifteen meters in diameter. The room's central feature immediately drew their attention—a raised platform containing what appeared to be control systems surrounding a transparent cylindrical column that extended from floor to ceiling.

Within the column, visible energy patterns shifted and flowed like luminescent smoke, occasionally coalescing into recognizable structures before dissolving again. The sight was mesmerizing, almost hypnotic in its fluid movements.

"It's a visualization system," Maya said, approaching cautiously. "Some kind of interface for observing quantum variance patterns. These control panels appear designed to modify parameters, adjust viewpoints."

Alice circled the platform, examining the technology with growing amazement. "This room was designed for direct observation and interaction with reality breaches."

The control panels featured an unusual integration of conventional switches and dials alongside more exotic interface elements—crystalline structures that responded to proximity, surfaces that shifted configuration based on user interaction. It was clearly designed for human operation, yet incorporated principles beyond standard human technology.

"I think I can activate the main observation system," Maya said, studying the controls. "Many of these elements correspond to quantum field theory principles, just using an unfamiliar interface design."

"Carefully," Alice cautioned. "We don't know if activation might trigger alerts elsewhere in the facility."

Maya nodded, proceeding with methodical precision. She adjusted several controls in sequence, monitoring responses through her own equipment before making additional changes. Gradually, the energy patterns within the central column stabilized, forming a more coherent visualization.

"I believe this is showing us the current state of the reality breach network throughout Daybridge," Maya explained, interpreting the patterns. "Each of these nodal points corresponds to a significant breach location."

Alice studied the visualization, recognizing the spatial arrangement. "Echo Alley is the central node. The other major breach points form a geometric pattern around it—exactly matching the paranormal hotspots I've documented over the years."

"And these smaller connections between nodes—" Maya indicated filament-like structures connecting the major points, "—appear to be the reality 'thin spots' you identified, the minor anomalies throughout Daybridge."

As they examined the visualization, a rhythmic pulsation became apparent—regular surges of energy flowing through the network at precisely timed intervals.

"The resonance amplifiers," Alice realized. "They're generating energy pulses to systematically widen the breaches."

Maya checked her instruments, correlating the pulses with her previous measurements. "The timing matches exactly with the activation pattern I documented—3:17 AM, 12:42 PM, and 8:05 PM daily."

She manipulated additional controls, expanding the visualization to show temporal patterns. "Based on this data, the expansion has accelerated dramatically in the past six months. Prior to that, the breaches were maintained at relatively stable parameters for decades."

"Something changed," Alice said. "Some new objective or directive."

Their analysis was interrupted by a sudden shift in the energy patterns—a disruption that rippled through the visualization like a stone dropped in still water. The quantum variance monitor emitted an alert tone, registering a significant spike in readings.

"Something's happening," Maya said, checking her instruments. "Quantum variance increasing beyond predicted parameters."

The central column's energy patterns intensified, colors shifting toward blue-violet wavelengths. Within the visualization, the Echo Alley node pulsed with increasing brightness.

"It's 3:17 AM," Alice noted, checking her watch. "The scheduled amplification cycle."

Maya attempted to adjust the controls, seeking better visibility of the process, but the system responded sluggishly to her commands. "The amplifiers are activating. Energy output is significantly higher than previous cycles."

As they watched, the visualization showed energy concentrating at Echo Alley, then radiating outward through the network of connected breach points. The quantum variance readings continued to climb, exceeding Maya's predicted thresholds.

"This is beyond scheduled expansion," Maya said, concern evident in her voice. "They're pushing the boundaries more aggressively than before."

Alice studied the pattern, noting how the energy flowed through the network. "They're not just widening the breaches—they're synchronizing them, creating a resonant effect across multiple breach points simultaneously."

The visualization suddenly shifted again, but in an unexpected way. The energy patterns separated into distinct layers, as if the system was now displaying multiple versions of the same network overlaid on each other—each with subtle variations in configuration.

"What's happening?" Alice asked, watching the multiplying patterns with growing concern.

Maya adjusted controls rapidly, attempting to clarify the display. "I think we're seeing multiple timelines simultaneously—adjacent realities where the breach network exists in slightly different configurations."

As they struggled to interpret the increasingly complex visualization, a new phenomenon manifested within the central column. Amidst the swirling energy patterns, a human figure began to coalesce—hazy at first, then gradually gaining definition.

Alice stepped back, instinctively reaching for equipment to document the manifestation. The figure continued to solidify—a woman in her mid-thirties with shoulder-length black hair, wearing what appeared to be a tactical uniform with insignia Alice didn't recognize.

As the manifestation stabilized, Alice found herself looking at a face that was simultaneously foreign and intimately familiar—her own features, albeit with subtle differences. Different hairstyle, different expression, different bearing—but unmistakably Alice Chen.

"Maya," Alice said quietly, "are you seeing this?"

"Quantum coherence forming a macro-scale manifestation," Maya confirmed, her scientific detachment momentarily overwhelmed by the sight before them. "A visualization of—"

"An adjacent timeline version of you," the figure completed, her voice emanating from the column with surprising clarity. "Federal Agent Alice Chen, Department of Temporal Security, Timeline Designation AR-117."

Alice stared at her doppelgänger, mind racing to process the implications. "You're... me? From another timeline?"

"A version of you who made different choices," Agent Chen confirmed. "Who pursued different paths but ultimately arrived at the same discovery—the reality breach network beneath Daybridge."

"How is this communication possible?" Maya asked, scientific curiosity overriding momentary shock. "The quantum dampening fields at Echo Alley prevented contact with Thomas Webb."

"The amplification cycle creates temporary windows of opportunity," Agent Chen explained. "Moments when the barriers between realities thin sufficiently for direct communication. I've been attempting to establish contact for several cycles, waiting for you to access the observation chamber."

Alice studied her counterpart carefully, noting differences that reflected divergent life choices—the disciplined posture of formal training, a small scar along the jawline she herself didn't possess, eyes that held a harder edge than her own.

"You said Department of Temporal Security," Alice noted. "The same organization that's controlling the breaches in my timeline? The one that eliminated Thomas Webb?"

Agent Chen's expression tightened. "The Department exists across multiple timelines, with varying directives and ethics depending on local governance. In some realities, including yours, it operates as a rogue agency pursuing dangerous expansion of the breach network. In others, like mine, we work to stabilize and protect reality interfaces."

"Why contact us now?" Alice asked, caution tempering her fascination with this manifestation of an alternate self.

"Because you're approaching a critical threshold," Agent Chen replied gravely. "In approximately fifty-four hours, the expansion in your timeline will reach irreversible parameters. When that happens, reality collapse becomes inevitable—not just for your timeline, but for adjacent realities connected through the breach network."

"Including yours," Maya concluded.

Agent Chen nodded. "The Department in your timeline is pursuing technology transfer—attempting to create stable passages between realities to extract advanced technologies and intelligence. They believe they can control the process, establish permanent corridors between selected timelines while maintaining overall stability."

"But they're wrong," Alice said, recalling Thomas Webb's warning.

"Catastrophically wrong," Agent Chen confirmed. "We've witnessed collapse scenarios in three monitoring timelines already. The pattern is consistent—once expansion exceeds a critical threshold, reality destabilization accelerates exponentially. Complete breakdown follows within 72 hours."

The implications settled over Alice with crushing weight. Not just Daybridge at risk, not just their timeline, but multiple realities connected through the breach network—potentially billions of lives across parallel existences.

"How do we stop it?" she asked, focusing immediately on practical action.

"The resonance amplifiers are the key," Agent Chen explained. "The Department has installed seven primary devices at major breach points throughout Daybridge, with secondary amplifiers at minor nodes. The entire network is controlled from a central facility beneath the original Project Resonance site."

"The warehouse district," Alice confirmed.

"Specifically, a sublevel chamber directly beneath Echo Alley," Agent Chen clarified. "That location houses the master control system and the primary power source for the amplifier network."

Maya adjusted her instruments, documenting everything. "How do we neutralize the amplifiers? Simply destroying them could potentially cause catastrophic feedback throughout the network."

"Correct," Agent Chen acknowledged. "Uncontrolled deactivation would likely accelerate collapse rather than prevent it. You need the shutdown sequence—a calibrated deactivation protocol that allows reality barriers to naturally restabilize."

"And you have this sequence?" Alice asked.

Agent Chen's image fluctuated briefly, energy patterns within the column destabilizing momentarily before resolidifying. "Transmission window destabilizing. Limited time remaining."

She gestured toward the control panel, where a data port suddenly illuminated. "Connect your device. I'm transferring technical specifications for the amplifier network, location coordinates for all devices, and the emergency shutdown protocol."

Maya quickly attached her equipment to the indicated port, initiating data transfer. "Receiving now."

Agent Chen turned back to Alice, her expression intense. "There's something else you need to know. About Margaret Chen—your grandmother, my great-aunt."

Alice stepped closer to the column. "What about her?"

"She didn't just discover the breach network—she understood its true origin." Agent Chen's image flickered again, the connection weakening. "Project Resonance didn't create the breaches. They were studying something much older, something that existed beneath Daybridge long before human settlement."

"What was it?" Alice pressed, sensing the connection was failing.

"The breach network is an artificial construct," Agent Chen said, her voice beginning to break up. "Created by entities that move between realities. Your grandmother called them Tr—"

The transmission cut off abruptly, Agent Chen's image dissolving into fragmentary energy patterns before disappearing entirely. The central column returned to its previous state of swirling, undefined patterns.

"Connection lost," Maya reported, checking her instruments. "The amplification cycle is complete. Quantum variance returning to baseline."

Alice stared at the now-empty column, mind racing with the implications of what they'd learned—and what had been cut off before completion. "Did you get the data transfer?"

Maya nodded, disconnecting her equipment. "Complete download. Technical specifications, location coordinates, shutdown protocols—everything she promised."

"Then we have what we need," Alice said, determination replacing shock. "We know where the amplifiers are located and how to deactivate them."

"But we also have new questions," Maya noted. "If the breach network isn't natural—if it was created by some form of interdimensional entities—that changes our understanding of what we're dealing with."

Alice nodded, processing the revelation that had been interrupted at its most critical point. "My grandmother knew. Whatever these entities are, she discovered them during Project Resonance, recognized the danger they posed, and spent decades preparing for this moment."

She turned to Maya, new resolve hardening her features. "We have the shutdown protocol and fifty-three hours to implement it. Let's get moving."

As they prepared to leave the observation chamber, Alice cast one final glance at the central column where her alternate self had briefly manifested—a federal agent fighting the same battle from within the very organization that threatened reality in Alice's timeline.

Different choices, different paths, but ultimately the same purpose. The symmetry wasn't lost on Alice as they navigated back through the alien corridors toward the surface, carrying the information that might save multiple realities from collapse.

The game had changed. What began as an investigation into strange voices in an alley had escalated into a race to prevent catastrophic reality failure across multiple timelines—with less than fifty-three hours remaining before the point of no return.

CHAPTER NINE: THE COLD WAR EXPERIMENT

"The data transfer included classified files from Agent Chen's timeline," Maya explained, spreading printouts across the motel room desk. "Historical records, technical documentation, personnel files—information that doesn't exist in our reality anymore."

Dawn light filtered through the thin curtains of the roadside motel room they'd checked into using cash and false names—a precaution against Department surveillance. After escaping the underground facility, they'd traveled to the outskirts of Daybridge, deliberately avoiding locations connected to either of them.

Alice studied a black-and-white photograph showing a group of scientists posed before an imposing concrete building. "Project Resonance research team, 1956," read the caption. Her grandmother stood in the center row—younger than Alice had ever seen her in family photos, expression serious but eyes bright with the intensity of discovery.

"Eight primary researchers," Maya noted, "plus support staff and military oversight. According to Agent Chen's files, the project began as a standard Department of Energy initiative investigating unusual electromagnetic readings in the Daybridge area."

"But they found something unexpected," Alice continued, examining project summaries. "Quantum fluctuations that couldn't be explained by conventional physics—what they eventually identified as thin points between parallel realities."

The documentation painted a fascinating picture of Cold War science colliding with phenomena beyond its comprehension. Initial readings had attracted government attention due to potential weapons applications—energy signatures that might be harnessed for defense purposes. But as the research progressed, the focus shifted dramatically.

"They discovered communication was possible through the thin points," Alice said, reading from a partially redacted report. "Initially just quantum-level information transfer, then eventually coherent data transmission between adjacent timelines."

"The intelligence implications were immediately obvious," Maya added. "Imagine gaining information from a timeline where history unfolded differently—advance knowledge of technological developments, political outcomes, military strategies."

Alice turned to the next document—a memo from military oversight to project leadership dated October 1957:

"Successful information acquisition from Timeline Designate B-12 has provided critical intelligence regarding Soviet rocket development programs. Continued expansion of communication protocols is authorized with highest priority. Concerns regarding barrier stability are noted but considered acceptable risk given strategic advantages of cross-timeline intelligence gathering."

The pattern was clear—scientific caution repeatedly overruled by military eagerness to exploit the breaches for intelligence advantages. As the project progressed, the researchers developed increasingly sophisticated methods for detecting, measuring, and eventually widening the natural reality thin spots throughout Daybridge.

"My grandmother tried to warn them," Alice said, finding a series of increasingly urgent memos from Margaret Chen to project leadership. "She recognized that artificial breach expansion was creating dangerous instability in the quantum barrier structure."

The final memo, dated February 1959, was blunt:

"Further expansion of Breach Point Alpha will create cascading destabilization across the entire network. Mathematical models indicate 94% probability of catastrophic barrier failure if current protocols continue. I formally request immediate project suspension and implementation of stabilization measures outlined in Appendix C."

Two weeks later, the "containment incident" occurred—an event so serious it led to immediate project termination and facility evacuation. The official records provided minimal details, citing only "unexpected energy manifestation requiring security protocols" and "temporary relocation of all personnel."

"What really happened?" Alice wondered, searching for clarity in the fragmented documentation.

Maya pointed to a personnel file from Agent Chen's timeline—a document that apparently didn't exist in their reality. "According to this, the incident involved unexpected manifestation of 'non-standard entities' through the primary breach point. Three researchers were lost during the event before emergency containment protocols were activated."

"Entities?" Alice echoed, recalling Agent Chen's interrupted revelation about the true origin of the breach network. "Not just energy or information transfer, but actual beings crossing between realities?"

"That appears to be the case," Maya confirmed grimly. "The project was officially terminated, the facility sealed, and all personnel reassigned with elevated security classifications."

"But that wasn't the end," Alice said, finding documentation of covert continuation. "A subset of the original project was maintained under deeper classification—renamed Project Looking Glass, with minimal personnel and direct oversight from a newly formed Department subdivision."

"The Department of Temporal Security," Maya concluded. "Born from this incident, established specifically to monitor and control reality breaches while exploiting their intelligence-gathering potential."

Alice examined the personnel transitions carefully, noting which researchers continued with the classified project and which were removed. Her grandmother's name appeared in neither category—instead, a brief notation indicated "voluntary resignation effective March 1959" followed by "continued classification limitations apply."

"She walked away," Alice murmured. "Refused to continue after the incident, even under classified conditions."

"A principled stand that likely saved her life," Maya observed. "Most of the original researchers who transitioned to Project Looking Glass died under suspicious circumstances within the following decade."

The pattern was familiar—the same systematic elimination Alice had observed with Thomas Webb. Researchers who learned too much or questioned methodologies disappeared through arranged accidents, sudden illnesses, or carefully constructed disappearances.

"There's one exception," Alice noted, identifying a name in the documentation. "Dr. Eleanor Voss, quantum mathematician. According to these records, she continued with Project Looking Glass until 1976, then died in a house fire that destroyed her research materials."

"Convenient," Maya said dryly.

"Too convenient," Alice agreed. "Especially since Agent Chen's timeline shows Dr. Voss defected from the project in 1975, went into protected status, and lived until 2018."

Maya's eyebrows rose. "You think she might still be alive in our timeline? That her death was fabricated like Thomas Webb's accident?"

"It's worth investigating," Alice said, already formulating search parameters. "If she truly defected and has been living under an assumed identity, she might have crucial information about the early development of the amplifier technology."

They spent the next three hours conducting parallel research—Maya analyzing the technical specifications of the resonance amplifiers while Alice pursued the Eleanor Voss lead. The motel's Wi-Fi was unreliable, forcing Alice to use cellular data connections through a series of anonymizing protocols she'd developed for sensitive investigations.

Public records showed minimal information about Eleanor Voss—basic birth documentation, academic achievements including a PhD in mathematical physics from Cornell University in 1951, employment records with the Department of Energy until 1976, then a death certificate from the house fire. No surviving family members were listed, no estate proceedings filed.

"It's thin," Alice noted. "Minimal documentation, just enough to establish a public record without substantive details."

"Consistent with constructed identity management," Maya agreed, looking up from her technical analysis. "Either for the original identity or for her new one if she did defect."

Alice expanded her search to academic publications, finding Voss's early papers on quantum field mathematics—work that had laid theoretical groundwork for understanding multidimensional interactions. The publications ended abruptly in 1959 when she joined Project Looking Glass, with no further contributions to public scientific literature.

"I need to cross-reference this with my paranormal case files," Alice said. "If Dr. Voss remained in Daybridge under a new identity, she might have intersected with phenomena I've investigated."

With her original files confiscated from her apartment, Alice relied on memory and backup documentation stored in cloud servers. She methodically reviewed cases involving witnesses or subjects with mathematical backgrounds, focusing particularly on older women who might correspond to Voss's age.

After nearly an hour of searching, a potential connection emerged—a case from four years earlier involving reported temporal anomalies at Lakeside Retirement Community. Alice had interviewed several residents who reported experiencing time slips within the facility's east wing. One resident in particular had provided unusually precise descriptions of the phenomena, using terminology that Alice now recognized as related to quantum field theory.

"Marianne Weaver," Alice read from her notes. "Retired mathematics professor, described temporal experiences as 'localized barrier permeability events' and correctly predicted their periodic recurrence based on mathematical patterns."

The case file included a photograph of the witness—a woman in her late eighties with silver hair and penetrating eyes that projected sharp intelligence despite her advanced age. Something about her facial structure, particularly around the eyes and cheekbones, resonated with the much younger Eleanor Voss from the Project Resonance photograph.

"It could be her," Alice said, comparing the images. "The age progression is plausible, and her background as a mathematics professor provides perfect cover for someone with her expertise."

"Can we locate her?" Maya asked, setting aside her technical analysis.

Alice checked her case notes. "Lakeside Retirement Community, Unit 217. Last contact four years ago."

"That's our next step then," Maya said decisively. "If she worked on Project Looking Glass until 1975, she would have direct knowledge of the amplifier technology development—possibly even the original designs."

Alice nodded, already formulating an approach strategy. "We need to be careful. If she's truly in hiding from the Department, she'll be extremely cautious about discussing her past."

"And if the Department has monitored your previous investigations," Maya added, "they might already have flagged this connection."

The possibility sent a chill through Alice. If the Department had thoroughly reviewed her case files after confiscation, they might have identified Marianne Weaver as Eleanor Voss—potentially putting the elderly mathematician at risk.

"We need to move quickly," Alice decided, gathering essential materials. "We have approximately forty-eight hours before critical threshold, and we still need to locate and neutralize seven primary amplifiers scattered throughout Daybridge."

Maya returned to her technical analysis. "The shutdown protocol requires sequential deactivation following specific timing parameters. Based on these specifications, we'll need at least six hours to complete the full network shutdown once we begin the process."

"Then we need Dr. Voss's insights to refine our approach," Alice said. "If anyone understands the fundamental design principles of the amplifiers, it would be one of their original creators."

They prepared to leave the motel, packing only essential equipment and the critical data from Agent Chen. As they worked, Maya outlined her technical findings.

"The amplifiers operate on quantum resonance principles—essentially creating harmonized energy fields that systematically weaken reality barriers at specific frequency patterns," she explained. "Each device contains three primary components: a quantum field generator, a resonance modulator, and a synchronization system that connects it to the central control facility."

"Can they be deactivated individually?" Alice asked.

"Yes, but only in the correct sequence," Maya cautioned. "Deactivating them in the wrong order would create destructive interference patterns throughout the network—potentially accelerating collapse rather than preventing it."

Alice considered this as they completed preparations. "We need to prioritize gathering information from Dr. Voss, then formulate a comprehensive deactivation strategy."

They left the motel through a rear exit, using a rideshare service with a pickup location several blocks away to further obscure their movements. The autumn morning had brought fog to Daybridge, providing additional concealment as they traveled toward the lakeside district where the retirement community was located.

Alice used the journey to brief Maya on their approach. "I've interviewed Marianne Weaver previously as a paranormal witness, so my return won't immediately seem suspicious. You'll pose as my research assistant, helping document temporal phenomena she previously reported."

"And if she is Eleanor Voss?" Maya asked.

"We'll need to establish trust quickly," Alice acknowledged. "Time is critical, but rushing could cause her to shut down completely if she's been in hiding for decades."

They arrived at Lakeside Retirement Community shortly before noon—a sprawling complex of connected buildings overlooking Daybridge's eastern shoreline. The facility projected comfortable affluence, with manicured grounds and modern architecture designed to appear residential rather than institutional.

At the reception desk, Alice presented her paranormal investigator credentials, explaining she was following up on previously documented phenomena. The administrator appeared mildly skeptical but not obstructive—likely accustomed to the occasional unconventional visitor for the community's residents.

"Ms. Weaver still resides in Unit 217," the administrator confirmed after checking records. "Though I should mention her health has declined somewhat since your last visit. She doesn't receive many visitors these days."

"We'll be respectful of her condition," Alice assured him. "This is purely a follow-up to complete our research documentation."

They were issued visitor badges and directed through the complex toward the east wing. As they walked, Alice noticed security cameras throughout the facility—standard for retirement communities, but potentially problematic if the Department had indeed made the connection between Marianne Weaver and Eleanor Voss.

"We should assume we have limited time before our presence is flagged in any monitoring systems," she murmured to Maya as they approached Unit 217.

Alice knocked gently on the door, receiving no immediate response. After a moment, she knocked again, slightly louder. This time, a voice responded—thin but clear, with the crisp diction of academic training.

"Who is it?"

"Marianne, it's Alice Chen," she replied. "The paranormal investigator who documented your temporal experiences four years ago. I've brought a colleague to help with some follow-up questions."

A long silence followed, stretching nearly thirty seconds before the door opened slightly, secured by a chain lock. A single sharp eye examined them through the narrow gap, assessment practically tangible in its intensity.

"You're not here about temporal anomalies," the elderly woman stated flatly. "Not after all this time."

Alice made a split-second decision to be direct. "No, Dr. Voss. We're here about Project Resonance and the quantum amplifiers currently destabilizing reality throughout Daybridge."

The eye widened almost imperceptibly, then narrowed with calculation. After another extended moment, the door closed, the chain rattled, and it reopened fully.

The woman who stood before them matched the photograph from Alice's case file but appeared more frail than she had four years earlier. Despite her physical diminishment, her eyes remained fiercely intelligent, missing nothing as she assessed her visitors.

"You found me," she said simply, neither confirming nor denying Alice's identification. "After all these years. Come in quickly before cameras capture too much of this interaction."

They entered the apartment, which belied its retirement community setting with its contents. While the furnishings were standard, the walls were covered with complex mathematical equations written directly onto whiteboards and taped papers. Multiple computers ran calculations, their screens displaying undulating patterns Alice recognized as quantum field visualizations similar to those they'd seen in the underground observation chamber.

Dr. Voss secured the door with multiple locks, then turned to face them fully.

"I wondered if Margaret's granddaughter would eventually find me," she said, studying Alice with unnerving intensity. "You have her eyes—and apparently her persistence."

The confirmation sent a jolt through Alice—not just that this was indeed Eleanor Voss, but that she had known Alice's grandmother well enough to recognize her features in her descendant.

"You knew she left me the quantum resonator," Alice said, removing the broken pendant from her pocket.

Dr. Voss nodded, approaching to examine the device with careful fingers. "One of several contingency measures we implemented after the 1959 incident. When the entities first manifested through the breach, we recognized the true danger—and the likelihood that the Department would pursue exploitation rather than containment."

"The entities," Maya repeated. "Agent Chen mentioned them before our connection was severed. What exactly came through the breach in 1959?"

Dr. Voss moved to a comfortable chair, gesturing for them to sit as well. Despite the urgency of their situation, Alice recognized the importance of allowing the elderly scientist to proceed at her own pace.

"We called them Traversers," Dr. Voss explained, her voice strengthening as she accessed long-sequestered knowledge. "Beings that exist primarily as quantum probability patterns rather than fixed matter—capable of moving between reality configurations with relative ease."

"Interdimensional entities," Maya translated into more familiar terminology.

"A simplification, but essentially correct," Dr. Voss acknowledged. "When we first detected the breach network beneath Daybridge, we assumed it was a natural phenomenon—quantum thin spots that happened to concentrate in this geographical location. It was only after the incident that we understood the truth."

She leaned forward, intensity burning through her frail exterior. "The breach network isn't natural at all. It's an artificial construct—a transit system created by the Traversers to facilitate movement between realities. Daybridge happens to sit at a junction point where multiple reality configurations converge, making it ideal for their purposes."

The revelation aligned with Agent Chen's interrupted explanation, confirming Alice's growing suspicion that they were dealing with something far beyond government experiments gone wrong.

"Project Resonance didn't create the breaches," Alice said. "It activated them."

"Precisely," Dr. Voss confirmed. "Our experiments essentially rang the doorbell on a system that had been dormant for centuries. When we began applying quantum resonance energy to study the thin spots, we inadvertently sent a signal through the network—a signal the Traversers recognized."

"And they responded by coming through," Maya concluded.

Dr. Voss nodded grimly. "Three researchers died in the initial manifestation—not killed as the official report claimed, but absorbed. The Traversers exist as probability patterns; when they interact with human consciousness, they can essentially merge with it, creating hybrid entities that retain human form but possess fundamentally altered consciousness."

Alice processed this disturbing information, connecting it to Thomas Webb's warning about reality collapse. "The Department continued the experiments despite this encounter?"

"The military oversight was fascinated by the implications," Dr. Voss said bitterly. "Entities that could move between realities, potentially carrying intelligence or technology. The project was officially terminated but secretly reconfigured as Looking Glass—with a dual mandate to study both the breach network and the Traversers themselves."

"While my grandmother walked away," Alice noted.

Dr. Voss's expression softened slightly. "Margaret understood the danger immediately. She recognized that continued interaction with the breach network would inevitably attract more Traversers—entities with goals and motivations we couldn't comprehend. She resigned despite significant pressure to continue."

"But you stayed," Maya observed, without judgment.

"I believed I could guide the research away from the most dangerous applications," Dr. Voss admitted. "A naive hope, as I eventually discovered. By 1975, it became clear that certain Department leadership had been compromised."

"Compromised?" Alice asked, dreading the answer.

"Hybridized," Dr. Voss clarified. "High-level officials who had direct contact with Traversers during controlled experiments began exhibiting altered decision-making patterns, pursuing breach expansion with increasing aggression while dismissing safety protocols."

The implications were staggering—not just a government agency pursuing dangerous technology, but one potentially influenced or controlled by interdimensional entities with unknown agendas.

"When I recognized what was happening, I gathered critical research data and engineered my exit," Dr. Voss continued. "Margaret helped arrange my new identity, using connections she'd maintained from her Project Resonance days. My death was convincingly staged, and Marianne Weaver was born—a retired mathematics professor with no connection to quantum physics or government research."

"But you continued monitoring the breach network," Alice noted, gesturing to the computers and equations surrounding them.

"As best I could with limited resources," Dr. Voss confirmed. "Over the decades, I developed methods to passively track quantum variance patterns throughout Daybridge. For most of that time, the breaches remained relatively stable—the Department appeared to be maintaining rather than expanding them."

"Until recently," Maya said.

Dr. Voss nodded gravely. "Approximately nine months ago, I detected a significant shift in methodology—aggressive expansion protocols implemented across all major breach points simultaneously. The pattern suggests preparation for something unprecedented."

"But why now, after decades of relative stability?" Alice wondered.

"I believe it relates to astronomical alignment," Dr. Voss said, turning to one of her whiteboards covered with calculations. "The Traversers' transit system appears sensitive to certain cosmic configurations—alignments that occur approximately every sixty-seven years. The last major alignment coincides with the 1959 incident when they first manifested."

"And another alignment is approaching," Maya concluded, quickly calculating the timeframe.

"Four days from now," Dr. Voss confirmed. "Based on my calculations, the Department is attempting to use this alignment to establish permanent passages between selected timelines—stable corridors that would allow continuous transfer of matter and information without the current limitations of temporary breaches."

"Which Thomas Webb's Resonance Cascade Theory predicted would lead to catastrophic reality collapse," Alice added.

"Thomas," Dr. Voss said softly, recognition in her voice. "Brilliant young man. In my timeline, he discovered my research notes decades after I'd supposedly died. The Department eliminated him once they realized what he'd learned."

"The same happened in our timeline," Alice confirmed. "And now they're approaching a critical threshold that Agent Chen warned could lead to irreversible reality destabilization."

Dr. Voss turned to her computers, typing commands that brought up visualization models similar to those they'd seen in the underground chamber. "Your timeline is approaching cascade failure more rapidly than I calculated. Based on these readings, you have approximately forty-five hours before critical threshold."

"We have the shutdown protocol," Maya said, producing the data transferred from Agent Chen. "Technical specifications for the amplifiers and the sequential deactivation procedure."

Dr. Voss examined the documentation with practiced efficiency, her age seemingly falling away as her scientific mind engaged with the technical details. "This is a functional protocol, but implementation will be extremely challenging. The Department will have security measures at each amplifier location."

"And we don't know which Department personnel might be hybridized with Traversers," Alice added, the concept still disturbing to contemplate.

"There are ways to identify them," Dr. Voss said, moving to a locked cabinet in the corner of the room. "Margaret and I developed detection methods during the early Looking Glass days."

She unlocked the cabinet, revealing equipment that appeared decades old yet remarkably sophisticated—technology that blended 1970s components with design elements similar to those they'd observed in the underground facility.

"Quantum resonance detectors," Dr. Voss explained, removing a device approximately the size of a paperback book. "Hybridized individuals maintain a connection to their native reality configuration, creating subtle quantum variance signatures around them. These detectors can identify those signatures at close range."

She handed the device to Alice. "It's calibrated to register Traverser quantum patterns specifically. Standard humans won't trigger it, nor will most technology."

"This could help us avoid compromised Department personnel during the shutdown operation," Alice said, examining the device carefully.

"There's something else you should know," Dr. Voss added, her expression growing more serious. "The Traversers aren't simply using the Department to expand the breach network. Based on energy pattern analysis, they appear to be preparing for large-scale transit—movement of significant numbers of their kind into our reality configuration."

"An invasion?" Maya asked, the scientific detachment in her voice slipping slightly.

"More like colonization," Dr. Voss clarified. "Their native reality appears to be degrading—entropy reaching critical levels. They're seeking stable configurations to inhabit, and our timeline presents a suitable option."

"And the Department is helping them," Alice said, anger edging her voice.

"The hybridized leadership is," Dr. Voss corrected. "Many Department personnel remain unaware of the true implications—believing they're simply developing advanced technology for national security purposes."

As they digested this information, a soft alert sounded from one of Dr. Voss's monitoring systems. She moved quickly to the computer, checking security feeds that apparently accessed the retirement community's surveillance network.

"We have a problem," she said, gesturing to the screen showing the facility's main entrance. "Department personnel have arrived—two agents at the front desk showing credentials."

Alice moved to view the feed, immediately recognizing the methodical efficiency of the agents' movements—the same professional bearing she'd observed in her alternate self during their brief encounter.

"How much time do we have?" she asked.

"Minutes at most," Dr. Voss replied, already moving toward another cabinet. "They'll need to navigate security protocols, but they'll have authorization that supersedes standard procedures."

She opened the cabinet, revealing a small safe which she quickly unlocked. From inside, she removed a thumb drive and several paper documents sealed in protective plastic.

"Margaret and I prepared contingencies decades ago," she explained, handing the materials to Alice. "This contains everything I've compiled on the Traversers, the breach network, and potential countermeasures beyond the shutdown protocol. If something happens to me, this information must survive."

"You're coming with us," Alice insisted. "We can help you relocate before they arrive."

Dr. Voss shook her head firmly. "I'm ninety-four years old, Ms. Chen. My running days are long past. Besides, my disappearance would immediately confirm your presence and accelerate their pursuit. You need time to implement the shutdown protocol."

"Dr. Voss—" Maya began to protest.

"Eleanor," the elderly scientist corrected with a small smile. "After all these decades, someone might as well use my real name again."

She moved to a closet, removing a small overnight bag that appeared pre-packed. "This contains additional equipment you'll need—modified resonance detectors, quantum field disruptors, and communication devices that operate outside standard electromagnetic frequencies."

Alice accepted the bag, recognizing the resolute determination in the scientist's expression. "What will you tell them?"

"That a paranormal investigator and her assistant asked routine questions about temporal anomalies I reported years ago," Eleanor replied simply. "They'll be suspicious but will have no concrete evidence of information transfer. Meanwhile, you'll have precious hours to begin the shutdown sequence."

The surveillance feed showed the agents completing administrative procedures, preparing to enter the residential section of the facility.

"You should leave through the service corridor," Eleanor instructed, moving to a side door within her apartment that Alice hadn't previously noticed. "It connects to the maintenance areas. Follow it to the east exit—it's minimally monitored and emerges near the staff parking area."

As they prepared to depart, Eleanor approached Alice directly, studying her face with intense focus. "You have her determination," she said quietly. "Margaret knew this day would come. She arranged everything—the resonator, the access points, the breadcrumbs—knowing you would eventually follow them."

"Why me?" Alice asked, the question that had haunted her since discovering her grandmother's elaborate preparations.

"Because in every timeline where the breach network exists, Alice Chen discovers it," Eleanor replied simply. "Different paths, different careers, different lives—but always the same discovery. Margaret saw this pattern during the original experiments—a quantum constant amid infinite variations. She knew her granddaughter would inevitably face this challenge, so she prepared accordingly."

The surveillance feed showed the agents entering the residential wing, moving purposefully toward the east section.

"Go," Eleanor urged. "You have forty-five hours to prevent reality collapse. Everything depends on successful implementation of the shutdown protocol."

Alice hesitated, reluctant to leave the elderly scientist to face Department interrogation alone.

"I've evaded them for nearly fifty years," Eleanor said with quiet confidence. "I can handle one more conversation. Now go—save our reality, and all the others connected to it."

With a final nod of respect and gratitude, Alice and Maya slipped through the service door into the maintenance corridor beyond. As the door closed behind them, Alice caught a final glimpse of Eleanor Voss—the last surviving member of Project Resonance, a woman who had spent decades in hiding to preserve crucial knowledge for this exact moment.

They moved quickly through the service areas, following Eleanor's directions toward the east exit. As they emerged into the staff parking area, the weight of responsibility settled fully across Alice's shoulders—forty-five hours to locate and deactivate seven quantum resonance amplifiers scattered throughout Daybridge, while evading Department personnel and potential Traverser hybrids.

The countdown to reality collapse had begun.

CHAPTER TEN: WITNESS TESTIMONY

The abandoned water treatment facility on Daybridge's industrial outskirts provided temporary sanctuary. Concrete walls three feet thick blocked standard surveillance signals, while the underground pump room offered both concealment and access to city infrastructure if quick evacuation became necessary.

Alice spread the materials from Eleanor Voss across a makeshift workstation—thumb drive contents displayed on Maya's laptop, paper documents carefully arranged by apparent significance. Nearby, Maya calibrated the quantum resonance detectors they'd received, familiarizing herself with the hybridized technology that blended 1970s components with more advanced design elements.

"Dr. Voss's documentation is extraordinary," Alice said, examining a handwritten journal containing observations spanning decades. "She's been systematically monitoring reality fluctuations throughout Daybridge since 1976, documenting patterns invisible to conventional observation."

The journal detailed hundreds of temporal anomalies, doppelgänger sightings, and object displacement events—many corresponding to cases in Alice's own paranormal investigation files, but recorded years or even decades before Alice had documented them. Eleanor Voss had maintained a comprehensive surveillance operation from her modest retirement community apartment, using equipment she'd apparently salvaged or reconstructed from Project Looking Glass resources.

"Her technical ingenuity is remarkable," Maya agreed, examining one of the modified detectors. "She adapted quantum monitoring technology from the 1970s into functional systems capable of detecting reality breaches with precision comparable to our modern equipment."

Alice turned to the thumb drive contents, organizing the files chronologically. The earliest documents dated from Project Resonance's inception in 1955—scanned copies of original research proposals, equipment requisitions, and theoretical frameworks for studying "non-standard electromagnetic phenomena" detected throughout Daybridge.

"The initial project wasn't focused on cross-timeline communication at all," Alice noted, reading the early documents. "They were investigating unusual energy readings that interfered with sensitive military equipment being tested near Daybridge."

"Accidental discovery," Maya said, joining Alice at the workstation. "Like many scientific breakthroughs—they were looking for one thing and stumbled onto something far more significant."

The documentation revealed how Project Resonance had evolved rapidly once researchers recognized the true nature of what they were detecting. Within six months, the focus had shifted entirely to studying what they termed "quantum boundary discontinuities"—locations where reality itself appeared thinner, allowing limited information transfer between adjacent probability fields.

"My grandmother's theoretical contributions were pivotal," Alice noted with a mixture of pride and concern. "Her mathematical framework for understanding quantum barrier permeability essentially created the field of cross-reality physics."

The project timeline showed accelerating discoveries throughout 1956 and 1957—first confirming the existence of parallel timelines, then establishing rudimentary communication, and finally developing technologies to deliberately widen the natural breach points for enhanced information transfer.

"The military applications were immediately apparent," Alice continued, finding documentation of intelligence operations utilizing breach information. "They began receiving technological insights, strategic intelligence, and warning of global events from adjacent timelines where history had unfolded slightly differently."

"The ultimate espionage advantage," Maya observed. "Information not just from foreign adversaries, but from alternative versions of reality itself."

The most disturbing documents detailed the February 1959 incident—the catastrophic breach expansion that had allowed Traverser entities to manifest physically in the Daybridge facility. Eleanor's personal notes provided clarity missing from official reports:

"The entities emerged through Breach Point Alpha at 3:17 AM during a scheduled expansion test. Unlike previous information transfers, these manifestations maintained coherent form within our reality parameters. Three researchers (Davidson, Phillips, Navarro) were directly exposed to the primary manifestation wave. They appeared physically unharmed but demonstrated immediate cognitive and behavioral alterations. Military Command classified the entities as 'potentially cooperative non-human intelligences' and ordered continued contact despite Margaret's strenuous objections."

Alice found her grandmother's final report to project leadership—a comprehensive analysis of the dangers posed by continued interaction with what she termed "extra-dimensional entities of unknown motivation and capability." The report included a passionate plea to seal the breaches permanently, warning that entities capable of traversing reality barriers posed existential risks beyond conventional threat assessment frameworks.

The report had been officially rejected. Project Resonance was publicly terminated, the facility sealed, and Margaret Chen officially reassigned to unrelated research. Behind the scenes, Project Looking Glass had continued with a subset of the original team—now focused specifically on establishing controlled communication with the Traverser entities.

"This confirms what Dr. Voss told us," Maya said, reviewing documentation of the project's covert continuation. "They didn't just discover the breach network—they awakened its creators."

Alice turned to later documents—Eleanor Voss's personal research conducted after her fabricated death in 1976. Unlike the formal scientific reports of Project Looking Glass, these materials reflected a single brilliant mind working with limited resources to understand an existential threat.

"She identified the hybridization process in detail," Alice noted, examining Voss's analysis of Traverser-human integration. "The entities don't simply possess or control humans—they merge quantum consciousness patterns, creating hybrid beings that retain human form and memory while incorporating Traverser perception and motivation."

Maya studied the technical specifications. "According to these measurements, hybridized individuals maintain quantum resonance connections to their origin reality—essentially existing in two planes simultaneously, which creates detectable energy signatures."

"That's what these detectors are calibrated to identify," Alice confirmed, indicating the devices Voss had provided. "They register the specific quantum variance pattern of consciousness existing across multiple reality configurations."

The documentation revealed how Eleanor had tracked the gradual infiltration of the Department of Temporal Security by hybridized personnel—starting with three researchers from the original incident, then expanding to include military oversight, project administration, and eventually reaching higher government echelons.

"By 1984, she estimated approximately seventeen percent of Department leadership had been hybridized," Alice read from a particularly troubling analysis. "Sufficient influence to guide policy and research direction while remaining below threshold for obvious detection."

"And their agenda?" Maya asked, the scientist in her seeking pattern and purpose.

Alice found a section of analysis titled "Traverser Motivations and Strategic Assessment." Eleanor's meticulous documentation presented a disturbing hypothesis:

"Based on quantum frequency analysis of breach communications and behavioral patterns of hybridized individuals, I believe the Traversers originate from a reality configuration experiencing terminal entropy decay. Their native dimensional plane is collapsing, forcing migration to stable alternative realities. The breach network beneath Daybridge represents an ancient transit system designed for mass relocation between reality configurations. Their current strategy appears focused on widening existing breaches to permit large-scale transit during the approaching astronomical alignment—essentially preparing our reality for colonization."

The implications were staggering—not merely scientific experimentation gone wrong or government agencies pursuing dangerous technologies, but an orchestrated infiltration preparing for mass transfer of interdimensional entities into their reality.

"Dr. Voss tracked their activities across decades," Alice continued, finding documented patterns of strategic manipulation throughout Daybridge's history. "Subtle reality alterations, timeline contaminations, gradual preparation of the breach network for eventual full activation."

The documentation included a map of Daybridge with dozens of locations marked as "manipulation sites"—places where Eleanor had detected deliberate reality alterations performed by hybridized agents or through technological means. Many corresponded to locations where Alice had investigated paranormal phenomena over the years.

"The warehouse district is just the central node," Maya noted, examining the pattern. "They've been modifying reality throughout Daybridge, creating a network of controlled instability."

"Weakening the fabric between realities in preparation for the full breach activation," Alice concluded.

One document particularly captured their attention—a technical analysis of what Eleanor termed "the final protocol." Based on energy pattern analysis and intercepted Department communications, she had determined that the current amplifier network was designed to create a permanent reality corridor during the upcoming astronomical alignment—a stable passage between their timeline and the Traversers' origin reality.

"She believed they're approaching endgame," Alice said, reading Eleanor's final assessments from just weeks earlier. "After decades of gradual preparation, they're now implementing the final phase—aggressive breach expansion to reach critical threshold precisely as the astronomical alignment peaks."

"Which would explain the accelerated timeline we're observing," Maya agreed. "They're not just testing limits—they're deliberately pushing toward a specific activation point."

Alice found a sealed envelope marked with her name—apparently prepared by Eleanor in anticipation that Alice would eventually discover her identity. Inside was a letter dated six months earlier:

My dear Alice,

If you are reading this, you have discovered what your grandmother, and I worked to prepare you for. Margaret recognized long ago that her granddaughter would inevitably confront the breach network, regardless of which life path you chose. In some timelines you approach it as a scientist, in others as a government agent, and in yours as an investigator of the paranormal. Different routes to the same destination.

What you must understand is that the Traversers recognized this pattern as well. They perceive reality differently than we do—seeing probability patterns across multiple timelines simultaneously. They identified you as a nexus point in their colonization strategy, someone who consistently discovers and potentially disrupts their plans across numerous reality configurations.

This is why Margaret gave you the quantum resonator—not merely to protect you from reality fluctuations, but to shield your consciousness from detection by Traverser perception. Without it, they would have identified and neutralized you years ago, as they have done in several adjacent timelines.

The resonance amplifiers currently expanding the breach network can be neutralized, but conventional deactivation will trigger failsafe protocols designed to accelerate breach expansion rather than halt it. The shutdown sequence provided by your alternate self is theoretically sound but incomplete—it addresses the technological components but not the quantum consciousness elements incorporated into the system.

To truly neutralize the network, you must address both aspects simultaneously. The technical shutdown must be accompanied by quantum consciousness disruption at the primary node—what your grandmother called "closing the door from both sides."

I have prepared the necessary modifications to the shutdown protocol based on my understanding of current amplifier technology. Implemented correctly, it will not merely deactivate the network but reestablish natural quantum barriers, potentially sealing the breaches permanently.

Be cautious, Alice. The Department has been seeking me for decades, knowing I possess this knowledge. They will recognize the threat you pose once you begin the shutdown sequence, and hybridized personnel will respond with lethal force if necessary.

Your grandmother believed in you. Across all timelines we observed, Alice Chen faces this moment with remarkable courage and determination. I have come to share her faith in you.

With hope for our reality and all others connected to it,

Eleanor Voss

Attached to the letter was a modified shutdown protocol—technical specifications that integrated Eleanor's understanding of Traverser quantum consciousness with the amplifier deactivation sequence provided by Agent Chen.

"This changes our approach," Alice said, showing Maya the modified protocol. "We're not just deactivating technology—we're disrupting a consciousness network that spans multiple realities."

Maya studied the modifications with her physicist's precision. "These adjustments account for quantum consciousness entanglement within the amplifier system. Brilliant adaptation—she understood aspects of the technology that even Agent Chen's version didn't address."

"Can we implement it?" Alice asked, focusing on practical execution.

"Yes, but it requires precise coordination," Maya explained. "The primary node in Echo Alley must be accessed simultaneously with the peripheral amplifiers. We'll need to split our efforts—one team deactivating the satellite amplifiers in sequence while another accesses the central control facility beneath the warehouse district."

Alice checked the countdown they'd established based on Eleanor's calculations—forty-two hours until critical threshold, when reality destabilization would become irreversible.

"We need additional resources," she acknowledged. "This operation requires more than two people, regardless of our expertise."

Maya nodded agreement. "Who can we trust with something of this magnitude? The Department has resources throughout conventional channels, and we can't know which personnel might be hybridized."

Alice considered their options, mentally reviewing potential allies from her years of paranormal investigation. "We need people who understand the stakes, have relevant skills, and have personally experienced reality anomalies—making them more likely to accept the truth of what we're facing."

She began listing candidates: Detective Rivera, whose professional skepticism was tempered by direct observation of Department interference; Eliza Weiss, whose brother's security access could provide crucial facility information; Dr. Cassandra Liu, who had witnessed Thomas Webb's removal decades earlier and might contribute valuable scientific expertise.

"A small team of specialized individuals," Alice continued, "each handling specific aspects of the coordinated shutdown."

"It's risky bringing more people into this," Maya cautioned. "Each additional person increases potential security vulnerabilities."

"More risky than attempting to simultaneously deactivate seven amplifiers with just two people?" Alice countered. "We need a team, and we need them quickly."

She began drafting messages to potential allies, using coded language established through previous paranormal investigations to communicate urgency without explicitly stating the situation. Each message included instructions for secure contact protocols and emergency contingencies if communication was compromised.

As Maya continued analyzing the modified shutdown sequence, Alice examined Eleanor's documentation of Traverser capabilities and limitations—crucial intelligence for understanding what they might face during the operation.

According to Eleanor's research, hybridized individuals maintained human physical limitations but possessed enhanced perceptual capabilities—specifically, the ability to detect quantum variance patterns invisible to standard human senses. They could essentially "see" reality fluctuations and identify individuals who had crossed between timelines or been exposed to breach energy.

Most concerning was their apparent ability to recognize certain thought patterns—particularly focused awareness of the breach network itself. Eleanor had developed specialized mental disciplines to shield her consciousness from detection, techniques she'd documented in detailed notes.

"Controlled thought fragmentation," Alice read from the methodology. "Deliberately maintaining multiple simultaneous cognitive threads to obscure specific knowledge regarding the breach network. Essentially creating mental static that prevents hybridized individuals from detecting focused awareness of their existence or capabilities."

"Metacognitive camouflage," Maya translated. "Fascinating adaptation. She developed psychological countermeasures based on understanding Traverser perception."

Alice studied the techniques, recognizing elements of meditation practices her grandmother had taught her as a child—exercises she'd always assumed were simply for concentration and mental discipline. Now she understood their true purpose—preparation for eventually confronting entities that could perceive human consciousness directly.

As they continued processing Eleanor's extensive documentation, responses began arriving from Alice's potential recruits. Detective Rivera simply replied: "Location secure. In position by 18:00." Dr. Liu requested verification through a specific mathematical question only Alice would know from their previous conversation. Eliza confirmed immediate access to facility schematics for all seven amplifier locations.

"They're responding," Alice noted with cautious optimism. "We might actually have a functional team within hours."

"Then we need to finalize the operational plan," Maya said, gesturing to Eleanor's modified shutdown protocol. "Based on these specifications, we need precisely coordinated access to all seven amplifiers, with the central node deactivated last in the sequence."

Alice turned to the facility schematics, studying the locations of each amplifier throughout Daybridge. "The Department will have security measures at each site, likely including hybridized personnel capable of detecting standard approach strategies."

"We'll need distraction protocols," Maya suggested. "Methods to divert attention from our primary objectives."

Alice nodded, already formulating tactical approaches based on her years of paranormal investigation fieldwork. "We create apparent breach activations at decoy locations—using Eleanor's equipment to generate quantum variance signatures that will draw Department response away from our true targets."

They spent the next hour developing a comprehensive operational plan, integrating Eleanor's technical modifications with practical execution strategies. The final approach involved three coordinated teams:

Team Alpha (led by Maya) would handle the sequential deactivation of five peripheral amplifiers, moving in a precise pattern that followed the modified shutdown protocol.

Team Beta (led by Detective Rivera with Dr. Liu's scientific support) would create diversionary quantum signatures at multiple locations throughout Daybridge, drawing Department resources away from the actual amplifiers.

Team Gamma (led by Alice) would access the central control facility beneath Echo Alley to implement the final shutdown sequence, including the quantum consciousness disruption component Eleanor had identified as essential for permanent breach closure.

"Synchronization is critical," Maya emphasized, reviewing the timeline. "Each amplifier must be deactivated in a precise sequence with specific timing intervals. Deviation could trigger failsafe protocols that accelerate breach expansion rather than halting it."

Alice checked her watch—6:17 PM. "We'll convene the full team at 8:00 PM at the location Rivera secured. That gives us twelve hours to prepare equipment, brief personnel, and position teams for coordinated deployment at dawn."

As they gathered their materials and prepared to relocate, Alice returned to Eleanor's letter, rereading the elderly scientist's assessment of her role in this interdimensional crisis. The concept that she represented a "nexus point" across multiple timelines—consistently discovering and confronting the breach network regardless of her life path—was simultaneously disturbing and oddly reassuring.

Her grandmother had known. Had prepared her through subtle guidance, specialized training, and the quantum resonator pendant—not just for Alice's protection, but because Margaret Chen had recognized her granddaughter's inevitable confrontation with forces beyond conventional understanding.

"Ready?" Maya asked, equipment packed and secured.

Alice nodded, tucking Eleanor's letter into her pocket. "As ready as anyone can be to save reality itself."

They left the water treatment facility through maintenance tunnels that connected to Daybridge's underground infrastructure—pathways Eleanor had documented as "surveillance-minimal transit routes." As they navigated the dimly lit passages, Alice felt the weight of accumulated knowledge settling into resolute determination.

In less than forty-two hours, the breach network would reach critical threshold—either collapsing into catastrophic reality failure or stabilizing into permanent corridors for Traverser colonization. Neither outcome was acceptable.

The countdown to implementation had begun.

CHAPTER ELEVEN: THE CONSPIRACY BOARD

The abandoned fire station had served as one of Rivera's unofficial operation centers for years—a property seized in a drug raid, held in administrative limbo through bureaucratic maneuvering, and conveniently absent from standard police inventory systems. Its location in Daybridge's aging industrial sector provided both isolation and multiple evacuation routes, while the former equipment bay offered ample space for their rapidly expanding operation.

Alice surveyed the transformation that had occurred over the past four hours. What had been an empty concrete space now resembled the command center for a specialized tactical operation—which, she reflected, was precisely what they had assembled.

The centerpiece was what Rivera had dubbed "the conspiracy wall"—a massive expanse of whiteboards and corkboards covering the station's main wall, where Alice had meticulously constructed a comprehensive visual representation of everything they knew. Photos, documents, maps, and timeline elements were connected by color-coded strings that traced relationships between people, places, events, and theoretical concepts.

"Seeing it all laid out like this is both impressive and terrifying," commented Dr. Cassandra Liu, the quantum physicist who had known Thomas Webb decades earlier. Now in her fifties, Liu had arrived carrying research materials and equipment from her university lab, explaining simply that she had "unfinished business with the Department."

"Visual representation helps identify patterns that might be missed in sequential analysis," Alice explained, attaching another document to the board. "Paranormal investigation often involves connecting seemingly unrelated phenomena that conventional approaches would categorize separately."

The board's organization reflected Alice's investigative methodology. The left section chronicled Project Resonance's evolution from 1955 through the 1959 containment incident, including photographs of key personnel, facility locations, and significant research developments. The center mapped the current breach network throughout Daybridge, with detailed schematics of each amplifier location and the quantum variance patterns Eleanor had documented over decades. The right section displayed the modified shutdown protocol, including technical specifications, timing sequences, and contingency measures.

Red strings connected events across these sections, showing how decisions made during Project Resonance had direct consequences for current reality destabilization. Blue strings traced the movement and influence of key personnel, including the researchers who had become hybridized following the 1959 incident. Green strings mapped locations throughout Daybridge where reality alterations had been documented, creating a disturbing pattern of systematic manipulation spanning decades.

"It's like a city-wide crime scene that's been developing for seventy years," Rivera observed, studying the patterns with a detective's trained eye. He had arrived with tactical equipment, secure communication devices, and city infrastructure access credentials that would prove essential for their operation.

"The amplifier network forms a precise geometric configuration," Maya noted, examining the mapped locations. "Seven points arranged in what Eleanor identified as a 'quantum resonance lattice'—designed to create synchronized energy pulses that systematically weaken reality barriers throughout the affected area."

Eliza Weiss approached the board, adding facility schematics for two amplifier locations she'd obtained through her brother's security credentials. "The Department has established consistent security protocols at each site—two-person teams, rotating eight-hour shifts, with additional personnel on standby within a five-minute response range."

Alice integrated this information into the operational timeline, adjusting team deployment strategies to account for security presence. "We'll need precisely coordinated diversions to draw personnel away from each amplifier in sequence, maintaining our deactivation schedule while minimizing direct confrontation."

As they refined the tactical approach, Maya continued analyzing Eleanor's technical documentation with Dr. Liu, the two physicists rapidly developing a shared understanding of the quantum principles involved.

"The breach isn't merely allowing information transfer between timelines," Maya explained, addressing the assembled team. "It's creating actual physical permeability between adjacent reality configurations—essentially allowing matter from one timeline to manifest within another."

"Like Thomas Webb's voice in Echo Alley," Alice noted.

"Or Agent Chen's manifestation in the underground chamber," Maya continued. "But the current expansion goes far beyond these limited phenomena. The amplifiers are systematically reducing quantum coherence requirements for cross-reality transfer, progressively lowering the energy threshold required for physical manifestation."

Dr. Liu indicated equations on the whiteboard. "According to Eleanor's calculations, when the breach network reaches critical threshold during the astronomical alignment, the energy requirement for complete physical transfer between timelines will temporarily drop to zero—creating what she termed a 'null barrier state' lasting approximately seventeen minutes."

"During which anything could pass between connected realities," Rivera translated into practical terms.

"Not just anything," Maya clarified grimly. "Everything. The pressure differential between reality configurations would create a cascading transfer effect—essentially a quantum flood from higher-pressure realities into lower-pressure ones."

Alice found the relevant section in Eleanor's documentation. "She described it as a 'reality breach cascade'—uncontrolled transfer of matter, energy, and consciousness patterns between timelines, potentially displacing or overwriting native elements in the receiving reality."

"That's their colonization strategy," Dr. Liu concluded. "Use the amplifier network to create a null barrier state during peak astronomical alignment, allowing mass transfer of Traverser entities into our reality configuration."

The implications settled heavily over the group—the scale and significance of what they were attempting to prevent becoming concrete rather than theoretical.

"Thirty-nine hours until critical threshold," Alice noted, checking the countdown clock they'd established based on Eleanor's calculations. "We deploy in teams at 0600 hours, beginning synchronized approach to peripheral amplifier locations while diversionary operations draw Department response to decoy sites."

Rivera examined the tactical overlay. "My contacts confirm increased Department activity throughout Daybridge—personnel deployments, equipment transfers, surveillance enhancement. They're preparing for something significant."

"The final phase of breach preparation," Alice concluded. "They'll be heightening security around all amplifier locations as we approach the alignment window."

"Which makes our operation exponentially more challenging," Eliza noted pragmatically.

Alice turned to the modified shutdown protocol Eleanor had provided, focusing the team on their primary objective. "The protocol requires sequential deactivation of peripheral amplifiers in counterclockwise order, following specific timing intervals between each shutdown. The central node beneath Echo Alley must be deactivated last, with the quantum consciousness disruption component implemented simultaneously."

"The consciousness component is where standard approaches would fail," Maya explained, indicating Eleanor's crucial modifications. "The amplifiers aren't purely technological—they incorporate quantum consciousness elements from hybridized individuals, essentially using Traverser perception capabilities to maintain cross-reality connections."

"How exactly does one disrupt quantum consciousness?" Rivera asked, the pragmatic detective seeking concrete methods rather than theoretical concepts.

Maya gestured to specialized equipment Eleanor had provided—devices that combined 1970s components with more advanced elements. "These modified resonators generate interference patterns specifically calibrated to disrupt Traverser consciousness frameworks without affecting human cognitive patterns."

"Essentially a quantum perception jamming system," Dr. Liu added. "It creates 'blind spots' in Traverser awareness, preventing them from maintaining the mental frameworks that support breach stability."

Alice checked her watch, noting the time for equipment distribution and final briefings. "Each team requires specific components for their aspect of the operation. Team Alpha needs precise timing synchronization for sequential amplifier deactivation. Team Beta requires quantum signature generators for diversionary operations. Team Gamma needs the consciousness disruption equipment for the central node."

As they organized equipment and finalized tactical approaches, Alice returned to the conspiracy board, studying the patterns she had documented. The connections revealed a disturbing symmetry—a seven-decade progression from accidental discovery to potential reality collapse, with deliberate manipulation by entities whose motivations and capabilities remained partly unknown despite Eleanor's extensive research.

Maya joined her at the board, the physicist's analytical mind complementing Alice's investigative perspective. "You know what's most disturbing about all this?" she said quietly. "The elegant patience of their approach. Decades of subtle influence, gradual technological development, systematic preparation—all converging on a seventeen-minute window of opportunity during a rare astronomical alignment."

"Planning on a timeline most humans can't comprehend," Alice agreed. "While government administrations changed, research priorities shifted, and personnel rotated, they maintained consistent progress toward a single objective."

"Because their perception transcends our experience of time," Maya noted. "Eleanor's research suggests Traversers perceive temporal dimensions differently—experiencing multiple timeframes simultaneously rather than sequentially."

Alice found the section of the board documenting her grandmother's role in both creating and attempting to counter Project Resonance's dangerous legacy. Margaret Chen had recognized the threat immediately following the 1959 incident, had walked away despite professional consequences, and had spent decades preparing countermeasures—including protection and guidance for her granddaughter.

"My grandmother understood what we were facing before anyone else," Alice said, tracing the connections. "She saw the pattern across timelines—how consistently the breach network would be exploited regardless of which specific individuals were involved."

"Because she recognized it wasn't just human ambition driving the process," Maya replied. "The Traversers identified our reality as suitable for colonization and have been systematically preparing it for decades—using hybridized humans as tools rather than partners."

"Which raises the question of what happens to our reality if they succeed," Alice said. "Eleanor's research indicates the Traversers' native configuration is experiencing terminal entropy decay. What does that suggest about their impact on host realities?"

Maya's expression darkened. "Resource depletion. Their quantum consciousness framework may gradually alter fundamental physical constants in the host reality to match their native configuration—essentially transforming our reality to match their preferences, regardless of consequences for native life forms."

"Terraforming on a reality-wide scale," Alice translated grimly.

Their discussion was interrupted by Rivera, who approached with updated intelligence from his police department contacts. "Department activity has escalated significantly in the past hour. They've established security cordons around all major breach points and are conducting systematic sweep operations throughout central Daybridge."

"Looking for us?" Alice asked.

"Unclear," Rivera replied. "But they're deploying specialized equipment and personnel with federal credentials that override local authority. Something big is happening."

Alice checked the astronomical alignment data Eleanor had provided. "The alignment begins in approximately forty-one hours, but preparatory adjustments to the amplifier network would need to start much earlier to establish proper resonance patterns."

"They're initiating preliminary configuration," Maya concluded. "Which means our window for successful intervention is narrowing."

Alice returned to the operational timeline, making necessary adjustments. "We accelerate deployment. Teams prepare for insertion at 0400 hours instead of 0600. We'll use the pre-dawn window when security rotations typically experience maximum fatigue."

The team acknowledged the updated schedule, returning to equipment preparation and final briefings. As they worked, Alice continued expanding the conspiracy board, integrating Rivera's latest intelligence with their existing understanding of Department operations.

The pattern that emerged was increasingly concerning—not just heightened security around known breach points, but systematic coverage of secondary locations throughout Daybridge. The Department appeared to be establishing a comprehensive security grid designed to detect and intercept any approach to amplifier locations.

"They're anticipating interference," Alice noted, mapping the deployment pattern. "Not just standard security, but specific countermeasures against anyone attempting to access the amplifier network."

"Which suggests they've identified us as a threat," Maya said. "Or at least recognized the possibility of organized opposition to their objectives."

Alice considered this, remembering Eleanor's warning that Traversers could perceive probability patterns across multiple timelines. "They may have observed similar intervention attempts in adjacent realities—seen versions of us attempting to disrupt the breach network in other timelines."

"Learning from alternate futures," Rivera said, grasping the concept despite its deviation from his usual investigative framework. "Implementing countermeasures based on what worked against them in other versions of events."

"Which means our approach needs to deviate from predictable patterns," Alice concluded. "We need strategies they won't anticipate based on alternate timeline experiences."

This realization prompted a comprehensive revision of their tactical approach. Instead of direct sequential operations following the most efficient path, they developed deliberately unpredictable movement patterns, non-standard communication protocols, and approach vectors that contradicted logical efficiency.

"Essentially, we're attempting to surprise entities that can perceive probability itself," Maya noted with grim humor. "No pressure."

As midnight approached, the team broke into specialized groups for final equipment testing and tactical rehearsal. Rivera and his security contacts practiced diversionary operations designed to draw Department response away from actual amplifier locations. Dr. Liu and Maya finalized the technical aspects of the shutdown sequence, ensuring precise timing coordination across all seven amplifiers. Eliza and her brother configured secure communication systems that would operate outside standard channels monitored by the Department.

Alice used this time to complete the conspiracy board, integrating final elements from Eleanor's documentation with their operational planning. The completed visual representation was both comprehensive and disturbing—a seven-decade progression of events culminating in the next forty-one hours, with reality itself hanging in the balance.

At the center of the board, connecting multiple elements across all sections, Alice placed a small family photograph—herself as a child with her grandmother Margaret Chen. The woman who had recognized the threat in 1959, who had spent decades preparing countermeasures, who had ensured her granddaughter would have the tools and knowledge necessary when the inevitable confrontation arrived.

Maya joined her, studying the completed board. "Your grandmother would be proud," she said quietly. "She trusted you would reach this point and made sure you'd be prepared when you did."

"I just hope her preparations are sufficient," Alice replied. "We're attempting to counter entities that have been manipulating reality for decades, using technology we barely understand, with less than two days remaining before critical threshold."

"Yet here we are," Maya noted, "assembled with precisely the right combination of knowledge, skills, and resources to potentially succeed. Across all the infinite probability branches, we've arrived at this specific configuration of circumstances."

"Almost as if someone arranged the variables," Alice said thoughtfully.

"Perhaps someone did," Maya suggested. "Eleanor's research indicated that quantum consciousness can influence probability patterns across multiple timeframes simultaneously. Perhaps your grandmother's preparations extended beyond conventional understanding of cause and effect."

The possibility resonated with Alice—that Margaret Chen's influence might transcend standard temporal limitations, guiding probability itself toward this specific culmination of circumstances. It seemed fitting for a woman who had pioneered understanding of quantum reality interfaces.

"Three hours until deployment," Rivera announced, approaching with final equipment distributions. "Everyone should rest while possible. Once the operation begins, we'll have no downtime until completion or failure."

As the team dispersed to utilize the former fire station's sleeping quarters, Alice remained at the conspiracy board, making final notations and connections. The comprehensive visual representation now told a complete story—from Project Resonance's innocent beginnings through decades of manipulation by interdimensional entities, culminating in their current desperate countermeasure operation.

Maya returned briefly, providing Alice with specialized equipment for the central node component of their mission. "The quantum consciousness disruption device requires direct interface with the primary control system beneath Echo Alley. Based on Eleanor's schematics, you'll need to access the central chamber while Team Alpha completes the peripheral amplifier shutdown sequence."

"Timing will be critical," Alice noted, reviewing the synchronized operation timeline.

"Down to the second," Maya confirmed. "Each amplifier deactivation creates a seventeen-second window during which the next in sequence must initiate shutdown. Deviation exceeding that interval triggers failsafe protocols that accelerate breach expansion rather than halting it."

Alice secured the equipment, mentally rehearsing the approach sequence for Echo Alley—the most heavily guarded location in the entire network. "The Department will prioritize central node protection above all peripheral amplifiers. We'll need multiple diversionary operations to create sufficient access opportunity."

"Rivera's team has prepared four separate distraction scenarios," Maya assured her. "Each designed to draw specific security response protocols away from the central facility."

They reviewed final details of the operation, ensuring all team members understood both their specific responsibilities and the overall sequence of events. The complexity of coordinating seven simultaneous operations across Daybridge while evading Department security would challenge even the most experienced tactical team—let alone their hastily assembled group of scientists, paranormal investigators, and a reluctant detective.

As Maya departed to make final equipment adjustments, Alice turned once more to the conspiracy board, focusing on the section documenting the Traversers themselves. Despite Eleanor's extensive research, fundamental questions remained unanswered—the entities' true nature, the full extent of their capabilities, and whether their colonization agenda might be addressed through means other than direct opposition.

Eleanor's notes suggested attempts at communication during Project Resonance had yielded limited understanding—the Traversers' consciousness framework operated on principles fundamentally different from human cognition, making meaningful exchange nearly impossible. They perceived reality as malleable probability patterns rather than fixed states, experienced time non-linearly, and appeared to value consciousness configurations over physical forms.

The containment incident in 1959 had demonstrated their ability to merge with human consciousness, creating hybrid entities that maintained human appearance while incorporating Traverser perception and motivation. This hybridization process represented neither possession nor replacement in conventional terms, but rather a fundamental integration of consciousness patterns across reality configurations.

What remained unclear was whether such integration could be reversed—whether hybridized individuals might be restored to their original consciousness configuration through the quantum disruption process they planned to implement. Eleanor's research offered tentative hope but no certainty.

Alice made a final notation on the board, then stepped back to absorb the complete picture they had assembled. The connections revealed both the enormity of what they faced and the unlikely confluence of circumstances that had brought them to this point—investigators of the paranormal, quantum physicists, law enforcement, and security specialists, united by direct experience with reality breaches and guided by the decades-long preparations of two brilliant women who had recognized the threat before anyone else.

"Two hours until deployment," Rivera announced, returning with secure communication devices for each team leader. "Final equipment check and synchronization in thirty minutes."

Alice nodded, gathering her personal gear for the operation. As she prepared, she touched the broken pendant containing the quantum resonator chip—her grandmother's first gift of protection, now integrated into the specialized equipment they would use to disrupt the breach network.

In less than forty-one hours, reality would either begin irreversible collapse or stabilize once more into its natural configuration. The countdown to intervention had nearly reached zero.

CHAPTER TWELVE: THE TEMPORAL STAKEOUT

The pre-dawn darkness shrouded Daybridge in silence broken only by distant industrial sounds and the occasional passing vehicle. Alice Chen positioned herself on the rooftop overlooking Echo Alley, establishing the observation post they had designated "Watchtower Alpha." From this vantage point, she could monitor Department security operations around the central breach point while remaining outside standard surveillance coverage.

The building—an abandoned textile warehouse three blocks from Echo Alley—provided both tactical advantages and symbolic resonance. According to Eleanor's documentation, it had once housed auxiliary monitoring equipment for Project Resonance, its rooftop used for tracking atmospheric effects of early breach experiments. Now it served a similar purpose, though with vastly different objectives.

Alice adjusted her equipment carefully—modified quantum variance detectors coupled with conventional surveillance gear, creating a hybrid monitoring system capable of tracking both physical security presence and the subtle reality fluctuations surrounding the breach point. Maya had calibrated the instruments to detect the specific energy signatures generated by the central amplifier, allowing precise monitoring of activation patterns.

"Watchtower Alpha established," Alice reported through the secure communication system. "Visual confirmation of four Department personnel at primary entrance points. Additional energy signatures suggest at least two hybridized individuals within the central chamber."

"Confirmed," came Rivera's response from his position coordinating the diversionary team. "Similar deployment patterns observed at peripheral sites. They've doubled standard security protocols at all amplifier locations."

Alice checked the synchronized operation timeline—thirty-seven hours until critical threshold, with amplifier deactivation sequence scheduled to begin in just under ninety minutes. Timing would be essential, with each team required to access their designated amplifier within specific windows coordinated across the entire network.

As she conducted final equipment checks, Alice activated the specialized monitoring system designed to detect communications through the breach itself—a modified version of her original recording equipment that had first captured Thomas Webb's voice in Echo Alley. Eleanor had enhanced the system using principles developed during Project Looking Glass, creating a passive receiver capable of detecting information transfer between connected timelines.

The system activated silently, scanning quantum frequencies beyond standard electromagnetic spectrum. For several minutes, it registered only background variance—the persistent "static" of reality thin points. Then, at precisely 4:17 AM, a pattern emerged—structured data transfer flowing through the breach in distinctive pulses.

Alice adjusted reception parameters, focusing on the information stream. Unlike her previous encounters with Thomas Webb or Agent Chen, this transmission wasn't directed communication intended for human recipients. Rather, it appeared to be automated data exchange—systematic information transfer between connected realities.

The monitoring system began decoding portions of the stream, converting quantum variance patterns into recognizable data formats. Fragmented information appeared on Alice's display—technical specifications, research summaries, strategic assessments—intelligence flowing through the breach in a carefully structured sequence.

"I'm detecting active data transfer through the central breach point," Alice reported, documenting the transmission patterns. "Automated information extraction, not direct communication. The

Department appears to be conducting systematic intelligence gathering from connected timelines."

"Can you determine what specifically they're accessing?" Maya asked from her position with Team Alpha, preparing for the peripheral amplifier shutdown sequence.

Alice studied the fragmented data, identifying patterns within the information stream. "Technical documentation primarily—quantum computing architectures, advanced materials science, propulsion system designs. They're extracting technological intelligence from timelines with more advanced development in specific sectors."

"Weaponizing the multiverse for technological advantage," Dr. Liu commented from her support position with Team Alpha. "Accessing innovations from alternate development paths without investing in the research process."

As Alice continued monitoring, a pattern emerged in the data extraction timing. The information flow intensified at precise seventeen-minute intervals, creating distinct transfer windows that corresponded to specific amplifier activation sequences.

"The transfer operates in synchronized pulses," Alice noted, documenting the pattern. "Each activation creates a seventeen-minute extraction window targeting specific information categories from designated timelines."

She expanded monitoring parameters, tracking energy fluctuations throughout the breach network as reflected through the central node. The visualization revealed a disturbing pattern—deliberate expansion and contraction cycles that systematically stretched reality barriers before allowing partial stabilization.

"They're stress-testing the barriers," Alice realized, observing the pattern across multiple cycles. "Progressively increasing expansion parameters while monitoring structural integrity of the quantum boundaries between timelines."

The tactical implications were immediately clear—the Department wasn't simply gathering intelligence through existing breach points but methodically preparing the entire network for something far more significant than information transfer.

As 4:34 AM approached—the timestamp Eleanor had identified as a primary activation cycle—Alice enhanced monitoring sensitivity, focusing on the central chamber beneath Echo Alley. The quantum variance readings began climbing steadily, indicating imminent amplifier activation.

What happened next exceeded all previous observations. At precisely 4:34 AM, the central amplifier initiated a synchronized activation sequence that cascaded through the entire network. Unlike the gradual expansions Alice had documented previously, this activation created a dramatic surge in quantum variance—a deliberate pushing of reality barriers beyond established parameters.

The monitoring system registered unprecedented energy levels flowing through the breach network, creating momentary connections between multiple timelines simultaneously rather than the controlled individual interfaces observed earlier. For approximately seventeen seconds, Daybridge existed at the center of a quantum nexus connecting several distinct reality configurations.

During this brief convergence, something extraordinary occurred. The monitoring system detected physical transfer between connected timelines—not merely information or energy, but actual matter transitioning through momentarily permeable reality barriers.

"Physical transfer detected," Alice reported urgently. "The Department isn't just extracting information—they're moving actual objects between timelines during peak activation cycles."

"What kind of objects?" Rivera asked, the concern evident in his voice despite the secure communication system's distortion.

Alice adjusted monitoring parameters, focusing on the quantum signatures of the transferred materials. "Technology components primarily—manufactured items with specific composition profiles. Based on variance patterns, they're extracting physical technology from more advanced timelines for reverse engineering."

"Technological theft across reality boundaries," Maya translated. "Acquiring advanced components they can't produce independently."

As the activation cycle completed, Alice documented the precise sequence—noting activation parameters, energy distribution patterns, and the systematic expansion of reality permeability during peak transfer windows. The data revealed a carefully calibrated process designed to progressively increase matter transfer capability while maintaining overall network stability.

"They're following a deliberate escalation protocol," Alice observed, recognizing the methodical approach. "Each activation cycle pushes boundary parameters slightly beyond previous thresholds, establishing new stability baselines before the next expansion."

"Conditioning the breach network for the final alignment event," Maya concluded. "When astronomical factors will naturally enhance quantum permeability, allowing them to exceed the critical threshold without triggering immediate collapse."

The monitoring system suddenly registered another form of transfer—distinct from both information extraction and technology acquisition. These signatures displayed consciousness patterns similar to those Eleanor had documented during Traverser manifestations, suggesting limited entity transfer between connected realities.

"I'm detecting consciousness transfer patterns," Alice reported, focusing monitoring equipment on this new phenomenon. "Quantum signatures consistent with Traverser manifestation, but at sub-physical integration levels—essentially consciousness probes testing permeability parameters."

"Advance scouts," Rivera translated into tactical terminology. "Assessing conditions before committing to larger-scale movement."

This development confirmed their understanding of the Traversers' ultimate objective—using the amplifier network to facilitate mass transfer during the approaching astronomical alignment. The current limited manifestations represented preliminary testing of the transit system they had spent decades preparing.

As Alice continued monitoring, another significant pattern emerged. The Department's security deployments shifted in synchronized response to each activation cycle, establishing defensive perimeters around successful transfer points while redirecting resources from less productive breach locations.

"They're optimizing resource allocation based on transfer success rates," Alice noted, tracking security movements throughout the network. "Prioritizing protection for breach points demonstrating highest matter transmission efficiency."

This observation provided critical tactical intelligence for their approaching intervention operation. By identifying which amplifier locations, the Department considered highest priority, they could anticipate security response patterns and adjust their approach vectors accordingly.

At 5:03 AM, the monitoring system detected something unexpected—a transmission directed specifically toward Alice's receiver rather than the automated data extraction process. Unlike the structured information transfer, this signal displayed characteristics of conscious communication similar to her previous interactions with Thomas Webb and Agent Chen.

Alice adjusted reception parameters, isolating the directed transmission from background variance. The communication clarified gradually, resolving into coherent language rather than raw data:

"To the observer monitoring this frequency—we detect your presence across multiple probability configurations. Temporal variance patterns suggest approaching intervention attempt targeting amplifier network. Be advised: Department security operations have been enhanced based on timeline intelligence indicating potential breach network disruption within approaching forty-hour window."

The message wasn't from Thomas Webb or Agent Chen but appeared to originate from a different timeline entirely—one aware of both the Department's activities and Alice's monitoring operation. Most concerningly, it confirmed their theory that the Department was gathering intelligence about their intervention plans from alternate timelines where similar attempts had already occurred.

Alice considered whether to respond, weighing the risks of engagement against potential intelligence benefits. After a brief analysis, she configured the system for minimal-footprint transmission using Eleanor's protocols for quantum consciousness shielding.

"Identify source timeline and affiliation," she transmitted, employing the verification protocols Eleanor had documented for cross-reality communication.

The response came after a seventeen-second delay—the standard transmission interval Eleanor had identified for stable cross-timeline communication:

"Designation Timeline J-73. Resistance coalition opposing Department colonization protocols. We have observed your intervention preparations across probability configurations. Be advised: Department has implemented countermeasures based on your previous attempt failures in adjacent timelines."

This confirmation of timeline monitoring sent a chill through Alice. The Department wasn't merely anticipating potential interference based on standard security protocols—they had observed actual intervention attempts by alternate versions of Alice and her team across multiple reality configurations.

"Request tactical intelligence regarding observed failure points in prior intervention attempts," Alice transmitted, recognizing the potential value of learning from alternate timeline experiences.

Another seventeen-second delay preceded the response:

"Primary failure vectors: 1) Sequential amplifier targeting allowing predictive security response; 2) Consciousness disruption components neutralized by hybrid defenders; 3) Timing synchronization compromised by Department quantum jamming systems activated at T-minus twenty minutes before critical threshold."

This information represented invaluable tactical intelligence—specific failure modes they hadn't anticipated, particularly the quantum jamming systems designed to disrupt their timing synchronization during the critical final phase of the operation.

"Can you provide countermeasure specifications for jamming systems?" Alice requested.

The response arrived with accompanying technical data:

"Transmitting quantum jamming countermeasure protocols. Implement frequency modulation pattern attached to maintain synchronization integrity. Critical advisory: Department has initiated Contingency Protocol Omega in three observed timelines where intervention approached success parameters."

"Define Contingency Protocol Omega," Alice transmitted, sensing this represented a significant escalation beyond standard security measures.

The seventeen-second delay felt particularly long as Alice awaited clarification of this ominous protocol. Finally, the response appeared:

"Controlled accelerated collapse of specific timeline segments to preserve central breach network integrity. Essentially sacrificing peripheral reality sections to maintain core transmission capabilities during the alignment window. In observed implementations, Department initiated targeted reality destabilization in geographic areas surrounding intervention team origins, effectively erasing operational support infrastructure and personnel resources."

The implications were horrifying—the Department was willing to deliberately collapse sections of reality itself to preserve their colonization objectives, essentially sacrificing portions of their own timeline to ensure successful Traverser transition during the alignment window.

"How is targeted collapse implemented?" Alice asked, needing to understand this contingency to develop potential countermeasures.

"Resonance inversion at selected amplifier nodes, creating localized reality destabilization cascades that propagate through connected spatial regions. Once initiated, collapse cannot be halted through standard amplifier deactivation protocols. Requires specialized quantum barrier reinforcement at boundary perimeters to contain spread."

Alice documented this critical intelligence, recognizing they would need to develop specific countermeasures against this contingency scenario. If the Department initiated targeted collapse in response to their intervention, the consequences could extend far beyond operational failure to catastrophic reality degradation throughout Daybridge.

As she prepared to request additional information, the quantum variance monitor registered a significant energy surge throughout the breach network—an unscheduled activation sequence initiating at all seven amplifier locations simultaneously.

"Energy surge detected across full network," Alice reported to all teams. "Unscheduled synchronized activation in progress. All amplifiers showing coordinated power increase exceeding previous parameters."

The monitoring system's displays shifted to warning indicators as quantum variance levels throughout Daybridge exceeded established baselines by significant margins. Reality itself seemed to shimmer visibly around Echo Alley, the air taking on a disturbing opalescent quality that registered clearly even through conventional optical equipment.

"They're conducting a full-scale network test," Maya responded, monitoring similar readings from her position. "Pushing all breach points simultaneously to establish final baseline parameters before the alignment sequence."

Alice focused monitoring equipment on the central chamber, tracking energy distribution patterns throughout the network. The visualization revealed a disturbing configuration—energy flowing from peripheral amplifiers toward the central node in a deliberate concentration pattern, creating unprecedented quantum variance intensity at Echo Alley.

For approximately thirty-four seconds, reality barriers throughout Daybridge thinned dramatically, creating momentary permeability between multiple connected timelines. During this window, the monitoring system detected significant matter transfer through the central breach point—substantial enough to register as distinct mass displacement rather than the limited component extraction observed earlier.

"Major transfer event in progress," Alice reported, tracking the quantum signatures. "Something substantial transitioning through central breach point during peak variance window."

The activation sequence concluded abruptly at 5:17 AM, energy levels declining rapidly as amplifiers returned to standby configurations. However, monitoring equipment continued detecting residual variance patterns consistent with persistent matter displacement—something had transferred through the breach and remained present in their reality.

Alice adjusted surveillance equipment, focusing conventional optics on the alley entrance while enhancing quantum variance detection sensitivity. The combined monitoring revealed unusual activity as Department personnel established enhanced security perimeters around Echo Alley, their movements suggesting protocol escalation beyond standard operations.

"Department security implementing containment procedures," Alice noted, observing the tactical pattern. "Configuration consistent with high-value asset protection rather than standard breach security."

"They brought something through," Rivera concluded. "Something significant enough to warrant special containment protocols."

Alice continued monitoring as dawn approached, tracking Department operations around Echo Alley while maintaining the cross-timeline communication channel. The timeline J-73 contact provided additional tactical intelligence regarding Department security protocols, including rotation schedules, response patterns, and vulnerability windows within the amplifier network.

Most valuable was confirmation that the approaching astronomical alignment represented a onetime opportunity for the Traversers' colonization objective. The specific configuration—occurring approximately every sixty-seven years—created natural quantum permeability enhancement that, when combined with the amplifier network's artificial expansion, would establish the null barrier state necessary for mass transit between realities.

"Astronomical alignment begins at 17:34 tomorrow," the contact confirmed. "Peak configuration occurs at precisely 18:17, creating a seventeen-minute window during which quantum barriers naturally thin to minimum resistance parameters. If amplifier network remains active during this window, null barrier state will manifest, allowing unrestricted matter transfer between connected timelines."

"And the Traversers are prepared for immediate transit during this window?" Alice asked.

"Affirmative. Based on observed timelines where colonization succeeded, approximately sixty thousand primary entities transition during the seventeen-minute window, establishing stable presence sufficient to maintain permanent breach apertures after alignment concludes."

The scale of the intended colonization exceeded their previous estimates, representing not merely exploratory manifestation but comprehensive reality infiltration—sufficient numbers to fundamentally alter the base configuration of their timeline following successful transition.

As 6:00 AM approached—the scheduled initiation time for their coordinated intervention operation—Alice completed final documentation of monitoring results and prepared for tactical deployment. The stakeout had provided critical intelligence regarding Department operations, amplifier activation patterns, and the specific threat timeline they faced.

"All teams, final status report," she requested through the secure communication system.

"Team Alpha in position," Maya confirmed. "Peripheral amplifier approach vectors established with countersurveillance measures active. Timeline synchronization confirmed against quantum variance patterns."

"Team Beta ready," Rivera reported. "Diversionary resources deployed at all designated locations. Initial activation sequence programmed for T-minus ten minutes to primary approach."

The remaining team members confirmed ready status, their positions established throughout Daybridge in preparation for the synchronized operation. Alice transmitted final adjustments based on stakeout intelligence, including enhanced countermeasures against the quantum jamming systems their cross-timeline contact had warned about.

"Operation timeline remains unchanged," Alice confirmed. "Synchronize to quantum variance pattern established during 5:17 activation sequence. That pattern provides optimal counterpoint for amplifier disruption timing."

As team members acknowledged the final instructions, Alice conducted one last scan of Echo Alley and the surrounding security perimeter. The Department had established comprehensive coverage, with both conventional personnel and what her equipment identified as hybridized individuals positioned at key access points.

Most concerning was the enhanced security around the central chamber itself—where whatever had transferred through during the 5:17 activation was now contained under protocols exceeding standard Department operations. This unexpected development would complicate their approach to the primary node, requiring tactical adjustments to their central chamber access strategy.

Alice transmitted final instructions to all teams, then prepared for descent from her observation post. The temporal stakeout had revealed far more than anticipated—confirming not only the Department's technological theft operations and Traverser colonization preparations, but also the existence of resistance movements across multiple timelines and the horrifying contingency measures the Department might implement if their intervention approached success.

As she gathered her equipment and prepared to join Team Gamma for the central node approach, Alice reflected on the pattern that had emerged during her observation of Echo Alley. The Department of Temporal Security wasn't merely studying reality breaches or even exploiting them for limited intelligence gathering—they were systematically preparing for comprehensive reality reconfiguration, willing to sacrifice portions of their own timeline to achieve objectives aligned with entities from beyond conventional existence.

The countdown to intervention had reached zero. In less than thirty-six hours, reality would either begin irreversible collapse, transform under colonization by interdimensional entities, or—if their coordinated operation succeeded—stabilize once more into its natural configuration.

The temporal stakeout had ended. The final confrontation was about to begin.

CHAPTER THIRTEEN: BREACH DYNAMICS

"Teams Alpha and Beta, initiate primary sequence," Alice transmitted through the secure communication system, initiating the operation they had meticulously planned over the past twelve hours. Dawn light had barely begun to illuminate Daybridge as coordinated movements commenced across the city—carefully timed approaches toward amplifier locations disguised within ordinary morning activities.

Alice moved through the underground maintenance tunnels that would provide her team access to the central facility beneath Echo Alley, leading the four-person unit designated Team Gamma. Dr. Liu accompanied her, carrying specialized equipment for the quantum consciousness disruption component of the shutdown protocol. Two security specialists recruited through Rivera's connections provided tactical support, their experience with Department operations proving invaluable for navigating the complex approach.

"First diversionary activation in three, two, one..." Rivera's voice came through the communication system, followed immediately by confirmation of energy signature deployment at a location two miles from their position. "Diversion Alpha active. Department security responding as anticipated."

Alice checked the tactical overlay displayed on her modified smartphone, tracking Department personnel movements throughout Daybridge. The diversionary quantum signatures—generated using equipment based on Eleanor's designs—created energy patterns mimicking amplifier activation anomalies, drawing security response away from their actual targets.

"Team Alpha approaching Amplifier Two," Maya reported from her position across the city. "Quantum variance readings consistent with standby configuration. No indication of enhanced security awareness."

Alice led her team deeper into the maintenance tunnel network, following the path Eleanor had documented decades earlier. According to the schematics, these service corridors connected to the original sublevel facility constructed during Project Resonance—providing access routes that bypassed modern security systems focused on surface-level approaches.

"Amplifier network showing standard operational patterns," Dr. Liu noted, monitoring the quantum field visualization system they'd configured based on Eleanor's technology. "No indication they've detected our approach vectors."

The tunnels grew narrower and older as they progressed, transitioning from modern municipal infrastructure to historical systems dating back to Daybridge's early development. The air became cooler, tinged with an electric quality that Alice had come to recognize as quantum variance leakage—the subtle bleed-through of energy from reality breach points.

"Approaching junction seven," Alice informed her team, consulting the modified mapping system. "Transition to original facility infrastructure in approximately thirty meters."

The passage ahead showed distinct architectural changes—conventional concrete giving way to the same pearlescent material they had encountered in the observation chamber. The walls incorporated the circuit-like patterns characteristic of technology beyond standard human development, confirming they had reached the original Project Resonance facility.

"First amplifier shutdown sequence initiated," Maya reported through the communication system. "Team Alpha has successfully accessed Amplifier Two and implemented phase one of the deactivation protocol."

Alice checked the synchronized timeline—the operation was proceeding exactly as planned, with Team Alpha beginning the sequential shutdown of peripheral amplifiers while Team Beta deployed diversionary measures to draw Department security away from active intervention sites.

"Department response patterns shifting," Rivera confirmed. "Security redeployment underway toward Diversions Alpha and Charlie. Reduced presence detected at Amplifiers Three and Five."

The coordinated operation represented their best chance of systematically deactivating the amplifier network before critical threshold—thirty-five hours and counting until the astronomical alignment created conditions for permanent breach expansion. Each amplifier required precise deactivation timing, following the carefully calculated sequence Eleanor had developed to bypass failsafe protocols that might otherwise accelerate breach expansion.

As Team Gamma approached the central facility beneath Echo Alley, Alice activated the quantum resonance detector provided by Eleanor—the specialized equipment designed to identify Traverser quantum signatures at close range. The device immediately registered multiple distinct patterns ahead, confirming hybridized presence within the central chamber.

"Five hybridized signatures detected," Alice informed her team quietly. "Concentrated in the primary control chamber approximately seventy meters ahead."

"Consistent with enhanced security following the 5:17 transfer event," Dr. Liu noted. "They're protecting whatever came through during that activation window."

Alice adjusted their approach strategy, directing the team toward a secondary access route Eleanor had identified—a maintenance passage designed for equipment servicing rather than personnel transit. The narrow corridor would limit their movement capabilities but offered approach vectors outside standard security coverage.

"Amplifier Two deactivation complete," Maya reported. "Energy dissipation proceeding within calculated parameters. Moving to Amplifier Four for next sequence phase."

Alice checked the quantum field visualization—the successful deactivation of the first peripheral amplifier had created subtle changes throughout the network, reducing overall quantum variance by approximately seven percent. The pattern confirmed Eleanor's shutdown protocol was functioning as designed, gradually reducing breach expansion without triggering failsafe acceleration.

Team Gamma reached the maintenance access corridor, transitioning to minimal movement protocols as they approached the central chamber perimeter. Alice deployed passive monitoring probes developed by Dr. Liu—microscopic quantum field sensors that transmitted real-time data about conditions within the chamber while remaining virtually undetectable by standard security systems.

The visualization revealed detailed chamber configuration—seven Department personnel, including the five hybridized individuals, surrounding a central platform containing what appeared to be specialized containment equipment. Within this containment field, energy patterns indicated something substantively different from standard matter or even Traverser quantum signatures.

"They're containing an intact quantum probability construct," Dr. Liu whispered, analyzing the readings. "Not merely information or technology transfer, but an actual probability matrix extracted from another timeline—essentially a fragment of alternate reality maintained in coherent form within our dimensional parameters."

The implications were staggering—the Department had progressed beyond extracting information or technology to removing actual segments of alternate realities for direct integration into their timeline. This development exceeded even Eleanor's predictions about their capability progression.

"Second diversionary activation implemented," Rivera reported. "Department security redirecting additional resources from peripheral amplifier locations. Temporary vulnerability window opening at Amplifiers Three and Seven."

"Team Alpha exploiting vulnerability at Amplifier Three," Maya confirmed. "Approaching deactivation access point with minimal opposition."

Alice studied the central chamber visualization, identifying potential approach vectors toward the primary control systems. According to Eleanor's documentation, the master shutdown sequence required direct access to the original control interface—the same system that had initiated Project Resonance's first contact with the breach network in 1956.

The visualization highlighted this interface—a crystalline structure incorporated into the chamber's central column, surrounded by more conventional technology added during subsequent decades of Department operations. Accessing this interface would require navigating through the chamber while avoiding detection by hybridized personnel capable of perceiving quantum variance patterns beyond standard human sensitivity.

"We need a targeted diversionary measure within the central facility itself," Alice determined, formulating an adjusted approach strategy. "Something to draw hybridized attention away from the primary control interface while we implement the master shutdown sequence."

Dr. Liu considered this challenge, then offered a solution based on Eleanor's technology. "We can modify one of the quantum resonance detectors to generate amplified Traverser signatures at a remote location within the facility. Hybridized individuals would instinctively investigate what would appear to be unauthorized entity manifestation."

"Implement the modification," Alice directed. "We'll position the device at maximum distance from our approach vector while maintaining control link for timed activation."

As Dr. Liu adapted the equipment, Alice continued monitoring the sequential amplifier shutdown progress across Daybridge. Team Alpha had successfully deactivated two peripheral amplifiers, with the approach to the third underway. The quantum field visualization showed a progressive reduction in breach network stability—precisely the controlled degradation pattern Eleanor's protocol was designed to create.

"Thirty-four hours, seventeen minutes until critical threshold," Dr. Liu noted, completing the equipment modification. "The astronomical alignment begins formal approach phase at that point, with reality barrier thinning accelerating geometrically as alignment progresses."

Alice checked the tactical overlay once more, confirming Department security distribution throughout Daybridge. The pattern revealed increasing concentration around peripheral amplifiers still in active status—exactly as they had anticipated when designing their sequential deactivation approach.

"Diversion device prepared," Dr. Liu confirmed, activating the modified resonance detector. "Remote deployment capability confirmed with seventeen-minute power sustainability."

Alice designated the optimal deployment location—a secondary storage chamber approximately fifty meters from their position, located opposite their planned approach vector to the central control interface. The small maintenance drones they had brought specifically for such contingencies would deliver the device while they maintained position outside direct security coverage.

"Team Alpha reports Amplifier Three deactivation sequence initiated," Maya's voice came through the communication system. "Seventeen-minute countdown to completion, followed by immediate transition to Amplifier Five approach."

"Department security implementing response pattern Delta," Rivera added. "Heightened alert status at remaining amplifier locations. They've recognized the sequential pattern."

This development had been anticipated in their planning—the Department would eventually detect the systematic amplifier deactivation and adjust security accordingly. The critical factor was maintaining sufficient progress before comprehensive countermeasures could be implemented.

Alice deployed the maintenance drone carrying the diversionary device, guiding it through narrow utility conduits toward the designated location. The drone's minimal quantum signature would register as standard maintenance automation to all but the most sensitive detection systems.

"Drone deployed," she confirmed as the small device disappeared into the conduit network. "Diversionary activation scheduled for T-minus three minutes to central chamber approach."

Team Gamma moved into final position for the central facility infiltration, each member confirming equipment readiness and protocol understanding. The quantum consciousness disruption component—the critical element that Eleanor had identified as essential for permanent breach closure—was secured in specialized shielding to prevent premature detection by hybridized personnel.

"Amplifier Three deactivation sequence progressing as calculated," Maya reported. "Quantum variance reduction measured at twenty-three percent across the network. Breach stability showing controlled degradation within optimal parameters."

Alice activated the final approach sequence, synchronizing team movements with the diversionary timeline. At precisely the designated moment, the modified resonance detector activated in the distant storage chamber, generating amplified Traverser quantum signatures that would immediately alert hybridized personnel to apparent unauthorized entity manifestation.

The chamber visualization confirmed immediate response—four of the five hybridized individuals redirecting toward the diversionary signature, leaving minimal security coverage at the central control interface. This created the narrow intervention window they required for master shutdown sequence initiation.

"Execute primary approach," Alice directed, leading Team Gamma through the maintenance access point into the central chamber's peripheral section.

They moved with practiced efficiency, using the specialized equipment Eleanor had provided to minimize their quantum variance signatures—essentially becoming less detectable to hybridized perception by dampening their reality interaction patterns. This technology, developed during Project Looking Glass but never implemented in Department operations, provided their critical advantage in approaching the central control interface.

The chamber itself exceeded expectations in both scale and complexity—a vast circular space extending vertically through multiple levels, centered around a crystalline column that pulsed with energies connecting to all seven amplifier locations throughout Daybridge. Surrounding this column, concentric rings of technology represented seven decades of progressive development—from the original Project Resonance equipment to modern Department systems integrating conventional and advanced components.

Most striking was the containment apparatus positioned near the column's base—a specialized field generator maintaining what Dr. Liu had identified as an extracted probability matrix from an alternate timeline. The contained material shifted constantly within its confinement, displaying characteristics of both energy and matter while conforming to neither classification entirely.

"Probability extraction technology," Dr. Liu whispered, recognizing the implications immediately. "They've developed methods to remove and contain fundamental reality components from alternate timelines—essentially harvesting probability itself."

Alice focused on their primary objective—the original control interface integrated into the crystalline column's base. According to Eleanor's documentation, this interface represented the most direct access point to the breach network's foundational systems, predating Department modifications and potentially bypassing security protocols implemented in subsequent decades.

Team Gamma navigated carefully toward this interface, using structural elements for concealment while monitoring hybridized personnel movements throughout the chamber. The diversionary signature continued drawing attention away from their approach vector, creating the essential intervention window they required.

"Amplifier Three deactivation complete," Maya reported through the secure communication system. "Network reconfiguring to compensate for reduced energy distribution. Temporary vulnerability detected at remaining amplifier locations as system attempts to establish a new equilibrium."

"Team Alpha exploiting vulnerability window to accelerate approach to Amplifier Five," Rivera added. "Department security implementing containment protocols at deactivated locations. Resources being redirected from active sites to secure neutralized amplifiers."

This security redistribution aligned perfectly with their operational strategy—creating progressive advantage as each amplifier deactivation forced the Department to allocate resources toward containment rather than protection of remaining active sites.

Alice reached the base of the crystalline column, accessing the original control interface while Dr. Liu prepared the quantum consciousness disruption component for integration. The interface itself appeared deceptively simple—a geometric arrangement of crystalline elements surrounding a central access point designed for direct consciousness interaction rather than conventional technological engagement.

"Interface access established," Alice confirmed quietly. "Preparing for master shutdown sequence integration."

Dr. Liu connected the specialized equipment containing Eleanor's modified protocol, establishing the quantum consciousness disruption field that would prevent Traverser influence during the shutdown process. This critical component—absent from standard deactivation approaches—addressed the fundamental consciousness elements incorporated into the breach network's operational framework.

"Disruption field active," Dr. Liu confirmed. "Seventeen-minute operational window before detection countermeasures can adapt to the pattern."

Alice initiated the master shutdown sequence, interfacing directly with the original Project Resonance systems while bypassing subsequent Department modifications. The crystalline column responded immediately—its energy patterns shifting from pulsing activation to controlled dissipation as the shutdown protocol began systematic breach network reconfiguration.

"Master sequence initiated," Alice reported to all teams. "Primary node entering controlled shutdown phase. Maintain peripheral deactivation timeline for optimal synchronization."

The quantum field visualization displayed remarkable changes throughout the breach network—energy patterns reconfiguring from expansion to contraction as the shutdown protocol progressively reestablished natural quantum barriers between connected timelines. The process followed exactly the pattern Eleanor had predicted, with reality interfaces gradually returning to their natural permeability parameters.

Then something unexpected occurred. The contained probability matrix near the column's base began responding to the shutdown sequence—its fluctuation patterns intensifying as energy redistribution affected the chamber's quantum field configuration. The containment system registered growing instability, generating alert patterns that would soon draw security attention regardless of their diversionary measures.

"The extracted probability construct is destabilizing," Dr. Liu noted with concern. "Containment systems weren't designed to maintain coherence during network shutdown. If it collapses within our timeline..."

She didn't need to complete the assessment—a probability matrix collapse would release enormous quantum energy throughout the chamber, potentially triggering catastrophic reality destabilization that could accelerate breach expansion rather than containing it.

"Can we modify the shutdown sequence to stabilize the construct?" Alice asked, already adjusting interface parameters based on real-time feedback.

"Not without compromising the primary protocol," Dr. Liu replied after quick analysis. "The probability construct fundamentally opposes natural barrier restoration. Its very existence requires sustained breach configuration."

Alice made a rapid tactical decision, directing the security specialists to prepare emergency containment measures using Eleanor's equipment. If they couldn't prevent the probability construct's collapse, they needed to contain its effects within manageable parameters.

"Hybridized personnel returning to central positions," one security specialist warned, monitoring chamber activity. "Diversionary effectiveness degrading as containment system alerts escalate."

Their intervention window was closing rapidly—the combination of containment system alerts and diminishing diversionary effectiveness would soon bring full security response to their position at the control interface. They needed to complete the master shutdown sequence before Department countermeasures could interrupt the process.

"Amplifier Five deactivation sequence initiated," Maya reported. "Network reconfiguration accelerating as cumulative shutdown effects propagate through remaining active nodes."

The master control interface displayed progressive shutdown indicators as the protocol Eleanor had designed systematically recalibrated quantum boundary parameters throughout Daybridge. The process was working precisely as intended—gradually reestablishing natural reality barriers while preventing the catastrophic collapse that uncontrolled deactivation would trigger.

However, the destabilizing probability construct threatened this delicate process. Its containment systems now showed critical alert patterns as the extracted timeline fragment struggled to maintain coherence within a reality increasingly hostile to its fundamental configuration.

"We need to isolate the construct from the master shutdown field," Alice determined, recognizing the critical interaction threatening their operation. "Create a localized stability bubble that shields it from network reconfiguration effects."

Dr. Liu quickly adapted their equipment, repurposing components of the quantum consciousness disruption system to establish an isolated field around the containment apparatus. This modification represented a significant risk—reducing the effectiveness of the disruption component while diverting resources from the master shutdown sequence.

"Field adaptation implemented," Dr. Liu confirmed. "Localized stability established around the probability construct. Containment integrity temporarily reinforced, but with reduced shutdown protocol efficiency."

The modification created essential breathing room—allowing the master shutdown sequence to continue while temporarily stabilizing the extracted probability construct. However, it also extended the required processing time for complete network deactivation, lengthening their exposure to Department security response.

"Hybridized personnel approaching central column," the security specialist warned. "Intercept imminent in approximately ninety seconds."

Alice adjusted the master shutdown sequence, accelerating critical components while allowing secondary systems to process at extended timelines. This modification concentrated essential barrier restoration parameters in the initial phase, ensuring fundamental protocol completion even if Department intervention interrupted later sequence elements.

"Amplifier Five deactivation complete," Maya reported. "Team Alpha transitioning to final peripheral nodes. Department security implementing comprehensive containment protocols throughout Daybridge."

The breach network visualization showed remarkable progress—quantum variance reduced by approximately sixty-four percent throughout Daybridge, with reality barriers progressively returning to natural configuration parameters. The master shutdown sequence was succeeding despite the unexpected complication of the probability construct, steadily reversing seven decades of artificial breach expansion.

Then Department security response reached critical mass. The remaining hybridized personnel identified their position at the control interface, implementing immediate countermeasures designed to interrupt the shutdown sequence. Energy weapons specifically designed to disrupt quantum field operations discharged toward their position, forcing emergency defensive measures that compromised optimal shutdown management.

"Maintain shutdown sequence integrity," Alice directed as the security specialists deployed countermeasures. "Priority is protocol completion regardless of opposition intensity."

The security team established defensive positioning, using specialized equipment to generate localized quantum field distortions that redirected energy weapon effectiveness while minimizing disruption to the shutdown sequence. This created essential operational continuity despite escalating Department response throughout the chamber.

"Amplifier Seven deactivation sequence initiated," Maya reported. "Final peripheral node entering shutdown protocol. Seventeen-minute countdown to network completion pending central node finalization."

The master shutdown sequence reached seventy percent completion, critical barrier restoration parameters successfully implemented throughout the breach network. Reality interfaces throughout Daybridge progressively returned to natural permeability configuration, quantum variance readings declining toward baseline parameters for the first time in decades.

Department security response intensified as they recognized the existential threat to their operations. Additional personnel entered the chamber, implementing specialized countermeasures designed to interrupt the shutdown sequence through direct interface override. These attempts encountered the quantum consciousness disruption field Dr. Liu had established, temporarily preventing effective intervention.

"Shutdown sequence reaching final implementation phase," Alice reported to all teams. "Maintain peripheral deactivation timeline for optimal synchronization. Eighty-three percent completion at central node."

The containment system housing the probability construct showed increasing stress patterns despite their stabilization efforts. The extracted timeline fragment fundamentally opposed the reality reconfiguration occurring throughout the chamber, its very existence predicated on sustained breach conditions now being systematically eliminated.

"Construct containment reaching critical parameters," Dr. Liu warned. "Stabilization field degrading as shutdown sequence progresses. Containment failure imminent within approximately three minutes."

This created an impossible operational dilemma—continuing the shutdown sequence would trigger catastrophic containment failure, while interrupting the protocol to stabilize the construct would compromise everything they had accomplished throughout the breach network.

Alice made the difficult decision based on Eleanor's research regarding probability construct behavior. "Maintain shutdown sequence integrity. Prepare for controlled containment failure with localized quantum field barriers to direct energy dispersion toward the central column."

This approach represented a significant risk—essentially channeling the enormous energy release from containment failure into the crystalline column itself, using the probability construct's collapse to actually accelerate final shutdown parameters rather than opposing them.

Dr. Liu immediately understood the strategy, reconfiguring their equipment to establish directional quantum field barriers around the containment system. "Dispersion channels configured. Energy redirection parameters established for optimal shutdown acceleration."

The master shutdown sequence reached ninety-one percent completion as Department security continued escalating countermeasures throughout the chamber. The hybridized personnel implemented increasingly desperate intervention attempts, recognizing the approaching point of irreversible breach network deactivation.

"Final peripheral amplifier entering terminal shutdown phase," Maya reported. "Network synchronization at ninety-four percent alignment with master sequence. Breach collapse proceeding within optimal parameters."

The quantum field visualization displayed remarkable transformation throughout Daybridge—reality interfaces returning to natural configuration after seven decades of artificial manipulation. The breach network that had allowed Traverser influence and Department exploitation was systematically dissolving, quantum barriers between timelines reestablishing their fundamental integrity.

As the shutdown sequence approached completion, the probability construct containment system reached critical failure parameters. The extracted timeline fragment could no longer maintain coherence within a reality returning to natural configuration, its fundamental opposition to established quantum boundaries triggering catastrophic destabilization.

"Containment failure in three, two, one..." Dr. Liu counted down, monitoring system collapse with scientific precision.

The containment field dissolved in a cascading energy release that would have triggered catastrophic reality fragmentation without their directional barriers. Instead, the carefully configured quantum field channels directed the enormous energy surge directly into the crystalline column—essentially using the probability construct's collapse to power the final phase of the shutdown sequence.

The crystalline column absorbed this energy surge, incorporating it into the master protocol in precisely the manner Alice had anticipated. Rather than opposing the shutdown sequence, the probability construct's collapse actually accelerated final implementation, driving quantum barrier restoration throughout the breach network at exponentially increased efficiency.

"Energy integration successful," Alice reported as the system responded exactly as intended. "Shutdown sequence accelerating toward completion. Ninety-seven percent network reconfiguration achieved."

Department security responded with final countermeasures, attempting to physically disconnect the control interface from the crystalline column. These efforts encountered quantum field barriers established by their security specialists, creating essential operational continuity for the seventeen seconds required to reach protocol completion.

"Shutdown sequence at ninety-nine percent," Alice reported, monitoring final implementation parameters. "Reality interface reconfiguration approaching completion throughout Daybridge breach network."

The crystalline column's energy patterns shifted from controlled dissipation to harmonized stabilization—the signature Eleanor had identified as indicating successful quantum barrier restoration. Throughout Daybridge, reality interfaces that had been artificially expanded for decades returned to their natural configuration, quantum variance readings declining to baseline parameters consistent with unmanipulated space-time.

"Master shutdown sequence complete," Alice confirmed as the interface displayed final implementation verification. "Breach network successfully deactivated with quantum barriers restored to natural configuration parameters."

The quantum field visualization confirmed this assessment—showing Daybridge returning to normal reality coherence for the first time since Project Resonance had initiated artificial breach expansion in 1956. The seven-decade legacy of reality manipulation had been successfully reversed, interdimensional colonization prevented mere hours before astronomical alignment would have enabled mass Traverser transit.

Department security operations throughout the chamber collapsed into disarray as hybridized personnel experienced sudden quantum consciousness disruption. With breach network deactivation, their connection to Traverser consciousness across reality barriers dissolved, leaving them momentarily disoriented as their perception frameworks reconfigured to standard human parameters.

"All teams, confirm status," Alice requested through the secure communication system.

"Team Alpha reports successful deactivation of all peripheral amplifiers," Maya responded. "Quantum variance readings returned to baseline throughout Daybridge. Reality interface integrity restored to natural parameters."

"Team Beta confirms Department security operations in disarray throughout the city," Rivera added. "Hybridized personnel experiencing widespread perceptual disruption. Systematic withdrawal from amplifier locations underway."

Alice directed Team Gamma to implement final containment measures around the central facility, ensuring Department personnel couldn't reactivate systems or implement emergency protocols. The crystalline column had entered self-stabilization mode—a process Eleanor had documented from the original Project Resonance research, essentially a return to dormant configuration following artificial activation.

"Thirty-three hours until astronomical alignment peak," Dr. Liu noted, checking the countdown they had established. "With the amplifier network deactivated and quantum barriers restored, the alignment will pass without enabling Traverser transit."

The breach network that had threatened reality stability for seven decades had been successfully neutralized, preventing both catastrophic collapse and interdimensional colonization. Project Resonance's dangerous legacy—amplified through decades of Department exploitation—had finally been contained through the combined efforts of individuals across multiple scientific disciplines and professional backgrounds.

As Team Gamma secured their equipment and prepared for extraction from the central facility, Alice took a final moment to observe the crystalline column returning to its natural state. The alien technology that had enabled communication between realities—technology that predated human civilization yet had been adapted for human purposes—gradually shifted into a dormant configuration, its luminescence fading as quantum energy dissipated throughout its structure.

"We've succeeded beyond optimal projections," Dr. Liu noted, reviewing final monitoring data. "Eleanor's modified protocol not only deactivated the breach network but appears to have implemented fundamental quantum barrier reinforcement throughout Daybridge. The natural thin points that originally attracted Project Resonance attention have been substantially stabilized."

This represented an outcome exceeding even their most optimistic projections—not merely temporary deactivation of artificial expansion, but actual reinforcement of the natural reality interfaces that had made Daybridge susceptible to manipulation in the first place.

"All teams, implement extraction protocols," Alice directed through the secure communication system. "Maintain operational security until confirmation of complete Department withdrawal from amplifier locations."

As Team Gamma navigated back through the maintenance access corridor, Alice reflected on the extraordinary confluence of circumstances that had enabled their success. The decades of preparation by Margaret Chen and Eleanor Voss, the specialized expertise of Maya and Dr. Liu, the tactical support from Rivera and his connections—all combining at precisely the right moment to counter a threat spanning multiple realities.

They had prevented catastrophic reality collapse mere hours before the astronomical alignment would have enabled mass Traverser transit into their timeline. The Department of Temporal Security's seven-decade project to exploit reality breaches for technological advantage had been systematically dismantled, their hybridized leadership suddenly disconnected from the interdimensional entities that had influenced their perception and motivation.

The breach network beneath Daybridge—once an active transit system for entities moving between realities—had returned to dormant configuration, its potential for both extraordinary discovery and existential threat temporarily contained through human intervention.

As Team Gamma reached the extraction point, Alice received confirmation of successful withdrawal from all amplifier locations throughout Daybridge. The operation had succeeded comprehensively, with minimal casualties and maximum effectiveness—an outcome that seemed almost impossibly fortunate given the forces they had confronted.

Perhaps, Alice reflected as they emerged into daylight, her grandmother's influence had extended beyond conventional understanding of cause and effect—guiding probability itself toward this specific culmination of circumstances. In a reality where quantum consciousness could perceive multiple timeframes simultaneously, perhaps Margaret Chen's preparations had transcended standard temporal limitations, arranging variables across decades to enable this precise moment of intervention.

Whatever forces had aligned to enable their success, the immediate threat had been neutralized. Reality barriers had been restored. The voices in Echo Alley had been silenced.

But as Alice well knew from years of paranormal investigation, silence rarely meant permanent resolution when dealing with phenomena beyond conventional understanding. The breach network might be dormant, but its existence remained—as did the entities who had created it for transit between realities.

Their victory was significant but potentially temporary. The Department of Temporal Security might be disrupted but not eliminated. The Traversers might be temporarily denied transit but not permanently deterred.

For now, however, reality had been preserved. Daybridge had been protected from both catastrophic collapse and interdimensional colonization. The immediate crisis had been resolved through the combined efforts of individuals who had recognized the threat and chosen to confront it despite overwhelming odds.

As Team Gamma rendezvoused with their colleagues at the designated extraction point, Alice allowed herself a moment of genuine relief. They had accomplished something extraordinary—preventing catastrophe through understanding rather than force, through cooperation across disciplines rather than institutional authority, through careful preparation rather than desperate reaction.

In that accomplishment lay hope for addressing whatever consequences might follow—whatever new challenges might emerge from the dormant technology beneath Daybridge, or the interdimensional entities temporarily denied access to their reality.

The paranormal investigator, the quantum physicist, the detective, and their allies had successfully confronted forces beyond conventional understanding. Whatever came next, they would face it with the knowledge and confidence gained through this remarkable intervention.

Reality had been preserved. The breach had been contained. The echoes had been silenced.

For now.

CHAPTER FOURTEEN: THE CONFRONTATION

Three days after the successful shutdown of the amplifier network, Alice Chen stood at the entrance to Echo Alley, watching Department personnel systematically dismantling monitoring equipment around the breach point. The astronomical alignment had passed without incident seventeen hours earlier—the critical window during which Traverser colonization would have occurred closing without the null barrier state they had prepared for decades to exploit.

"They're conducting comprehensive withdrawal," Maya observed from beside her, monitoring quantum variance patterns with equipment modified from Eleanor's designs. "Removing all evidence of operational presence while maintaining minimal observation capability."

The Department's response to their intervention had been surprisingly measured—neither the aggressive counterstrike Alice had anticipated nor the complete abandonment that seemed equally plausible. Instead, they had implemented what appeared to be pre-established contingency protocols for scenario-specific continuation following major operational compromise.

"They're adapting rather than retreating," Alice noted, recognizing the methodical approach that suggested long-term strategy rather than reactive crisis management. "Reconfiguring for sustained observation while developing new implementation vectors."

Their successful shutdown operation had neutralized the immediate threat of Traverser colonization and reality collapse, but the Department of Temporal Security itself remained—an organization with seven decades of accumulated resources, specialized knowledge, and strategic objectives that transcended any single operational setback.

"Quantum variance readings have stabilized at seventeen percent above natural background," Maya reported, studying measurement data from the modified sensors. "The breach network remains dormant but not eliminated. Essentially, we've returned it to pre-amplification status similar to its configuration before Project Resonance activation."

This assessment aligned with Eleanor's predictions—their intervention had successfully deactivated the artificial expansion of natural reality thin points, but couldn't eliminate the fundamental breach network that predated human civilization. The Traverser transit system remained intact beneath Daybridge, dormant but potentially subject to future reactivation under appropriate conditions.

"We've won a battle, not the war," Alice said, articulating what both of them understood. "We've prevented immediate catastrophe, but the underlying conditions remain essentially unchanged."

Their current position—observing Department operations from concealed vantage points throughout central Daybridge—represented phase one of what Alice had designated "Operation Oversight." Having successfully prevented reality collapse and interdimensional colonization, they had transitioned to systematic documentation of Department response patterns to inform long-term countermeasures against potential reactivation attempts.

The team that had implemented the shutdown operation had mostly dispersed—Rivera returning to his police duties with heightened awareness of Department activities throughout Daybridge, Dr. Liu resuming her university research with new perspectives on quantum reality interfaces, Eliza and her security contacts maintaining vigilance within institutional frameworks. Only Alice and Maya remained fully committed to ongoing monitoring operations, their specialized expertise most relevant to tracking potential breach reactivation indicators.

"They've established new monitoring configurations at all seven amplifier locations," Maya noted, reviewing data from distributed sensors they had placed throughout Daybridge. "Passive observation systems rather than active manipulation technology. They're studying the shutdown effects rather than immediately attempting reversal."

This approach suggested something Alice found both reassuring and concerning—the Department appeared to be genuinely analyzing what had happened rather than blindly pursuing reactivation. This indicated a more sophisticated adaptive capability than they had anticipated, potentially signifying long-term strategies beyond the immediate colonization objective they had disrupted.

"They're learning," Alice observed. "Analyzing our countermeasures to develop more effective approaches for future implementation."

As they continued observation, Alice's secure communication device activated—a specialized system Eleanor had designed for quantum-encrypted information transfer invulnerable to conventional interception. The incoming communication originated from their secure operations center established in Eleanor's former residence at Lakeside Retirement Community, where they had relocated following successful amplifier network shutdown.

"Quantum variance spike detected at Echo Alley," came Dr. Liu's voice through the secure connection. "Seventeen percent amplitude increase over stabilized baseline, duration approximately thirty-four seconds before return to current parameters."

This development was concerning—the first significant energy fluctuation since their shutdown operation three days earlier. While the breach network remained dormant overall, this isolated spike suggested potential instability within the restored quantum barriers.

"Transmitting detailed measurement data," Dr. Liu continued. "Pattern analysis indicates organized information transfer rather than random fluctuation—essentially a directed communication attempt through the dormant breach point."

Alice and Maya exchanged concerned glances. A directed communication attempt suggested deliberate activation rather than natural variance—someone or something attempting to establish connection through the dormant breach network despite their shutdown intervention.

"Implementing enhanced monitoring protocols," Maya responded, activating specialized equipment designed to capture quantum variance patterns with maximum fidelity. "Preparing for potential repeated transmission attempt."

They observed Department personnel responding to the same energy fluctuation—security elements establishing perimeter control while technical specialists deployed advanced monitoring equipment around Echo Alley. The response pattern confirmed that Department systems had detected the same variance spike, triggering established protocols for potential breach reactivation scenarios.

"Second variance spike initiating," Dr. Liu reported through the secure connection. "Amplitude increasing to twenty-three percent above baseline. Pattern consistency suggests deliberate transmission rather than random fluctuation."

Alice activated their modified receiver system—specialized equipment developed from Eleanor's designs combined with components from Alice's original paranormal investigation tools. The hybrid technology was specifically calibrated to detect and decode information transfer through reality interfaces, essentially eavesdropping on communications between connected timelines.

The receiver activated successfully, capturing quantum variance patterns and converting them to interpretable data formats. Unlike the automated information extraction they had observed during their temporal stakeout, this transmission displayed characteristics of directed communication—structured information deliberately formatted for human comprehension.

"Transmission origin tracking suggests Timeline J-73," Dr. Liu reported after analyzing the pattern characteristics. "Consistent with the resistance coalition contact from our previous cross-timeline communication."

This identification was both surprising and concerning—Timeline J-73 represented the alternate reality where resistance elements had provided tactical intelligence regarding Department countermeasures during their shutdown operation planning. That they would attempt communication after successful shutdown suggested ongoing developments requiring cross-timeline coordination.

The receiver completed preliminary decoding, converting quantum variance patterns into text format displayed on their specialized equipment:

"To resistance elements in Timeline K-17: Urgent advisory regarding breach network status. Department operations in our timeline indicate coordinated reactivation protocol implementation across multiple connected realities. Evidence suggests synchronized approach to bypass individual timeline shutdown countermeasures through distributed activation sequence. Recommend immediate enhanced monitoring of dormant amplifier locations with particular focus on quantum resonance harmonics consistent with external activation attempts."

The message contained technical specifications for monitoring parameters specifically designed to detect the described reactivation approach—essentially an early warning system for identifying cross-timeline activation attempts before they reached implementation threshold.

"They're attempting coordinated reactivation across multiple timelines simultaneously," Maya translated, immediately grasping the strategic implications. "Using distributed activation protocols to gradually establish resonance patterns that could eventually reactivate our dormant network through external influence rather than direct local intervention."

This approach represented sophisticated adaptation to their shutdown countermeasures—essentially attempting to reactivate Daybridge's breach network through accumulated influence from connected timelines rather than direct manipulation within their reality. The strategy might potentially bypass the quantum barrier reinforcement their intervention had established.

"Implementing recommended monitoring parameters," Maya confirmed, reconfiguring their equipment to detect the specific resonance patterns identified in the cross-timeline communication. "Distributing updated detection protocols to all observation points throughout Daybridge."

Alice considered the strategic implications of this development. The Department's measured withdrawal and reconfigured monitoring suddenly appeared in a different context—not merely adaptation to operational setback, but preparation for an entirely different activation approach coordinated across multiple reality configurations simultaneously.

"They're more organized than we anticipated," Alice noted grimly. "Coordinating across timelines to implement distributed strategies that transcend individual reality limitations."

This level of cross-timeline coordination suggested sophisticated communication capabilities despite their shutdown of the amplifier network—alternative channels or technologies enabling Department operations to maintain contact across reality barriers even with the primary breach network dormant.

As they processed these implications, their monitoring equipment detected Department personnel implementing what appeared to be transmission protocols at Echo Alley—essentially attempting to respond to the cross-timeline communication they had intercepted. The technical specialists had deployed specialized equipment directly at the breach point, generating carefully calibrated energy patterns designed to temporarily enhance quantum permeability without triggering comprehensive reactivation.

"They're attempting response transmission," Maya observed, adjusting their monitoring equipment to capture this interaction. "Localized permeability enhancement specifically configured for minimal-footprint communication rather than physical transfer."

Their receiver captured this transmission attempt, decoding the quantum variance patterns into a comprehensible format:

"Timeline K-17 Department command acknowledges advisory. Implementing coordinated monitoring protocols across all dormant amplifier locations. Reactivation sequence Alpha-Seven remains primary implementation objective with the seventeen-day preparation timeline confirmed. Technical specifications for resonance harmonization follow in the secondary transmission packet."

The Department's response revealed critical intelligence—confirmation of active reactivation planning with specific timeline parameters and implementation methodology. The reference to "Reactivation sequence Alpha-Seven" suggested a pre-established contingency protocol designed specifically for recovery following shutdown countermeasures like those they had implemented.

"They already had contingency protocols prepared," Alice noted with grudging respect for their operational foresight. "Specific methodologies developed for breach network reactivation following exactly the type of intervention we implemented."

"Seventeen-day preparation timeline," Maya highlighted the most immediately concerning element. "They're not regrouping for long-term reconsideration—they're implementing accelerated reactivation protocols with specific completion parameters."

This timeline significantly altered their strategic considerations. Rather than the extended observation and incremental countermeasure development they had planned, they now faced imminent reactivation attempts requiring immediate intervention to maintain the shutdown status they had achieved at significant risk.

Alice activated the secure communication system, contacting their operations center at Lakeside Retirement Community. "Dr. Liu, we've intercepted Department communication confirming accelerated reactivation protocols. Seventeen-day implementation timeline with cross-timeline coordination. We need an immediate full team recall for countermeasure development."

"Understood," came the physicist's response. "Initiating secure contact protocols for all team members. Will prepare facility for the comprehensive strategy session within three hours."

As they prepared to withdraw from their observation position, the quantum variance monitor detected another spike at Echo Alley—significantly larger than the previous communications, reaching thirty-four percent above stabilized baseline. This energy signature exceeded parameters consistent with information transfer, suggesting something more substantial attempting to interact through the dormant breach point.

"Major variance event in progress," Maya reported, focusing monitoring equipment on the phenomenon. "Pattern indicates active breach interface rather than communication attempt—essentially something pushing against the quantum barriers from an adjacent timeline."

Department personnel responded with obvious alarm, security elements establishing enhanced perimeter control while technical specialists implemented what appeared to be emergency containment protocols. Their response pattern suggested this development exceeded anticipated parameters, potentially representing uncontrolled breach activity rather than regulated communication.

The quantum variance spike continued intensifying, reaching forty-seven percent above baseline—approaching levels that might temporarily overcome the reinforced barriers their shutdown protocol had established. The energy pattern displayed characteristics of conscious direction rather than random fluctuation, suggesting a deliberate attempt to establish a physical interface rather than merely transfer information.

"Active breach attempt in progress," Alice determined, recognizing the pattern from Eleanor's documentation of Traverser manifestation attempts. "Something is trying to physically transition through Echo Alley despite dormant network status."

Their monitoring equipment captured extraordinary data as the energy pattern reached critical intensity. For approximately seventeen seconds, reality itself visibly distorted around Echo Alley—the air taking on the opalescent quality characteristic of barrier permeability, physical surroundings demonstrating subtle displacement patterns consistent with overlapping spatial configurations.

Then, with shocking suddenness, a figure materialized at the center of Echo Alley—emerging through momentarily permeable reality barriers despite the dormant status of the breach network. The figure appeared human but moved with the distinctive fluidity Eleanor had documented as characteristic of hybridized individuals, suggesting Traverser consciousness integration within human form.

Department personnel immediately implemented containment protocols, security elements establishing tactical positions around the materialized figure while technical specialists deployed specialized equipment designed to prevent further manifestation. Their response demonstrated both preparation for this contingency and significant concern regarding its implications for containment integrity.

Alice and Maya maintained observation from their concealed position, recording comprehensive data regarding both the manifestation itself and Department response protocols. The monitoring equipment continued capturing quantum variance patterns throughout the event, providing crucial information about breach dynamics during this unexpected development.

The manifested figure appeared to communicate with Department personnel, though distance prevented direct audio capture of this interaction. Body language suggested authoritative direction rather than compliance, with Department security elements responding to apparent instructions from the manifested individual despite their containment protocols.

"That's not standard Department response to unauthorized manifestation," Alice noted, recognizing deviation from established protocols. "They're treating this individual as command authority rather than containment priority."

"Quantum signature analysis suggests hybridized configuration consistent with high-level Department leadership," Maya added, studying the monitoring data. "Essentially a senior official with Traverser consciousness integration manifesting from an adjacent timeline where they maintained operational capability despite local shutdown."

This development suggested something deeply concerning—Department leadership maintaining cross-timeline operational continuity despite their successful shutdown intervention. If hybridized command elements could physically transition between connected realities, their local countermeasures might prove insufficient against coordinated multi-timeline strategies.

As they continued observation, the manifested figure directed Department personnel to deploy specialized equipment directly at the Echo Alley breach point. The technology appeared significantly advanced beyond standard configurations they had documented previously, suggesting capabilities developed specifically for post-shutdown reactivation scenarios.

"They're implementing direct barrier manipulation," Maya determined, analyzing energy patterns generated by the deployed technology. "Attempting to establish localized permeability enhancement that could potentially bypass our shutdown countermeasures through precisely targeted quantum field modification."

This approach represented sophisticated adaptation to their intervention—essentially attempting to create controlled "windows" through the reinforced quantum barriers rather than comprehensive network reactivation. Such a methodology might potentially reestablish limited cross-timeline access without triggering the widespread instability their shutdown protocol had been designed to prevent.

"If successful, this approach could create stable access points without full network reactivation," Maya continued, concern evident in her assessment. "Essentially surgical breach restoration rather than comprehensive reactivation—potentially flying under detection thresholds for the monitoring systems we've established."

Alice recognized the strategic implications immediately. Rather than attempting direct reversal of their shutdown intervention, the Department appeared to be implementing precision countermeasures designed to establish limited cross-timeline access while avoiding detection parameters based on full network activation. This methodology might potentially restore essential operational capabilities while minimizing observable disturbance to quantum barrier integrity.

"We need to adapt our countermeasures to address targeted permeability enhancement rather than comprehensive reactivation," Alice determined, already formulating adjusted monitoring parameters. "Distributed detection systems focused on localized barrier manipulation rather than network-wide energy distribution."

As they prepared to withdraw and implement these adjustments, Department personnel completed equipment deployment at Echo Alley. The specialized technology activated with distinctive energy signatures, generating precisely configured quantum field modifications focused directly at the dormant breach point.

The effect was immediate and alarming. Reality distortion intensified around Echo Alley, creating visible spatial displacement that extended approximately seventeen meters in all directions from the central breach point. Within this affected area, multiple reality configurations appeared to temporarily overlap—creating the disturbing visual effect of several different versions of the warehouse district simultaneously occupying the same spatial coordinates.

"They're forcing localized reality overlay," Maya reported, monitoring equipment capturing extraordinary data during this phenomenon. "Creating deliberate configuration overlap between adjacent timelines without full barrier dissolution."

This methodology represented a significant advancement beyond previous Department capabilities—essentially establishing controlled reality intersection without comprehensive breach expansion. The approach created limited windows between connected timelines while maintaining overall barrier integrity, potentially enabling selective cross-timeline operations without triggering catastrophic instability.

Most concerning was the apparent stability of the configuration—the overlapping reality segments maintaining coherent integration rather than destructive interference. This suggested sophisticated understanding of quantum boundary dynamics beyond what they had anticipated in Department operational capabilities.

"The hybridized commander is providing technical direction beyond local timeline development," Maya assessed, observing the manifested figure's interaction with Department technical specialists. "Essentially importing advanced methodology from alternate reality configurations where they maintained operational continuity despite resistance intervention."

This cross-timeline knowledge transfer represented exactly the strategic advantage they had feared—Department operations leveraging parallel development across multiple realities to accelerate recovery from countermeasures implemented in any individual timeline. The approach essentially transformed separate reality configurations into distributed operational resources, sharing advances across connected timelines to overcome local limitations.

As the reality overlay stabilized around Echo Alley, something unprecedented occurred. Multiple versions of the same location became simultaneously accessible—different configurations of the warehouse district existing in parallel within the affected area. Department personnel established operational positions throughout this overlapping reality complex, essentially securing access to multiple timeline configurations simultaneously.

"They're establishing a controlled reality intersection nexus," Maya determined, comprehending the strategic objective behind this approach. "Creating stable access to multiple timeline configurations without full breach network reactivation."

This methodology effectively bypassed their shutdown countermeasures by establishing limited but stable cross-timeline access without requiring comprehensive network reactivation. The approach focused extremely precise reality manipulation at the original breach point rather than attempting to reverse the amplifier network shutdown throughout Daybridge.

"We need to intervene immediately," Alice decided, recognizing the critical threat this development represented. "If they establish stable reality intersection capability, they can potentially restore cross-timeline operations despite our shutdown of the amplifier network."

They quickly gathered their monitoring equipment and prepared for direct intervention—a significant escalation from their planned observation activities, but necessary given the unexpected development at Echo Alley. The specialized countermeasure technology they had prepared for potential reactivation attempts would need immediate deployment to address this unanticipated methodology.

"Contact Rivera and request tactical support at Echo Alley," Alice directed through the secure communication system. "We need immediate intervention capability with specialized equipment deployment."

As they coordinated response options, the reality overlay at Echo Alley continued stabilizing—multiple timeline configurations maintaining coherent intersection within the affected area. Department personnel established what appeared to be systematic transition protocols between overlapping reality segments, essentially creating navigable pathways between connected timeline configurations.

Most concerning was the apparent two-way nature of these pathways—personnel moving between reality configurations in both directions rather than merely accessing alternate timelines from their original position. This suggested the Department had established genuine cross-timeline transit capability despite the dormant status of the broader breach network.

"They've created a localized transit nexus," Maya assessed, recognizing the strategic implications. "Essentially a quantum intersection hub allowing controlled movement between connected timelines without requiring full network activation."

This development fundamentally altered their tactical considerations. Rather than preventing network reactivation, they now faced the challenge of neutralizing an already-established reality intersection point—a significantly more complex objective requiring direct confrontation with Department operations actively utilizing the created nexus.

"We need the quantum field disruptors Eleanor provided," Alice determined, referencing specialized technology designed to destabilize artificial reality manipulations. "Direct application at the intersection perimeter should progressively collapse the established overlay configuration."

As they finalized intervention preparations, something unexpected emerged from the reality intersection at Echo Alley. Multiple figures materialized from different timeline configurations—individuals with varied appearance but similar movement patterns suggesting hybridized status. These figures congregated around the central breach point, creating what appeared to be a coordinated cross-timeline operation team.

"They're assembling hybridized personnel from multiple connected timelines," Maya observed with growing concern. "Essentially creating a composite operation team leveraging specialized capabilities from different reality configurations."

This represented precisely the strategic advantage they had feared when implementing the shutdown operation—Department capability to coordinate across reality barriers despite local countermeasures, leveraging parallel development across multiple timelines to overcome intervention in any individual configuration.

Alice recognized they faced a critical decision point. Their planned observation and incremental countermeasure development was clearly insufficient against this accelerated cross-timeline coordination. Direct intervention had become necessary despite significantly elevated risk parameters and uncertain outcome probability.

"We need to implement immediate confrontation protocols," Alice determined, activating the full team recall through their secure communication system. "Department operations have established localized reality intersection capability requiring direct neutralization response."

As they coordinated team deployment, Maya continued monitoring the developing situation at Echo Alley. The reality intersection had stabilized into what appeared to be a permanent configuration—multiple timeline versions simultaneously accessible within the affected area, with established transition protocols enabling controlled movement between connected reality segments.

Most concerning was the systematic equipment transfer occurring through this intersection point—specialized technology moving between timeline configurations in what appeared to be deliberate resource consolidation. This methodology effectively circumvented one of the primary advantages of their shutdown intervention, allowing Department operations to leverage technological development across multiple realities despite local limitations.

"They're implementing cross-timeline resource consolidation," Maya reported, documenting the equipment transfer patterns. "Essentially pooling technological capabilities from multiple reality configurations to accelerate operational recovery in our timeline."

This approach represented sophisticated adaptation to their countermeasures—essentially treating connected timelines as distributed resource networks rather than separate operational theaters. By establishing controlled intersection capability, Department operations could leverage parallel development across multiple realities to overcome intervention effects in any individual timeline.

As team members began arriving at their coordination point near Echo Alley, Alice outlined the tactical situation and intervention objectives. Rivera provided critical intelligence regarding Department security deployment throughout central Daybridge, while Dr. Liu analyzed the quantum physics implications of the established reality intersection.

"The intersection methodology they've implemented is actually quite brilliant," Dr. Liu acknowledged with reluctant professional admiration. "Rather than attempting to reactivate the full breach network, they've established precisely targeted reality overlay at the original breach point—essentially creating a controlled intersection of multiple timeline configurations without requiring comprehensive barrier dissolution."

"Can we neutralize it?" Alice asked, focusing on practical intervention capability rather than theoretical assessment.

"Yes, but with significant complications," Dr. Liu responded, studying the monitoring data they had captured. "The stabilized intersection has established self-sustaining quantum resonance patterns. Direct disruption would trigger cascading reality reconciliation throughout the affected area—essentially forcing overlapping configurations to resolve into singular spatial parameters."

"Which means what exactly?" Rivera asked, translating the technical assessment into practical implications.

"Forcing everything from multiple timeline configurations to suddenly exist in single reality parameters," Maya explained. "Entities, objects, energy patterns—all competing for spatial occupation rights within conventional physics frameworks."

"That sounds... messy," Rivera observed with characteristic understatement.

"Potentially catastrophic," Dr. Liu confirmed. "Such forced reconciliation could trigger localized reality collapse within the affected area—essentially quantum annihilation as incompatible configurations attempt simultaneous occupation of identical spatial coordinates."

This assessment created significant tactical complications. Direct neutralization of the established reality intersection could potentially trigger the very catastrophe they had implemented the shutdown operation to prevent—localized reality collapse that might propagate through connected spatial regions if not properly contained.

"We need an alternative approach," Alice determined, already formulating adjusted intervention parameters. "Something that gradually degrades intersection stability rather than forcing immediate reconciliation."

Maya considered this requirement, reviewing the specialized equipment Eleanor had provided for various contingency scenarios.

"The quantum field modulators could potentially achieve this objective—essentially introducing progressive destabilization patterns that gradually reduce intersection coherence without triggering catastrophic reconciliation."

This approach would require direct application within the affected area—placing team members in immediate proximity to both Department security operations and the reality intersection itself. The risk parameters exceeded standard intervention thresholds, but alternatives appeared increasingly limited as Department cross-timeline coordination continued expanding through the established nexus.

"We need to implement immediately," Alice decided, recognizing the escalating threat as additional hybridized personnel continued emerging through the reality intersection. "Further delay allows additional resource consolidation that will exponentially increase intervention difficulty."

The team quickly organized specialized equipment for the neutralization operation, with Maya and Dr. Liu configuring the quantum field modulators for optimal destabilization parameters. Rivera coordinated tactical approach vectors with his security contacts, establishing distraction protocols to create necessary intervention windows through Department security coverage.

As preparations concluded, Alice conducted final team briefing—outlining primary objectives, contingency protocols, and extraction procedures following successful implementation. The operation represented a significant escalation from their previous observation stance, directly confronting Department operations actively utilizing cross-timeline capabilities.

"Primary objective is controlled degradation of reality intersection stability," Alice emphasized, ensuring all team members understood the delicate balance required. "We're not attempting immediate neutralization, but rather progressive destabilization that allows natural barrier restoration without catastrophic reconciliation."

With final preparations complete, the team-initiated approach protocols—utilizing distributed distraction measures to create intervention windows through Department security coverage around Echo Alley. The quantum field modulators were configured for sequential deployment at specific coordinates surrounding the reality intersection, creating overlapping destabilization fields that would gradually reduce configuration coherence.

Alice led the primary insertion team, utilizing Eleanor's quantum variance dampening technology to reduce detection probability by hybridized personnel operating within the intersection perimeter. This approach allowed careful advancement toward deployment positions despite active Department security throughout the affected area.

As they navigated through the outer perimeter of the reality intersection, Alice experienced firsthand the extraordinary phenomenon they had previously observed from a distance. Multiple timeline configurations overlapped within the affected area, creating the disorienting experience of seeing several different versions of the same location simultaneously occupying identical spatial coordinates.

The warehouse district appeared in various developmental stages across connected timelines—some configurations showing advanced urbanization, others maintaining industrial characteristics, some displaying evidence of significant conflict or environmental degradation. These overlapping reality segments created a fragmentary landscape where consistent navigation required careful attention to configuration boundaries and transition points.

Most disconcerting were the occasional entities moving between reality segments—individuals with the distinctive movement patterns of hybridized personnel, navigating the intersection complex with practiced familiarity suggesting extensive experience with cross-timeline operations. These personnel appeared to be implementing systematic protocols throughout the connected configurations, establishing what resembled permanent operational infrastructure within the reality intersection itself.

"They're not treating this as temporary capability," Alice noted quietly to Maya as they advanced toward primary deployment positions. "They're establishing permanent operational infrastructure within the intersection complex—essentially creating a persistent cross-timeline nexus despite our shutdown of the broader network."

This approach represented significant strategic adaptation—rather than attempting to reverse their shutdown countermeasures throughout Daybridge, Department operations had simply established alternative methodology focused at the original breach point. The approach effectively circumvented their intervention while maintaining essential cross-timeline capabilities.

As they reached designated deployment positions surrounding the central intersection point, Alice observed something deeply concerning—what appeared to be preparations for expanded intersection parameters beyond the current affected area. Department technical specialists were deploying specialized equipment at the perimeter boundaries, suggesting a methodology for progressive extension of the reality overlay throughout surrounding portions of Daybridge.

"They're preparing for intersection expansion," Alice informed team members through the secure communication system. "Accelerate deployment timeline for quantum field modulators. Priority is containing current parameters before expansion implementation."

Team members acknowledged this directive, accelerating equipment deployment at designated coordinates surrounding the reality intersection. The quantum field modulators were designed to establish overlapping destabilization fields that would gradually reduce configuration coherence without triggering catastrophic reconciliation—essentially introducing controlled degradation rather than forced neutralization.

As Alice prepared to deploy the primary modulator at her designated position, movement at the central intersection point captured her attention. The original hybridized figure who had first manifested through Echo Alley was directing what appeared to be final preparation phases for intersection expansion—coordinating technical specialists from multiple timeline configurations in synchronized deployment patterns.

"Primary expansion sequence initiating," Maya reported through the secure communication system. "Field measurements indicate seventeen percent parameter increase implemented at intersection boundaries. Modulator deployment must complete before second expansion phase."

Alice accelerated deployment procedures, activating the primary quantum field modulator at her designated position. The specialized technology initiated as designed, generating subtle destabilization patterns that began propagating through the established reality intersection. The effect wasn't immediately visible but registered clearly on monitoring equipment—quantum coherence gradually declining throughout the affected area as the modulation field established influence parameters.

Similar reports came from other team members as additional modulators activated at designated coordinates surrounding the intersection complex. The combined effect created overlapping destabilization fields that systematically reduced configuration stability without triggering immediate reconciliation—exactly the controlled degradation they had intended.

Department technical specialists detected this intervention almost immediately, monitoring equipment registering the subtle destabilization patterns propagating throughout the intersection complex. Their response was immediate and coordinated—hybridized personnel implementing countermeasures designed to reinforce quantum coherence against the introduced destabilization fields.

"Countermeasures detected at multiple positions," Maya reported, monitoring field measurements throughout the affected area. "Department technical response implementing coherence reinforcement protocols to maintain intersection stability."

This development had been anticipated in their planning—Department operations would naturally attempt to preserve the established reality intersection against neutralization efforts. The quantum field modulators had been specifically designed to generate destabilization patterns resistant to standard countermeasures, progressively adapting to reinforcement attempts while maintaining controlled degradation protocols.

What they hadn't anticipated was direct intervention by the hybridized command figure coordinating operations at the central intersection point. This individual appeared to recognize the destabilization methodology immediately, implementing specialized countermeasures that demonstrated intimate familiarity with the very technology they were deploying.

"Primary hybrid implementing targeted countermeasures directly aligned with our modulation patterns," Maya reported with evident concern. "They recognize our specific technology and methodology—essentially implementing perfectly calibrated response protocols."

This suggested something deeply troubling—the hybridized commander possessed knowledge of their specific countermeasure technology, potentially acquired through cross-timeline intelligence gathering from reality configurations where similar intervention attempts had already occurred. This represented precisely the strategic advantage they had feared when confronting operations with multi-timeline coordination capability.

"Adjust modulation frequencies to secondary parameters," Alice directed, implementing contingency protocols they had established for exactly this scenario. "Transition to asynchronous destabilization patterns to prevent coordinated countermeasure effectiveness."

Team members acknowledged this directive, adjusting modulator configurations to implement the more complex destabilization methodology. This approach sacrificed efficiency for resistance to coordinated countermeasures, essentially creating unpredictable destabilization patterns that couldn't be neutralized through single-vector response protocols.

As this adjustment implemented throughout their deployment network, something unexpected occurred at the central intersection point. The hybridized commander appeared to directly address their intervention attempt, turning toward Alice's position despite her utilization of quantum variance dampening technology designed to prevent detection.

"Alice Chen," the figure stated with disturbing clarity despite significant distance. "Your intervention patterns are consistent across seventeen documented timeline configurations. Perhaps we should discuss more productive approaches than this perpetual cycle of disruption and recovery."

The direct address was deeply unsettling—not merely identifying Alice specifically but suggesting familiarity with her intervention attempts across multiple reality configurations. This implied sophisticated cross-timeline intelligence gathering far exceeding what they had anticipated in Department operational capabilities.

Most concerning was the hybridized commander's apparent awareness of their specific location despite quantum variance dampening technology—suggesting perceptual capabilities that transcended conventional detection limitations. This development significantly altered tactical considerations, as concealment measures they had relied upon for operational security appeared compromised by enhanced hybrid perception.

"Maintain modulator deployment protocols," Alice directed team members through the secure communication system. "Continue implementation regardless of direct engagement attempts."

The hybridized commander appeared to anticipate this response, directing Department personnel to adjust security positions throughout the intersection complex. Rather than attempting to locate and neutralize all team members, they established containment perimeters around deployed modulators—essentially isolating the destabilization technology while maintaining overall intersection integrity.

"They're implementing targeted containment rather than comprehensive neutralization," Maya reported, monitoring Department response patterns through distributed sensors. "Essentially isolating our modulators within localized stability fields while maintaining broader intersection coherence."

This approach demonstrated sophisticated tactical adaptation—treating their intervention as a technical challenge rather than a security threat, implementing precisely calibrated countermeasures rather than overwhelming response. The methodology suggested operations directed by strategic intelligence rather than reactive protocols, consistent with leadership possessing cross-timeline coordination experience.

As Department countermeasures progressively isolated their deployed modulators, the hybridized commander approached Alice's position directly—navigating through overlapping reality configurations with practiced efficiency suggesting extensive experience with intersection dynamics. Despite continued utilization of quantum variance dampening technology, Alice's position appeared clearly identifiable to the hybrid's enhanced perception.

"Your persistent opposition to Department operations demonstrates remarkable consistency across reality configurations," the hybridized commander stated, stopping approximately seventeen meters from Alice's position. "While individual methodologies vary, the fundamental pattern remains identical—Alice Chen confronting breach manipulation despite overwhelming probability disadvantage."

The statement contained disturbing implications—suggesting observation of multiple versions of Alice across connected timelines, all apparently engaged in similar opposition to Department operations despite varying specific circumstances. This cross-reality pattern recognition represented sophisticated intelligence gathering capabilities transcending individual timeline limitations.

"Perhaps this perpetual opposition cycle might benefit from direct engagement rather than continued countermeasure deployment," the hybrid continued, making no immediate move to approach closer or implement security response. "Your concerns regarding breach network utilization may be addressed through collaborative protocols rather than binary opposition frameworks."

The approach was unexpected—suggesting negotiation rather than neutralization despite Alice's active intervention against Department operations. This methodology departed significantly from documented Department response patterns, potentially indicating strategic adaptation based on cross-timeline outcome analysis.

Alice maintained operational focus despite this unexpected engagement attempt, continuing modulator adjustments to maximize destabilization effectiveness against implemented countermeasures. The specialized equipment was progressively adapting to isolation protocols, generating penetrating destabilization patterns that propagated beyond containment parameters.

"Your technology is impressive," the hybrid acknowledged, observing these adjustments with evident professional assessment. "Eleanor Voss's quantum field manipulation designs demonstrate remarkable effectiveness across multiple application scenarios. However, isolation protocols will achieve containment within approximately seventeen minutes regardless of adaptation parameters."

This statement contained another disturbing revelation—specific knowledge of Eleanor's involvement in their countermeasure development, suggesting intelligence gathering extending to team composition details across connected timelines. Such comprehensive awareness significantly complicated operational security for any intervention attempt against cross-timeline coordination capabilities.

As Department countermeasures continued progressively isolating their deployed modulators, Alice recognized the tactical situation was deteriorating toward potential failure parameters. Despite sophisticated technology and careful implementation, their intervention appeared increasingly insufficient against Department operations leveraging cross-timeline resources and intelligence.

In this critical moment, Maya implemented their contingency protocol—activating the specialized system Eleanor had designed specifically for scenarios where conventional countermeasures proved insufficient against Department response capabilities. This technology operated on fundamentally different principles than the quantum field modulators, essentially introducing what Eleanor had termed "reality reconciliation catalysts" throughout the intersection complex.

Unlike the modulators' gradual destabilization approach, these catalysts created focal points for natural barrier restoration—essentially accelerating the reality system's inherent tendency toward configuration reconciliation without forcing immediate collapse. The methodology leveraged fundamental quantum principles Eleanor had identified during Project Resonance, essentially working with natural barrier dynamics rather than imposing artificial manipulation.

The effect was subtle but profound. Throughout the reality intersection, quantum coherence patterns began shifting toward natural configuration parameters—overlapping reality segments gradually reconciling toward baseline timeline stability without catastrophic disruption. The process didn't force immediate neutralization but rather accelerated natural reconciliation processes that would eventually restore standard reality coherence.

The hybridized commander recognized this intervention immediately, directing urgent countermeasures throughout the intersection complex. However, the catalyst methodology operated on principles fundamentally different from standard destabilization approaches, making conventional response protocols largely ineffective against the accelerated reconciliation process.

"Eleanor's final contingency," the hybrid noted with what appeared to be genuine admiration despite operational opposition. "Reality reconciliation catalysts operating on fundamental quantum principles rather than imposed manipulation frameworks. Genuinely elegant approach to complex barrier dynamics."

This assessment contained yet another disturbing implication—intimate familiarity with Eleanor's research extending to contingency technologies she had developed specifically for worst-case scenarios. Such detailed knowledge suggested intelligence gathering capabilities that somehow transcended Eleanor's careful operational security despite decades of concealment.

As reality reconciliation accelerated throughout the intersection complex, Department personnel implemented increasingly desperate countermeasures—deploying specialized technology directly at catalyst locations in attempts to neutralize the reconciliation process. These efforts demonstrated sophisticated technical capability but fundamental misalignment with the catalyst methodology, essentially attempting to counter natural processes rather than imposed manipulation.

"Their approach demonstrates the fundamental limitation of Department operations," Maya observed, monitoring reconciliation progression throughout the affected area. "They persist in treating reality as something to be manipulated rather than understood—imposing artificial configurations rather than working with natural quantum dynamics."

This philosophical distinction highlighted the fundamental difference between their approach and Department methodology—essentially cooperation with natural reality systems versus imposition of artificial manipulation. Eleanor's reconciliation catalysts represented this principle in technological form, accelerating natural processes rather than forcing external reconfiguration.

As reconciliation progressed throughout the intersection complex, overlapping reality segments began gradually resolving toward baseline configuration—multiple timeline versions progressively reconciling toward single coherent parameters. The process maintained controlled progression rather than catastrophic collapse, allowing gradual resolution without triggering destructive interference patterns.

The hybridized commander directed final containment attempts while simultaneously implementing what appeared to be controlled withdrawal protocols—essentially securing critical resources while preparing for intersection neutralization. This approach suggested pragmatic adaptation rather than desperate resistance, preserving operational capabilities despite intervention success.

"They're implementing strategic withdrawal rather than maximum resistance," Alice noted, recognizing the tactical significance of this response. "Preserving cross-timeline coordination capability despite localized intersection neutralization."

This methodology demonstrated sophisticated operational perspective—treating their successful intervention as a temporary setback rather than definitive defeat, preserving essential capabilities for continued operations despite current location compromise. The approach suggested long-term strategic frameworks transcending individual operational outcomes.

As reality reconciliation reached advanced stages throughout the intersection complex, the hybridized commander addressed Alice directly once more—communication seemingly important enough to prioritize despite ongoing withdrawal operations.

"Your intervention is temporarily successful," the hybrid acknowledged without apparent hostility despite operational opposition. "Reality reconciliation will neutralize this specific intersection configuration within approximately seventeen minutes. However, breach network fundamentals remain unchanged throughout Daybridge. Alternative methodology will simply establish reconfigured access protocols at different coordinates."

This statement contained both tactical information and strategic implication—acknowledging current intervention success while simultaneously indicating continued Department capability for alternative implementation approaches. The message essentially confirmed Alice's earlier assessment that they had won a battle rather than the war, with fundamental conditions remaining essentially unchanged despite successful countermeasures.

"Perhaps consider that opposition without understanding serves neither objective effectively," the hybrid continued, this communication appearing genuinely important rather than merely tactical distraction. "Department operations pursue stability across reality configurations rather than exploitation frameworks you've attributed to our objectives. The breach network represents existential protection rather than control methodology."

This claim directly contradicted everything they had learned about Department operations and Traverser objectives—suggesting protective rather than exploitative motivation behind seven decades of reality manipulation. The assertion seemed calculated to introduce doubt regarding their fundamental understanding of what they opposed, potentially compromising intervention commitment through strategic narrative manipulation.

"Reconciliation reaching final implementation phase," Maya reported, monitoring progression throughout the intersection complex. "Reality configuration returning to baseline parameters with controlled resolution of overlapping segments. Intersection neutralization approximately seventy percent complete."

Department withdrawal operations continued with methodical efficiency—personnel and critical equipment transitioning from the affected area through remaining stable pathways before intersection neutralization rendered them inaccessible. The approach demonstrated practiced protocols suggesting extensive experience with operational adaptation to changing field conditions.

As reconciliation progression approached completion parameters, the hybridized commander made a final communication attempt—this message delivered with apparent urgency despite continued withdrawal coordination.

"Alice Chen exists as a nexus point across connected reality configurations," the hybrid stated with disturbing specificity. "Your consistent opposition to Department operations represents probability constant despite variable circumstances. Consider that such pattern consistency might itself indicate significance beyond individual perception frameworks."

This cryptic statement echoed Eleanor's assessment regarding Alice's role across multiple timelines—suggesting the Department had independently recognized the same pattern consistency Eleanor had documented decades earlier. The implication that Alice represented some form of "probability constant" contained disturbing suggestions about reality dynamics beyond conventional understanding.

"In seventeen documented timeline configurations where Alice Chen successfully neutralizes Department operations, subsequent reality dissolution occurs within seventy-two hours of intervention completion," the hybrid continued, this information delivered with apparent concern rather than tactical manipulation intent. "Consider that opposition without understanding may achieve precisely the catastrophe you believe you're preventing."

With this final disturbing claim, the hybridized commander completed withdrawal from the affected area—transitioning through remaining stable pathways before intersection neutralization rendered them inaccessible. The statement lingered with troubling implications, suggesting potential consequences beyond their current understanding of breach network dynamics.

Reality reconciliation completed its progression throughout the intersection complex, quantum coherence returning to baseline parameters as overlapping timeline segments resolved into a single configuration reality. The warehouse district surrounding Echo Alley returned to normal appearance, multiple reality versions reconciling into the singular configuration native to their timeline.

"Intersection neutralization complete," Maya confirmed, monitoring equipment showing quantum variance readings returning to stabilized baseline throughout the affected area. "Reality coherence restored to natural parameters with no evidence of remaining overlap configurations."

Their intervention had succeeded in neutralizing the Department's reality intersection capability at Echo Alley, preventing establishment of permanent cross-timeline access despite shutdown of the broader amplifier network. The reconciliation catalysts had performed exactly as Eleanor had designed, accelerating natural barrier restoration without triggering catastrophic collapse.

Yet the hybridized commander's final communication lingered with disturbing persistence—the claim that successful intervention against Department operations had consistently preceded reality dissolution across multiple documented timeline configurations. While potentially representing nothing more than strategic deception to undermine intervention commitment, the specific details suggested concerning possibility of legitimate warning.

"We need to implement enhanced monitoring throughout Daybridge," Alice directed as team members regrouped following successful intervention. "Comprehensive quantum variance tracking with particular focus on natural breach points independent of Department amplifier locations."

This approach represented a significant expansion of their monitoring operations—extending beyond Department technology to the fundamental breach network that predated human civilization. If the hybrid's disturbing claim contained legitimate warning rather than tactical deception, they needed comprehensive understanding of baseline reality dynamics following Department operation neutralization.

As team members implemented these expanded monitoring protocols, Alice reflected on the extraordinary sequence of events that had brought them to this point—from paranormal investigation of voices in Echo Alley to direct confrontation with interdimensional entities utilizing human organizations for reality manipulation. Throughout this progression, her grandmother's preparation and Eleanor's guidance had proved consistently prescient, anticipating developments that seemed impossible to predict through conventional analysis.

Perhaps the hybridized commander's cryptic reference to Alice as "nexus point" across connected reality configurations contained more significance than immediately apparent. If her grandmother had recognized this pattern consistency decades earlier, implementing preparation measures specifically calibrated for this eventual confrontation, might the Department have similarly identified pattern significance through cross-timeline observation?

The possibility that their successful intervention might itself represent predictable probability pattern with documented consequences across multiple reality configurations was deeply unsettling. Had they been so focused on preventing Department operations that they'd overlooked fundamental dynamics of the breach network itself? Might opposition without complete understanding potentially trigger unintended consequences despite righteous intervention motivation?

As enhanced monitoring systems activated throughout Daybridge, Alice recognized they had entered new operational territory—no longer merely countering Department manipulation but potentially addressing fundamental reality dynamics beyond conventional understanding. The breach network beneath Daybridge remained dormant but not eliminated, its true nature and purpose still partially obscured despite everything they had learned.

The hybridized commander's final warning—disturbing yet delivered with apparent genuine concern—suggested possibilities they couldn't simply dismiss as tactical deception. Across seventeen documented timeline configurations, successful neutralization of Department operations had supposedly preceded reality dissolution within seventy-two hours. Whether a legitimate warning or strategic manipulation, this claim demanded serious consideration given potential catastrophic implications.

"All monitoring systems active," Maya confirmed as expanded detection networks initialized throughout Daybridge. "Comprehensive quantum variance tracking established at all identified natural breach points. Baseline readings appear stable with no evidence of progressive destabilization."

For now, reality appeared to be maintaining integrity following their successful intervention. The Department's reality intersection had been neutralized, cross-timeline access temporarily prevented, colonization objectives disrupted. Yet fundamental questions remained unanswered, the breach network's true nature and purpose still partially obscured despite everything they had learned.

Alice Chen—paranormal investigator, reluctant interdimensional crisis manager, apparent "nexus point" across connected reality configurations—faced the unsettling possibility that successful opposition might itself represent merely another predictable probability pattern within vastly more complex dynamics than any human understanding had yet comprehended.

The voices in Echo Alley had been silenced once more. But the fundamental mystery they represented remained incompletely resolved, with disturbing implications stretching across multiple connected realities.

For now, they maintained vigilance—monitoring, analyzing, preparing for whatever might follow their successful intervention. The next seventy-two hours would either validate or disprove the hybridized commander's disturbing warning, potentially revealing whether their opposition had truly prevented catastrophe or merely altered its specific manifestation parameters.

Reality itself hung in the balance, its fundamental integrity dependent on dynamics that transcended conventional understanding despite their best efforts to comprehend the extraordinary forces they had confronted.

CHAPTER FIFTEEN: CASE CLOSED?

Forty-eight hours after their successful neutralization of the Department's reality intersection at Echo Alley, Alice Chen stood at the observation window of their monitoring center at Lakeside Retirement Community. The specialized equipment Eleanor had assembled over decades now operated at maximum capacity, tracking quantum variance patterns throughout Daybridge with unprecedented precision.

"Still no evidence of progressive destabilization," Maya reported, analyzing the comprehensive data streams displaying on multiple monitors. "Quantum variance readings remain consistent at all identified natural breach points. No indications of reality dissolution as suggested by the hybridized commander."

This assessment provided cautious reassurance regarding the most immediately concerning aspects of the warning they had received. Despite the claim that successful intervention against Department operations had consistently preceded reality dissolution across multiple timeline configurations, their enhanced monitoring showed no evidence of such catastrophic progression within their reality.

"Seventy-two hours was the specified timeframe," Alice noted, checking the countdown they had established following the hybridized commander's warning. "Twenty-four hours remain before we can reasonably conclude the warning represented tactical deception rather than legitimate concern."

The team had maintained continuous monitoring operations throughout this critical window, utilizing Eleanor's specialized equipment to track quantum variance patterns across all identified natural breach points throughout Daybridge. The comprehensive coverage provided real-time data regarding reality stability parameters, allowing immediate detection of any progressive degradation that might indicate approaching dissolution.

"Department operations have established new monitoring configurations at seven locations throughout Daybridge," Dr. Liu reported, reviewing intelligence gathered through distributed sensor networks. "All passive observation systems rather than active manipulation technology. They appear to be studying natural breach dynamics rather than attempting immediate reactivation."

This approach suggested something interesting about the Department response to their intervention—a focus on understanding rather than immediate countermeasures, essentially a research-oriented stance rather than operational recovery. The pattern indicated strategic reassessment rather than tactical resistance, potentially signifying fundamental reconsideration of methodologies following multiple intervention successes.

"They're learning," Maya observed, recognizing the significance of this approach. "Adapting to intervention outcomes by enhancing fundamental understanding rather than simply implementing technological countermeasures."

As they continued monitoring both quantum variance patterns and Department activities throughout Daybridge, Alice reflected on the extraordinary sequence of events that had transformed her understanding of reality itself. What had begun as a paranormal investigation of mysterious voices in Echo Alley had progressively revealed interdimensional entities, government exploitation of reality breaches, and fundamental questions about the nature of existence across multiple connected timelines.

Throughout this progression, her grandmother's preparation and Eleanor's guidance had proved consistently prescient—anticipating developments that seemed impossible to predict through conventional analysis. The quantum resonator pendant, the specialized equipment, the tactical intelligence regarding Department operations—all provided precisely when needed most, suggesting preparation extending far beyond standard contingency planning.

The hybridized commander's cryptic reference to Alice as "nexus point" across connected reality configurations continued resonating with disturbing implications. If her role in confronting the breach network represented a probability constant rather than circumstantial involvement, what might that suggest about reality dynamics beyond conventional understanding? Could her consistent opposition to Department operations across multiple timelines actually represent a predetermined pattern within vastly more complex systems than human comprehension had yet achieved?

"Incoming transmission detected at Echo Alley," Maya reported suddenly, monitoring equipment registering distinctive energy patterns at the original breach point. "Quantum variance signature consistent with directed communication rather than random fluctuation."

This development was concerning given their successful neutralization of the Department's reality intersection at that location. The breach network remained dormant following amplifier shutdown, with natural quantum barriers restored to standard permeability parameters. Any communication attempt through these reinforced barriers suggested capabilities exceeding what they had anticipated in potential opposition forces.

"Analyzing transmission pattern," Dr. Liu continued, focusing specialized equipment on the energy signature. "Characteristics consistent with Timeline J-73 contact from previous cross-timeline communication. Appears to be utilizing a minimal-footprint methodology designed specifically for transmission through reinforced quantum barriers."

This identification provided crucial context—the resistance coalition that had provided tactical intelligence during their shutdown operation planning rather than Department-affiliated entities attempting reactivation protocols. The transmission methodology demonstrated a sophisticated understanding of quantum barrier dynamics, essentially establishing minimal connection without compromising overall integrity.

Alice activated their modified receiver system, calibrating reception parameters to capture the incoming communication without enabling expanded connection. The specialized equipment Eleanor had designed provided capability for controlled information transfer while maintaining essential barrier integrity, essentially creating a secure communication channel without enabling physical transit potential.

The receiver successfully decoded the incoming transmission, converting quantum variance patterns into a comprehensible format:

"To resistance elements in Timeline K-17: Urgent advisory regarding breach network status. Department operations across connected timelines have initiated coordinated observation protocols following intersection neutralization. Pattern suggests implementation of 'Deep Analysis' contingency referenced in secured communications. Recommend extreme caution regarding natural breach dynamics following Department operational neutralization."

The message contained concerning implications—suggesting a coordinated Department response across multiple connected timelines rather than isolated adaptation within their specific reality. The reference to "Deep Analysis" contingency suggested pre-established protocols specifically designed for scenarios following successful resistance intervention, potentially indicating sophisticated adaptation strategies rather than operational retreat.

Most concerning was the warning regarding natural breach dynamics following Department neutralization—essentially supporting aspects of the hybridized commander's disturbing claim rather than contradicting it. The suggestion that caution was warranted regarding breach behavior following intervention success indicated potential legitimacy to concerns about unintended consequences.

"Requesting clarification regarding natural breach dynamics following Department neutralization," Alice transmitted through the secure channel, utilizing Eleanor's minimal-footprint methodology to maintain barrier integrity during communication.

The response arrived after a brief transmission delay, converted into a comprehensible format through their specialized receiver:

"Department operations have historically provided a stabilizing influence on natural breach dynamics despite exploitation objectives. Artificial manipulation created a partially compensatory effect against the underlying instability inherent in the breach network architecture. In three documented timeline configurations where Department neutralization achieved complete operational cessation, progressive reality degradation followed despite successful intervention implementation."

This information provided disturbing validation of the hybridized commander's warning—suggesting Department operations, despite problematic exploitation objectives, had inadvertently created stabilization effects on the underlying breach network. The implication that successful intervention might actually remove essential stabilization influence represented precisely the unintended consequence scenario they had feared.

"Can you provide specifications regarding degradation progression and potential countermeasures?" Alice requested, recognizing the critical importance of this intelligence for addressing potential stability complications following their successful intervention.

The response contained both technical specifications and a strategic assessment:

"Degradation typically initiates at natural breach points independent of artificial amplifier locations. Progressive quantum barrier erosion accelerates geometrically once initiated, creating expanding instability zones that eventually trigger catastrophic reconciliation events. In Timeline R-34, limited success achieved through implementation of the 'resonance stabilization framework' developed by Maya Chen, essentially creating artificial quantum barrier reinforcement without enabling exploitation capabilities."

This information contained both concerning confirmation of degradation risk and potential solution methodology—specifically referencing technology Maya had developed in an alternate timeline configuration. The reference to "resonance stabilization framework" suggested a specialized approach to quantum barrier reinforcement that maintained integrity without enabling exploitation capabilities similar to Department operations.

"Maya, does this reference mean anything to you?" Alice asked, turning to her colleague with the transmission displayed.

Maya studied the reference with evident surprise. "Conceptually, yes. I've been developing theoretical frameworks for quantum barrier stabilization without manipulation capability—essentially technology that reinforces natural reality interfaces without creating exploitation potential. However, I haven't reached the implementation stage in our timeline."

"Yet apparently your alternate self in Timeline R-34 successfully developed functioning technology based on these same theoretical principles," Alice noted, recognizing the significance of this cross-timeline development parallel.

"Quantum resonance theory suggests consistent development patterns across connected timelines despite circumstantial variations," Dr. Liu explained, understanding the implications immediately. "Essentially, Maya Chen develops similar theoretical frameworks across multiple reality configurations, with implementation timeline representing the primary variable rather than the fundamental approach."

This pattern consistency across connected realities suggested a possibility for accelerated development based on cross-timeline information exchange—essentially leveraging parallel research across multiple configurations to overcome individual timeline limitations. If Maya's alternate self had successfully implemented stabilization technology that maintained barrier integrity without enabling exploitation, perhaps a similar approach could be rapidly developed within their timeline.

"Request technical specifications for resonance stabilization framework implemented in Timeline R-34," Alice transmitted, recognizing the potential value of this cross-timeline intelligence exchange.

The response contained detailed technical documentation—essentially providing implementation blueprints for technology Maya had conceptualized but not yet developed within their timeline. The specifications outlined a sophisticated approach to quantum barrier reinforcement that worked with natural reality dynamics rather than imposing artificial manipulation, essentially stabilizing interfaces without creating exploitation potential.

"This is extraordinary," Maya acknowledged, reviewing the technical specifications with growing excitement. "The implementation methodology aligns perfectly with my theoretical framework but incorporates several development stages I hadn't yet reached. The approach essentially creates selective permeability enhancement that reinforces barrier integrity while allowing minimal-footprint information transfer without physical transit capability."

"Can you implement this technology based on these specifications?" Alice asked, recognizing the potential solution to their current dilemma.

"Yes, with approximately seventeen hours development timeline," Maya confirmed after careful assessment. "The fundamental components already exist within our current equipment inventory. Primary development requirement involves configuration adaptation rather than new technology creation."

This possibility represented a potential resolution to the concerning scenario they faced—the ability to implement stabilization measures that would prevent progressive reality degradation following Department neutralization without recreating exploitation capability. The approach would essentially maintain quantum barrier integrity through methods fundamentally different from Department operations, working with natural reality dynamics rather than imposing artificial manipulation.

"Priority implementation," Alice directed, recognizing the critical importance of this development given their current monitoring data. "Utilize all available resources to accelerate the timeline where possible."

As Maya began adaptation work with assistance from Dr. Liu, Alice continued monitoring both quantum variance patterns throughout Daybridge and Department activities following their successful intervention. The enhanced detection network showed subtle but measurable changes in natural breach dynamics—nothing approaching critical instability, but definite indications of progressive adjustment following amplifier network shutdown.

Most interesting was the Department response to these changes—their new monitoring configurations focused specifically on natural breach points rather than artificial amplifier locations, essentially studying fundamental network dynamics rather than technological manipulation parameters. This approach suggested sophisticated understanding potentially exceeding what they had attributed to Department operations, indicating greater awareness of natural breach behavior than previously assumed.

"Department monitoring activities demonstrate an interesting pattern," Alice noted, studying their deployment configurations throughout Daybridge. "They're essentially implementing the same enhanced observation protocols we established following the hybridized commander's warning."

"Suggesting they genuinely anticipated potential stability complications following amplifier network neutralization," Maya observed, continuing adaptation work while participating in ongoing assessment. "Their operations may have been more knowledgeable about fundamental breach dynamics than we previously recognized."

This possibility created uncomfortable implications regarding their opposition to Department operations. If the organization genuinely understood stability requirements for natural breach points, its activities might have incorporated protective elements despite problematic exploitation objectives. The hybridized commander's claim that "Department operations pursue stability across reality configurations rather than exploitation frameworks" suddenly seemed potentially more complex than simple tactical deception.

As they continued monitoring both breach dynamics and Department activities, Rivera arrived with updated intelligence regarding the organizational response following their successful intervention. His police department contacts had provided valuable information about institutional reconfiguration occurring within federal agencies connected to Department operations.

"They're implementing comprehensive organizational restructuring," Rivera reported, sharing documentation indicating significant administrative changes. "Essentially transitioning from classified military-adjacent operations to a research-oriented institutional framework with civilian oversight components."

This development suggested a fundamental reorientation rather than simply a tactical adjustment—essentially transforming operational methodology at the institutional level rather than merely adapting field procedures. The transition from classified military protocols to a research framework with civilian oversight represented a significant shift in approach to breach network interaction.

"They're adapting at a fundamental organizational level," Alice noted, recognizing the significance of this change. "Not simply

adjusting tactical operations but restructuring the institutional
framework to incorporate different operating principles."

As they processed these developments, Maya continued accelerated
implementation of the resonance stabilization framework based on
specifications from Timeline R-34. The technology was progressing
rapidly through development phases, with component integration
demonstrating promising results in preliminary testing scenarios.

"Initial implementation achieving ninety-four percent alignment
with theoretical parameters," Maya reported, monitoring performance
metrics during component testing. "The stabilization field
demonstrates selective permeability exactly as specified—essentially
reinforcing quantum barrier integrity while maintaining
minimal-footprint information transfer capability."

This technological approach represented a sophisticated balance
between competing objectives—preventing potential reality
degradation following Department neutralization without recreating
the exploitation capability that had made their intervention necessary.
The resonance stabilization framework would essentially maintain
quantum barrier integrity through methods fundamentally different
from Department operations, working with natural reality dynamics
rather than imposing artificial manipulation.

"Deployment timeline estimate?" Alice asked, balancing
development requirements against monitoring data indicating subtle
progression in natural breach dynamics throughout Daybridge.

"Approximately seven hours to field-ready configuration," Maya
responded after careful assessment. "Primary integration phase
completing with minimal adaptation requirements. Deployment
methodology already established through existing sensor network
infrastructure."

This timeline provided a reasonable safety margin against potential
stability complications based on monitoring data progression. While
natural breach dynamics showed measurable changes following

amplifier network shutdown, current progression remained well within manageable parameters without indicating an approaching critical instability.

As development continued, Alice received communication from an unexpected source—official Department channels rather than clandestine contact. The communication arrived through conventional means, essentially formal organizational outreach rather than operational engagement:

"Ms. Chen, following recent events involving quantum variance stabilization throughout Daybridge, the Department of Advanced Scientific Research (formerly Temporal Security Division) requests consultation regarding optimal monitoring protocols for natural phenomena previously under operational jurisdiction. Our organizational restructuring incorporates civilian scientific oversight with particular emphasis on a collaborative approach to phenomenon management rather than unilateral containment methodologies."

The communication represented an extraordinary institutional adaptation—not merely a tactical adjustment but a fundamental reorientation of organizational approach. The reference to "Department of Advanced Scientific Research" indicated a complete rebranding from military-adjacent classification to a civilian scientific framework, suggesting a genuine structural transformation rather than a cosmetic modification.

Most significant was the explicit acknowledgment of Alice's expertise and implied recognition of her intervention legitimacy—essentially establishing a collaborative consultation framework rather than an oppositional relationship. This approach suggested sophisticated institutional learning rather than mere tactical repositioning, potentially indicating a genuine reassessment of fundamental operational principles.

"They're offering collaborative engagement rather than continued opposition," Alice noted, recognizing the strategic significance of this development. "Essentially acknowledging our intervention legitimacy while establishing a potential framework for a coordinated approach to breach dynamics management."

"Interesting strategic adaptation," Rivera observed with professional assessment. "Rather than continuing resource-intensive opposition against demonstrated intervention capability, they're incorporating your expertise into a reconfigured operational framework. Essentially converting a potential adversary into a consultant while maintaining institutional continuity."

This approach demonstrated sophisticated organizational evolution—adapting to intervention outcomes by transforming operational methodology rather than merely implementing tactical countermeasures. The transition from classified military protocols to a civilian research framework with collaborative consultation elements represented a fundamental shift in approach to breach network interaction.

As they considered an appropriate response to this unexpected outreach, Maya completed the primary development phase for the resonance stabilization framework. The technology had progressed rapidly through implementation stages, component integration achieving performance metrics exceeding initial projections based on cross-timeline specifications.

"Stabilization framework ready for field deployment," Maya confirmed, final testing demonstrating optimal functionality parameters. "The system generates precisely calibrated quantum resonance fields that reinforce natural barrier integrity without creating exploitation potential. Essentially maintaining stability while preventing manipulation capability."

This technological approach represented the ideal resolution to the complex situation they faced—addressing potential stability complications following Department neutralization without recreating problematic exploitation capability. The resonance stabilization framework worked with natural reality dynamics rather than imposing artificial manipulation, essentially reinforcing quantum barriers while maintaining minimal information transfer without physical transit potential.

"Deployment locations?" Alice asked, focusing on practical implementation strategy.

"Seven primary natural breach points throughout Daybridge," Maya responded, indicating locations on the comprehensive mapping system. "The framework operates through a distributed resonance network rather than a centralized amplification system—essentially creating a collaborative stability field through synchronized node operation rather than a hierarchical control structure."

This distributed approach represented a fundamental difference from the Department methodology—a collaborative network rather than centralized control, distributed stability rather than hierarchical manipulation. The framework essentially established a cooperative relationship with natural reality dynamics rather than imposing an artificial configuration, reinforcing inherent stability rather than creating dependent manipulation.

"Implement deployment immediately," Alice directed, recognizing both the technical merits and philosophical alignment of this approach. "Prioritize Echo Alley as the primary stabilization point given historical significance as the original breach location."

As team members began field deployment operations, Alice formulated a response to the Department's unexpected outreach. The situation presented complex strategic considerations—balancing legitimate concerns regarding organizational trustworthiness against potential benefits of a collaborative approach to breach dynamics management.

After careful consideration, Alice composed a measured response that established clear parameters while allowing potential constructive engagement:

"Your organizational restructuring represents an appropriate adaptation following recent events. Collaborative approach to natural phenomenon management aligns with optimal methodologies for addressing complex reality dynamics. However, verification protocols require implementation before substantive engagement can proceed. I propose neutral-site consultation following confirmation of complete transition from exploitation methodologies to genuine research frameworks with appropriate ethical oversight mechanisms."

This response established a reasonable engagement pathway while maintaining necessary caution regarding organizational trustworthiness following seven decades of problematic operations. The approach essentially created a potential collaborative framework while requiring verifiable transformation rather than merely accepting proclaimed changes at face value.

As this communication was transmitted through formal channels, Maya reported successful initial deployment of the resonance stabilization framework at three primary breach points throughout Daybridge. The technology was functioning exactly as designed, generating precisely calibrated quantum resonance fields that reinforced natural barrier integrity without creating exploitation potential.

"Stabilization fields operating at ninety-seven percent theoretical efficiency," Maya confirmed, monitoring performance metrics through the distributed sensor network. "Natural quantum barriers showing an immediate reinforcement response without artificial manipulation characteristics. Essentially perfect implementation of selective permeability enhancement."

The monitoring network displayed remarkable transformation throughout deployed locations—quantum variance patterns stabilizing into optimal configuration that maintained natural reality interfaces while preventing progressive degradation. The approach worked precisely as intended, reinforcing barrier integrity through methods fundamentally different from Department operations.

Most significant was the effect at Echo Alley—the original breach point where their extraordinary journey had begun with the investigation of mysterious voices echoing through the narrow passage. The stabilization field established perfect equilibrium at this location, maintaining natural barrier integrity while allowing minimal-footprint information transfer without physical transit capability.

"Echo Alley stabilization achieved optimal parameters," Maya reported with evident satisfaction. "The quantum interface has established a perfect equilibrium configuration—essentially maintaining natural barrier integrity while allowing controlled information exchange without exploitation potential."

This technological implementation represented the ideal resolution to the complex situation they faced—preventing potential reality degradation following Department neutralization without recreating problematic exploitation capability. The resonance stabilization framework essentially established a new relationship with the breach network, working cooperatively with natural dynamics rather than imposing artificial manipulation.

As deployment operations continued at the remaining breach points throughout Daybridge, Alice received a response to her communication with the restructured Department organization. The message demonstrated interesting institutional adaptation, essentially accepting verification requirements while proposing a specific implementation methodology:

"Your verification requirements are entirely reasonable following historical operational parameters. We propose an independent oversight committee comprising recognized experts from relevant scientific disciplines with complete access to organizational transformation documentation and ongoing research protocols. Additionally, we acknowledge your established jurisdiction regarding

Echo Alley specifically, recognizing both historical significance and demonstrated expertise in managing this particular phenomenon."

This response contained an extraordinary institutional concession—explicit acknowledgment of Alice's jurisdiction regarding Echo Alley, essentially formalizing her authority over the location where their involvement had originally begun. The recognition represented a remarkable organizational adaptation, transforming from opposition to explicit acknowledgment of established expertise and jurisdictional authority.

"They're officially recognizing your authority over Echo Alley," Rivera noted with evident surprise at this institutional concession. "Essentially formalizing your jurisdiction over the original breach point while transitioning broader operations to a collaborative research framework."

This development created a potential resolution framework that balanced competing priorities—maintaining necessary oversight regarding natural breach dynamics while preventing a return to problematic exploitation methodologies. The approach essentially established specialized jurisdiction parameters that acknowledged demonstrated expertise while creating accountability structures for organizational transformation.

As they processed this development, Maya reported complete deployment of the resonance stabilization framework at all seven primary breach points throughout Daybridge. The technology was functioning optimally across the entire network, generating synchronized stabilization fields that maintained natural barrier integrity throughout the breach network.

"Comprehensive stabilization achieved throughout Daybridge," Maya confirmed, monitoring network-wide performance metrics. "All natural breach points showing optimal equilibrium configuration with enhanced barrier integrity and selective permeability maintenance. Essentially perfect implementation across the entire network."

The monitoring system displayed a remarkable transformation throughout Daybridge—quantum variance patterns stabilizing into an optimal configuration that maintained natural reality interfaces while preventing both progressive degradation and exploitation potential. The approach had successfully addressed potential stability complications following Department neutralization without recreating problematic manipulation capability.

"Countdown threshold passed," Dr. Liu noted, checking the timer they had established following the hybridized commander's warning. "Seventy-two hours since intervention completion with no evidence of progressive destabilization. Quantum barriers maintaining optimal integrity parameters throughout the monitoring network."

This milestone provided significant reassurance regarding the most immediately concerning aspects of the warning they had received. Despite the claim that successful intervention against Department operations had consistently preceded reality dissolution across multiple timeline configurations, their implementation of the resonance stabilization framework appeared to have successfully prevented such progression within their reality.

With the stabilization technology successfully deployed and the Department organizational transformation establishing a potential collaborative framework, Alice recognized they had reached a critical decision point regarding the long-term approach to breach network management. The situation presented an opportunity for a fundamental reconfiguration of the relationship with these extraordinary phenomena—establishing a new paradigm based on understanding rather than exploitation, cooperation rather than control.

After careful consideration, Alice formulated a comprehensive response to the Department's restructuring proposal, establishing clear parameters for potential collaborative engagement:

"I accept provisional recognition of specialized jurisdiction regarding Echo Alley specifically, contingent upon implementation of an independent oversight committee with verification authority regarding organizational transformation. Additionally, I propose the establishment of the 'Daybridge Quantum Research Initiative' as a civilian scientific framework for studying natural breach dynamics through a collaborative methodology with appropriate ethical protocols and transparent operation requirements."

This proposal essentially created a new institutional framework for approaching breach network dynamics—a civilian scientific initiative rather than a classified government operation, transparent research rather than secret exploitation, collaborative understanding rather than unilateral control. The approach represented a fundamental paradigm shift in the relationship with these extraordinary phenomena.

The response from the restructured Department demonstrated remarkable institutional adaptation, essentially accepting the proposed framework while suggesting a specific implementation methodology:

"The Daybridge Quantum Research Initiative represents the optimal approach to natural phenomenon management through a collaborative scientific methodology. We propose an integrated research framework with civilian oversight, transparent protocols, and explicit ethical guidelines regarding cross-reality interaction. Your specialized jurisdiction over Echo Alley is formally acknowledged, with an additional proposal that you consider accepting the research director position within the broader initiative structure."

This response represented extraordinary institutional evolution—not merely accepting Alice's authority over Echo Alley but proposing an expanded leadership role within a comprehensive research initiative. The approach essentially transformed a former adversarial relationship into a collaborative research framework with civilian leadership and transparent operational protocols.

"They're offering you directorship of the entire research initiative," Maya noted, recognizing the significance of this proposal. "Essentially transitioning from the opposition to placing you in a leadership position regarding comprehensive breach network research throughout Daybridge."

This development created a potential resolution framework that aligned scientific understanding with appropriate ethical guidelines while preventing a return to problematic exploitation methodologies. The approach essentially established a collaborative research initiative under civilian leadership with transparent operational protocols and independent oversight mechanisms.

"Interesting strategic adaptation," Rivera observed with professional assessment. "Rather than attempting to neutralize your opposition capability, they're incorporating your expertise into the leadership structure while maintaining institutional continuity through transformation rather than dissolution. Genuinely sophisticated organizational evolution."

After careful consideration, Alice formulated a measured response, accepting the provisional framework while establishing clear verification requirements before committing to a formal leadership role.

"I accept the provisional consultation role regarding initiative development while verification protocols confirm genuine organizational transformation. Echo Alley jurisdiction formally established with immediate implementation of research protocols utilizing a resonance stabilization framework for maintaining quantum barrier integrity while enabling controlled information exchange without exploitation capability."

This approach established a constructive engagement pathway while maintaining the necessary verification requirements before formal leadership commitment. The framework created immediate research protocols at Echo Alley utilizing the successfully deployed stabilization technology while broader initiative development proceeded through collaborative consultation with appropriate oversight mechanisms.

As this communication was transmitted through formal channels, Maya conducted a comprehensive assessment of the resonance stabilization framework performance throughout Daybridge. The technology continued functioning optimally across the entire network, maintaining a perfect equilibrium configuration at all natural breach points.

"Stabilization framework demonstrating remarkable effectiveness," Maya confirmed, reviewing seven-day performance projections based on current metrics. "The quantum interfaces have established self-sustaining equilibrium patterns that should maintain indefinitely with minimal maintenance requirements. Essentially perfect implementation of selective permeability enhancement."

This technological success represented the ideal resolution to the complex situation they had faced—preventing potential reality degradation following Department neutralization without recreating problematic exploitation capability. The resonance stabilization framework essentially established a new relationship with the breach network, working cooperatively with natural dynamics rather than imposing artificial manipulation.

Most significant was the configuration at Echo Alley—the original breach point maintained perfect equilibrium parameters that allowed minimal-footprint information transfer while preventing physical transit capability. This arrangement essentially enabled controlled research regarding cross-timeline communication while preventing exploitation potential that had characterized Department operations.

One week after the successful deployment of the stabilization framework, Alice stood at the entrance to Echo Alley, observing the transformed research operation that had replaced clandestine Department activities. Civilian scientists conducted careful studies of quantum variance patterns using transparent protocols and shared methodologies, their approach fundamentally different from the secret exploitation that had characterized seven decades of military-adjacent operations.

The Daybridge Quantum Research Initiative had established a preliminary operational framework with remarkable efficiency—transparent protocols, civilian oversight, ethical guidelines regarding cross-reality interaction. The approach represented a fundamental paradigm shift in the relationship with these extraordinary phenomena, essentially creating a new institutional model based on understanding rather than exploitation.

Alice's specialized jurisdiction over Echo Alley had been formally established through both Department acknowledgment and municipal recognition, essentially creating legitimate research authority where previously only clandestine operations had existed. This arrangement allowed the implementation of carefully calibrated protocols utilizing the resonance stabilization framework to maintain quantum barrier integrity while enabling controlled information exchange for legitimate scientific purposes.

Most extraordinary was the cross-timeline communication network gradually establishing through this carefully managed interface—research collaboration with parallel scientific initiatives across connected realities, essentially creating distributed knowledge development transcending individual timeline limitations. The approach represented a remarkable transformation from exploitation to collaboration, secret manipulation to transparent exchange.

"The stabilization framework continues performing beyond theoretical projections," Maya reported, joining Alice at the entrance to Echo Alley. "Seventeen days of continuous operation with zero degradation in performance metrics. The quantum interfaces have established self-sustaining equilibrium patterns that appear capable of indefinite maintenance with minimal support requirements."

This technological success represented the perfect implementation of their balanced approach—maintaining quantum barrier integrity while enabling controlled information exchange without exploitation capability. The resonance stabilization framework worked with natural reality dynamics rather than imposing artificial manipulation, essentially establishing a cooperative relationship with the breach network rather than exploitative control.

"The research initiative is progressing remarkably well," Maya continued, reviewing preliminary scientific outcomes from the transformed operation. "Cross-timeline collaboration has already yielded significant advances in quantum field theory that would have required decades of isolated development within individual reality configurations."

This collaborative knowledge development represented extraordinary potential for scientific advancement through ethical information exchange rather than exploitative manipulation. The approach essentially transformed problematic military operations into a legitimate research initiatives with appropriate ethical guidelines and transparent protocols.

"Case closed?" Maya asked with a slight smile, referencing Alice's typical terminology for completed paranormal investigations.

Alice considered this question carefully, reflecting on their extraordinary journey from paranormal investigation to interdimensional crisis management. They had successfully prevented reality collapse and interdimensional colonization, neutralized exploitative Department operations, implemented stabilization technology maintaining quantum barrier integrity, and established a legitimate research initiative with appropriate ethical guidelines.

By conventional standards, these outcomes would certainly justify "case closed" designation—successful resolution of the immediate crisis with appropriate long-term management protocols established. The voices in Echo Alley had been explained, the threat neutralized, and stable research parameters implemented.

Yet Alice recognized something more profound had emerged through their extraordinary experience—fundamental questions about reality itself that transcended simple case resolution parameters. The breach network beneath Daybridge represented merely a visible manifestation of a vastly more complex system connecting multiple reality configurations through principles exceeding conventional understanding.

"Not closed," Alice responded thoughtfully, "but transformed. We've established a new relationship with phenomena fundamentally beyond complete understanding—working with rather than against forces connecting multiple reality configurations through dynamics we're only beginning to comprehend."

This perspective represented a more sophisticated approach than simple binary resolution—acknowledging an ongoing relationship with extraordinary phenomena requiring continuous adaptation rather than a onetime solution. The framework essentially established sustainable engagement protocols appropriate to phenomena inherently transcending conventional understanding.

"Appropriate assessment," Maya acknowledged with a thoughtful nod. "We haven't 'solved' the breach network so much as established an ethical relationship with it—maintaining stability while enabling legitimate research without recreating exploitative manipulation."

As they observed the transformed research operation at Echo Alley, Alice reflected on the extraordinary confluence of circumstances that had brought them to this point—from paranormal investigation of mysterious voices to fundamental reconfiguration of humanity's relationship with interdimensional phenomena. Throughout this progression, her grandmother's preparation and Eleanor's guidance had proved consistently prescient, anticipating developments that seemed impossible to predict through conventional analysis.

Perhaps most profound was the recognition that their journey represented merely an initial engagement with forces fundamentally transcending conventional understanding. The breach network beneath Daybridge connected multiple reality configurations through principles exceeding current scientific frameworks, essentially linking countless variations of existence through quantum dynamics humanity was only beginning to comprehend.

"The hybridized commander's claim that I represent 'nexus point' across connected reality configurations seems increasingly plausible," Alice noted, considering the pattern consistency that had emerged throughout their extraordinary experience. "My grandmother's preparation, Eleanor's guidance, our successful intervention—all suggest orchestrated probability rather than random circumstance."

"Quantum consciousness theory suggests certain individuals may function as probability anchors across connected timelines," Maya responded, considering this possibility from a scientific perspective. "Essentially maintaining a consistent pattern implementation despite circumstantial variations between reality configurations."

This concept—that Alice's role in confronting the breach network represented a probability constant rather than circumstantial involvement—contained profound implications regarding reality dynamics beyond conventional understanding. If her consistent opposition to Department operations across multiple timelines actually represented a predetermined pattern within a vastly more complex system, what might that suggest about existence itself?

"Perhaps 'case closed' represents a fundamentally inadequate framework for approaching phenomena inherently transcending conventional understanding," Alice suggested, formulating a more appropriate conceptual model. "Better to establish 'case managed' designation—acknowledging an ongoing relationship requiring continuous adaptation rather than a onetime resolution."

This perspective represented a sophisticated evolution in Alice's approach to paranormal investigation—recognizing certain phenomena require sustainable engagement protocols rather than simple resolution parameters. The framework essentially established a continuous relationship model appropriate to manifestations inherently exceeding conventional understanding.

As they continued observing the transformed research operation at Echo Alley, Alice's secure communication device activated—a specialized system Eleanor had designed for quantum-encrypted information transfer invulnerable to conventional interception. The incoming communication originated from their secure operations center at Lakeside Retirement Community, where Dr. Liu maintained comprehensive monitoring of quantum variance patterns throughout Daybridge.

"Interesting development at monitoring station seven," came Dr. Liu's voice through the secure connection. "Quantum variance pattern suggesting directed communication attempt through a stabilized interface. Signature characteristics unlike any previously documented timeline configuration."

This development represented a potential new connection through the carefully managed interface they had established using the resonance stabilization framework. The selective permeability enhancement maintained quantum barrier integrity while allowing minimal-footprint information transfer for legitimate research purposes, essentially enabling controlled communication without exploitation capability.

"Implementing reception protocols," Alice confirmed, activating specialized equipment designed for secure cross-timeline communication. "Maintaining stabilization field integrity while establishing minimal-footprint connection parameters."

The receiver successfully established a connection through the stabilized interface, maintaining quantum barrier integrity while enabling controlled information exchange. The incoming communication resolved gradually, converting quantum variance patterns into a comprehensible format:

"To probability nexus designation 'Alice Chen' in timeline classification K-17: Communication established through stabilized interface utilizing resonance framework implementation. Confirmation requested regarding successful resolution of Department exploitation operations while maintaining breach network stability parameters."

The message originated from an unfamiliar timeline designation, suggesting a connection with a reality configuration beyond the previously established communication network. The reference to "probability nexus designation" aligned with the hybridized commander's description of Alice's role across connected realities, essentially confirming pattern consistency transcending individual timeline configurations.

"Confirmed successful neutralization of Department exploitation operations," Alice responded through the secure connection. "Resonance stabilization framework implemented throughout the Daybridge breach network, maintaining quantum barrier integrity while enabling controlled information exchange without exploitation capability."

The response arrived after a brief transmission delay, converted into a comprehensible format through their specialized receiver:

"Congratulations on a successful implementation. Timeline K-17 represents the seventh reality configuration achieving optimal resolution parameters through probability nexus intervention. Pattern consistency suggests designated probability anchors successfully maintaining critical path implementation across the connected reality spectrum despite significant circumstantial variation."

This communication contained extraordinary confirmation of the pattern consistency they had theorized—essentially validating the concept that Alice functioned as a "probability anchor" across connected timelines, maintaining consistent intervention patterns despite circumstantial variations between reality configurations. The reference to "seventh reality configuration achieving optimal resolution" suggested coordinated probability management rather than isolated coincidence.

"Request clarification regarding probability nexus designation and coordinated resolution pattern," Alice transmitted, seeking a better understanding of these extraordinary implications.

The response contained both confirmation and expansion of these concepts:

"Probability nexus designations represent consciousness patterns maintaining consistent implementation vectors across multiple connected timelines despite circumstantial variation. Essentially, individuals who reliably achieve specific outcome parameters regardless of differentiated reality configurations. Your designation as 'Alice Chen' consistently implements successful breach network stabilization across numerous reality configurations through varying methodologies but identical fundamental approach parameters."

This explanation validated their theoretical understanding while expanding conceptual framework regarding cross-timeline consciousness patterns. The suggestion that certain individuals maintained consistent implementation vectors regardless of circumstantial variations between reality configurations contained profound implications regarding existence itself—essentially indicating organized probability management transcending conventional understanding of reality dynamics.

"Is this pattern consistency a natural phenomenon, or a deliberately orchestrated implementation?" Alice asked, seeking clarification regarding the fundamental nature of these extraordinary dynamics.

The response provided a fascinating perspective regarding this critical question:

"Both simultaneously. Natural quantum consciousness resonance creates consistent pattern implementation across connected timelines. However, certain probability nexus designations demonstrate awareness of this consistency, essentially utilizing cross-timeline pattern recognition to implement guided probability management. Your grandmother 'Margaret Chen' represents a primary example of conscious probability management across multiple reality configurations."

This explanation contained extraordinary confirmation of their theoretical understanding regarding Margaret Chen's preparation extending beyond conventional limitations. The suggestion that her grandmother had consciously implemented probability management across multiple timelines—essentially orchestrating circumstances transcending individual reality configurations—validated Alice's developing comprehension of her remarkable preparation measures.

"The quantum resonator pendant," Alice noted to Maya as they processed this extraordinary communication. "Her specialized training protocols, Eleanor's carefully timed intervention—all representing conscious probability management implemented across multiple connected timelines."

"Essentially, your grandmother recognized pattern consistency across reality configurations and deliberately enhanced implementation probability through strategic preparation measures," Maya translated, comprehending these remarkable implications. "Extraordinary application of quantum consciousness principles transcending conventional temporal limitations."

This understanding transformed their perspective regarding their successful intervention against Department operations and subsequent establishment of ethical research protocols. Rather than representing isolated circumstances, their actions potentially formed part of coordinated probability implementation across multiple connected realities—essentially maintaining critical pattern consistency transcending individual timeline configurations.

"Request information regarding broader breach network purpose beyond currently understood parameters," Alice transmitted, seeking enhanced comprehension of the extraordinary system they had encountered.

The response provided a fascinating perspective extending far beyond their current understanding:

"The breach network represents an ancient transit system designed by consciousness evolution several probability iterations beyond current development parameters. Essentially, infrastructure created by entities existing several reality layers beyond your current perception framework. The original purpose involved non-destructive consciousness migration between reality configurations experiencing entropic cascade failure—essentially an evacuation system for civilizations facing terminal reality dissolution."

This explanation contained extraordinary implications regarding the breach network's true nature and purpose—essentially infrastructure created by entities far beyond current human development parameters for managing consciousness migration between threatened reality configurations. The system represented technology so advanced it appeared virtually indistinguishable from natural phenomena despite artificial origin parameters.

"Department exploitation represents a fundamental misapplication of technology designed for consciousness preservation rather than material advantage," the communication continued. "Your successful implementation of ethical research protocols while maintaining stability parameters represents an appropriate evolutionary approach to infrastructure fundamentally exceeding current understanding capabilities."

This perspective validated their transformed relationship with the breach network—essentially establishing ethical engagement protocols appropriate to technology fundamentally transcending current comprehension frameworks. Their approach of maintaining stability while enabling legitimate research without exploitation represented appropriate evolutionary interaction with systems exceeding conventional understanding.

As they processed this extraordinary communication, Alice recognized they had established an appropriate relationship with phenomena fundamentally beyond complete comprehension—working with rather than against forces connecting multiple reality configurations through principles exceeding current scientific frameworks. The transformed research initiative represented an ideal approach to these extraordinary dynamics, maintaining stability while enabling ethical knowledge development without exploitative manipulation.

"Case transformed," Alice stated with renewed conviction, formulating an appropriate designation for their extraordinary experience. "We haven't 'solved' the breach network but established an ethical relationship with it—maintaining stability while enabling legitimate research appropriate to phenomena fundamentally transcending current understanding capabilities."

This perspective represented a sophisticated evolution in approach to extraordinary phenomena—recognizing certain manifestations require sustainable engagement protocols rather than simple resolution parameters. The framework essentially established a continuous relationship model appropriate to dynamics inherently exceeding conventional understanding.

The Daybridge Quantum Research Initiative continued developing with remarkable effectiveness—transparent protocols, civilian oversight, ethical guidelines regarding cross-reality interaction. Alice's specialized jurisdiction over Echo Alley enabled implementation of a carefully calibrated research utilizing the resonance stabilization framework to maintain quantum barrier integrity while allowing controlled information exchange for legitimate scientific purposes.

Cross-timeline collaboration gradually expanded through this carefully managed interface—research coordination with parallel scientific initiatives across connected realities, essentially creating distributed knowledge development transcending individual timeline limitations. The approach represented a remarkable transformation from exploitation to collaboration, secret manipulation to transparent exchange.

Most profound was the recognition that their extraordinary journey represented merely an initial engagement with forces fundamentally transcending conventional understanding. The breach network beneath Daybridge connected multiple reality configurations through principles exceeding current scientific frameworks, essentially linking countless variations of existence through quantum dynamics humanity was only beginning to comprehend.

Alice Chen—paranormal investigator, interdimensional crisis manager, apparent "probability nexus" across connected reality configurations—had established an appropriate relationship with phenomena fundamentally beyond complete understanding. Not case closed, but case transformed—ongoing engagement with extraordinary forces connecting multiple realities through principles humanity was only beginning to comprehend.

The voices in Echo Alley continued speaking, but now through carefully managed research protocols rather than clandestine exploitation operations. The breach network remained active but stabilized, maintained through ethical engagement rather than manipulative control. The department had transformed from military-adjacent secrecy to transparent civilian research, exploitation replaced by collaborative understanding.

Reality itself continued flowing through its countless configurations, probability nexus designations maintaining pattern consistency across connected timelines, consciousness gradually evolving toward enhanced understanding of existence fundamentally exceeding current comprehension capabilities.

Not case closed, but case transformed—exactly as it should be when confronting phenomena truly beyond conventional understanding.

EPILOGUE: THE DETECTIVE'S JOURNAL

Three months after establishing the Daybridge Quantum Research Initiative, Alice Chen sat in her newly constructed office overlooking Echo Alley. The space represented perfect integration of her dual roles—combining the practical functionality of a paranormal investigator's workspace with the scientific resources necessary for her position as research director. One wall displayed her extensive case files in a meticulously organized archival systems, while another housed specialized monitoring equipment tracking quantum variance patterns throughout Daybridge.

The central desk—handcrafted from reclaimed wood salvaged during the warehouse district renovation—supported both conventional investigation tools and the specialized communication system Eleanor had designed for secure cross-timeline interaction. This hybrid workspace symbolized Alice's unique position bridging multiple worlds—paranormal investigator, interdimensional researcher, probability nexus across connected realities.

"Final archival components completed," Alice noted, adding the comprehensive Echo Alley documentation to her secured case management system. The file contained an extraordinary accumulation of evidence, analysis, and implementation protocols—essentially complete documentation of their journey from initial investigation through Department neutralization to establishment of an ethical research framework.

Unlike standard case files stored in conventional formats, the Echo Alley documentation required specialized security protocols reflecting its extraordinary contents. The primary archive resided in quantum-encrypted storage developed through collaboration between Maya and Timeline J-73 specialists, essentially creating secure information repository invulnerable to conventional intrusion attempts.

Most important was the distributed security framework Alice had implemented following Eleanor's contingency protocols—multiple partial copies maintained by trusted associates throughout Daybridge, each containing sufficient information for comprehensive understanding while requiring coordinated access for complete implementation capability. This approach ensured critical knowledge preservation regardless of potential compromise attempts against any individual storage location.

Rivera maintained security oversight for physical documentation components, utilizing specialized secure storage within police department facilities while maintaining official separation from institutional knowledge frameworks. Maya preserved technical specifications for stabilization technology implementation, ensuring capability regeneration if current systems experienced catastrophic compromise. Dr. Liu maintained comprehensive quantum theory documentation connecting practical implementations with fundamental physics principles, essentially preserving conceptual frameworks necessary for understanding operational methodologies.

This distributed knowledge preservation system represented sophisticated application of Eleanor's contingency planning—ensuring critical information maintained resilience against potential compromise attempts while remaining accessible to authorized implementation teams if necessary. The approach essentially created sustainable protection frameworks appropriate to knowledge fundamentally transcending conventional security parameters.

As Alice completed final documentation protocols, the specialized communication system activated—indicating incoming transmission through the stabilized interface at Echo Alley. The system utilized the resonance stabilization framework to maintain quantum barrier integrity while enabling controlled information exchange without exploitation capability, essentially creating secure cross-timeline communication network for legitimate research purposes.

"Incoming communication from Timeline R-34," Maya reported, monitoring connection parameters while implementing security protocols. "Quantum signature consistent with established research coalition contact. Transmission utilizing standard minimal-footprint methodology through stabilized interface."

This connection represented part of the cross-timeline research collaboration gradually developing through carefully managed interfaces—essentially creating distributed knowledge development transcending individual reality limitations. The approach enabled legitimate scientific coordination without compromising barrier integrity or enabling exploitation capabilities that had characterized Department operations.

The receiver successfully established a secure connection, converting quantum variance patterns into a comprehensible format:

"To Research Director Chen, Timeline K-17: Quarterly coordination report from Daybridge Quantum Coalition, Timeline R-34. Research implementation proceeding according to established protocols with seventeen participant timelines now maintaining synchronized data exchange through stabilized interfaces. Attached technical documentation includes unified breach network mapping across connected configurations, demonstrating remarkable consistency despite significant circumstantial variation between reality parameters."

This communication represented exactly the ethical research collaboration they had established following Department neutralization—transparent coordination between parallel scientific initiatives across connected realities, essentially creating distributed knowledge development while maintaining appropriate security protocols and ethical guidelines.

The attached technical documentation contained extraordinary information regarding breach network configuration across multiple connected timelines—essentially comprehensive mapping demonstrating remarkable consistency despite significant circumstantial variation between reality parameters. The unified analysis revealed the network's fundamental architecture transcended individual reality configurations, maintaining core structural integrity regardless of specific local manifestation characteristics.

"The mapping consistency is remarkable," Maya noted, reviewing the cross-timeline documentation with evident scientific appreciation. "Despite significant variation in surface development patterns, the fundamental network architecture maintains almost perfect alignment across all seventeen participating timelines. Essentially confirming the breach network predates current reality configurations rather than representing parallel development within individual timelines."

This confirmation aligned with information they had received regarding the network's true nature and origin—essentially ancient infrastructure created by consciousness evolution several probability iterations beyond current development parameters. The system represented technology so advanced it appeared virtually indistinguishable from natural phenomena despite artificial origin parameters.

"Implementing unified mapping integration with our current research frameworks," Alice directed, recognizing the extraordinary value of this cross-timeline collaboration. "Priority focus on identifying potential connection nodes beyond currently documented parameters."

As Maya integrated this information with their existing research frameworks, Alice reviewed recent developments within the Daybridge Quantum Research Initiative. The transformed organization continued functioning with remarkable effectiveness—transparent protocols, civilian oversight, ethical guidelines regarding cross-reality interaction. The approach represented a fundamental paradigm shift in relationship with these extraordinary phenomena, essentially creating new institutional model based on understanding rather than exploitation.

Most significant was the cross-timeline communication network gradually expanding through carefully managed interfaces—research collaboration with parallel scientific initiatives across connected realities, essentially creating distributed knowledge development transcending individual timeline limitations. The approach represented a remarkable transformation from exploitation to collaboration, secret manipulation to transparent exchange.

The resonance stabilization framework continued performing beyond theoretical projections—maintaining perfect equilibrium parameters at all natural breach points throughout Daybridge. The technology worked with natural reality dynamics rather than imposing artificial manipulation, essentially establishing a cooperative relationship with the breach network rather than exploitative control.

As Alice completed her quarterly assessment documentation, the specialized communication system activated once more—indicating incoming transmission through different parameters than standard research collaboration channels. The quantum signature displayed characteristics associated with the probability nexus communication network that had gradually developed following their discovery of cross-timeline pattern consistency.

"Incoming transmission through probability nexus channel," Maya noted, identifying the distinctive signature patterns. "Quantum characteristics suggest Timeline M-17 origin with priority designation protocols active."

This specialized communication channel operated through different principles than standard research collaboration networks—utilizing direct probability resonance between nexus designations rather than conventional quantum variance transmission.

The approach essentially created secure communication capability between probability anchors across connected timelines, enabling coordination beyond institutional frameworks.

The receiver successfully established a secure connection, converting probability resonance patterns into a comprehensible format:

"To Probability Nexus Designation 'Alice Chen', Timeline K-17: Priority advisory from counterpart designation in Timeline M-17. Investigation initiated regarding anomalous entity manifestation patterns demonstrating characteristics inconsistent with standard breach network transit protocols. Preliminary analysis suggests origin parameters potentially external to established multiverse configuration framework. Recommend implementation of enhanced monitoring protocols focused on dimensional boundary characteristics beyond standard variance parameters."

This communication contained disturbing implications regarding potential threats transcending currently understood reality frameworks—essentially entities originating from dimensional parameters beyond established multiverse configuration. The suggestion that manifestation patterns demonstrated characteristics inconsistent with standard breach network transit protocols indicated phenomena potentially operating through principles fundamentally different from currently understood interdimensional dynamics.

"Requesting additional specification regarding anomalous manifestation characteristics," Alice transmitted through the secure probability nexus channel, seeking enhanced comprehension of these concerning developments.

The response arrived through direct probability resonance, bypassing conventional transmission limitations:

"Entity manifestation demonstrates three consistent characteristics distinguishing from standard breach network transit: 1) No detectable quantum variance preceding manifestation despite significant mass transfer; 2) Complete immunity to standard containment protocols including resonance stabilization frameworks; 3) Apparent violation of conservation principles regarding information integrity during transdimensional transfer."

These characteristics described phenomena fundamentally different from anything they had encountered through breach network interactions—essentially entities operating through principles transcending currently understood reality frameworks. The complete absence of quantum variance preceding manifestation despite significant mass transfer represented particularly concerning violation of established interdimensional transit principles.

"Have you established communication or determined objective parameters?" Alice inquired, seeking critical information regarding potential threat assessment.

"Limited communication achieved through probability resonance rather than conventional methodologies," came the response. "Entity self-identifies as 'Observer' with stated purpose involving 'probability stream integrity assessment' across multiple dimensional layers. Preliminary interaction suggests perception framework operating through principles fundamentally transcending current understanding capabilities."

This description suggested entities operating through consciousness parameters vastly exceeding current human development—essentially beings perceiving reality through frameworks so advanced they appeared virtually incomprehensible through conventional understanding capabilities. The reference to "probability stream integrity assessment" indicated potential monitoring function across multiple dimensional layers beyond established multiverse configuration.

"Any indication of hostile intent or interference objectives?" Alice asked, focusing on practical threat assessment despite the extraordinary philosophical implications.

"No direct evidence of hostile intent detected," the response clarified. "However, stated assessment parameters include identification of 'probability anomalies requiring correction' without specific definition regarding implementation methodology. Potential concern involves subjective interpretation of 'correction' requirements from perception framework fundamentally exceeding our understanding capabilities."

This assessment suggested complex potential threat parameters—entities potentially lacking direct hostile intent but operating through perception frameworks so advanced their actions might appear incomprehensible or potentially harmful from human understanding perspective. The undefined "correction" methodology represented particular concern given potential capability disparities between entity operational parameters and current human defense frameworks.

"Implementing enhanced monitoring protocols," Alice confirmed, already formulating appropriate response strategies. "Coordinating cross-timeline observation network with a particular focus on dimensional boundary characteristics beyond standard variance parameters."

As she initiated these enhanced monitoring measures, Alice recognized they faced potential challenges fundamentally transcending previous experience parameters—essentially entities operating through principles beyond current understanding capabilities potentially manifesting across multiple connected timelines simultaneously. The situation required coordinated response strategies utilizing the cross-timeline networks they had established following their successful breach network stabilization.

"Maya, we need to implement interdimensional observation protocols beyond standard variance parameters," Alice directed, already formulating comprehensive monitoring framework. "Essentially expanding detection capabilities beyond breach network dynamics to identify potential manifestations operating through alternate dimensional transit principles."

"Utilizing the probability resonance detection system Eleanor provided in her contingency resources," Maya suggested, immediately comprehending the appropriate technological approach. "The framework was specifically designed for identifying phenomena operating through principles transcending conventional quantum variance parameters."

This specialized technology—part of Eleanor's extraordinary contingency resources—represented exactly the appropriate detection capability for addressing potential manifestations operating beyond standard breach network transit protocols. The system utilized probability resonance detection rather than conventional quantum variance monitoring, essentially identifying pattern disruptions across dimensional boundaries rather than specific energy signatures within established parameters.

As they implemented these enhanced monitoring protocols, Alice activated the cross-timeline coordination network they had established following their discovery of probability nexus designations across connected realities. This approach essentially created distributed observation capability transcending individual timeline limitations, enabling comprehensive monitoring across multiple reality configurations simultaneously.

"Initiating Interdimensional Detective Network protocols," Alice transmitted through secure probability resonance channels, establishing formal activation of the coordinated observation framework they had developed precisely for addressing threats potentially manifesting across multiple connected timelines simultaneously.

This network represented an extraordinary evolution in Alice's approach to paranormal investigation—essentially distributed observation capability coordinating multiple versions of herself across connected reality configurations. The approach utilized direct probability resonance between nexus designations to establish secure communication capability transcending conventional limitations, enabling real-time coordination beyond institutional frameworks.

Confirmation responses arrived from seven distinct timeline configurations, each representing probability nexus designation "Alice Chen" within their respective reality parameters. The unified network established comprehensive monitoring coverage across connected realities, essentially creating distributed observation capability that transcended individual timeline limitations.

"Interdimensional Detective Network active," Maya confirmed as coordination protocols completed initialization. "Distributed observation framework established across seven confirmed timeline configurations with synchronized monitoring parameters focused on dimensional boundary characteristics beyond standard variance parameters."

This coordinated approach represented ideal response strategy for addressing potential threats operating through principles transcending conventional understanding capabilities. The distributed network essentially created comprehensive monitoring coverage that no individual timeline could achieve independently, leveraging parallel development across connected realities to enhance overall detection capabilities.

As enhanced monitoring systems activated throughout their timeline, Alice completed final documentation within her detective's journal—essentially personal record separate from official research documentation, containing observations, assessments, and philosophical reflections regarding their extraordinary experiences.

"The Echo Alley case represents a fundamental transformation in my understanding of reality itself," Alice wrote, articulating personal perspective beyond institutional documentation parameters. "What began as an investigation of mysterious voices has progressively revealed existence framework fundamentally transcending conventional comprehension capabilities. The multiverse isn't merely a theoretical concept but a practical reality requiring appropriate engagement protocols reflecting phenomena inherently exceeding complete understanding."

This philosophical perspective represented a sophisticated evolution in Alice's approach to paranormal investigation—recognizing certain phenomena require sustainable engagement protocols rather than simple resolution parameters. The framework essentially established continuous relationship model appropriate to manifestations inherently exceeding conventional understanding.

"Most profound is the recognition that consciousness itself transcends individual reality configurations," Alice continued, documenting developing philosophical framework based on extraordinary experiences. "Probability nexus designations maintaining pattern consistency across connected timelines suggest existence fundamentally exceeding conventional dimensional limitations. We perceive reality through necessarily limited frameworks while participating in dynamics vastly more complex than current understanding capabilities can fully comprehend."

As she completed these reflections, the specialized communication system activated once more—this time indicating conventional contact through secure channels rather than cross-timeline transmission. The incoming communication originated from Rivera, utilizing the encrypted connection they had established following Department neutralization.

"Potential case requiring your specific expertise," came the detective's characteristically concise message. "Situation at Meridian Park demonstrating unusual parameters beyond conventional explanation frameworks. Witness reporting interaction with entity claiming transdimensional origin with appearance shifting between multiple distinct configurations simultaneously. Standard investigation protocols revealing no evidence despite multiple consistent testimonials from credible observers."

This description suggested phenomena potentially connected to the anomalous manifestation patterns their probability nexus counterpart had warned about—essentially entities potentially operating through principles transcending standard breach network transit protocols. The reported appearance shifting between multiple distinct configurations simultaneously aligned with characteristics consistent with perception frameworks fundamentally exceeding current understanding capabilities.

Almost simultaneously, the probability resonance channel activated with incoming transmission from Timeline M-17—their counterpart providing urgent update regarding developing situation:

"Priority advisory: Entity designated 'Observer' has initiated manifestation protocols within your timeline parameters. Quantum signature detected at location designation 'Meridian Park' approximately seventeen minutes ago. Manifestation characteristics consistent with previously documented parameters—no preceding variance despite significant mass transfer, immunity to standard containment protocols, apparent violation of conservation principles regarding information integrity."

This confirmation established a direct connection between Rivera's reported situation and the anomalous entities their interdimensional network had been established to monitor. The coinciding reports from conventional police investigation and cross-timeline advisory created comprehensive situation assessment transcending individual observation limitations.

"Responding to Meridian Park situation," Alice confirmed through both conventional and probability resonance channels, already gathering specialized equipment developed specifically for addressing phenomena operating beyond standard parameters. "Implementing observation protocols designed for entities potentially transcending conventional dimensional frameworks."

The specialized equipment included Eleanor's probability resonance detector—technology specifically designed for identifying phenomena operating through principles beyond standard quantum variance parameters. The system utilized a fundamentally different detection methodology, essentially monitoring pattern disruptions across dimensional boundaries rather than specific energy signatures within established parameters.

"I'll coordinate cross-timeline observation through the network while you conduct direct investigation," Maya offered, establishing optimal division of responsibilities given their respective expertise parameters. "Essentially maintaining comprehensive monitoring across connected realities while you implement direct engagement protocols within our specific timeline configuration."

This approach leveraged their complementary capabilities—Alice's investigative expertise combined with Maya's technical proficiency in maintaining cross-timeline coordination. The methodology essentially created optimal response framework utilizing both direct engagement and distributed observation simultaneously.

As Alice prepared for departure to Meridian Park, she reviewed final notes within her detective's journal—documentation representing personal perspective beyond institutional frameworks, essentially philosophical reflection regarding their extraordinary journey from conventional investigation to interdimensional coordination.

"Perhaps most remarkable is the recognition that 'case closed' represents fundamentally inadequate framework for approaching phenomena inherently transcending conventional understanding," she wrote, articulating evolved conceptual model based on extraordinary experiences. "Reality itself exists as a continuous process rather than discrete parameters, with consciousness potentially representing fundamental component rather than an emergent property. Our investigations don't merely solve discrete mysteries but progressively reveal existence framework fundamentally exceeding conventional comprehension capabilities."

This perspective represented a sophisticated evolution in Alice's approach to paranormal investigation—recognizing certain phenomena require continuous engagement protocols rather than discrete resolution parameters. The framework essentially established sustainable relationship model appropriate to manifestations inherently transcending conventional understanding.

As she completed these reflections, Alice closed the journal and secured it within specialized protection systems developed through cross-timeline collaboration. The detective's journal represented extraordinary accumulation of knowledge, experience, and philosophical development—essentially documenting progressive evolution from conventional paranormal investigator to interdimensional probability nexus coordinating response strategies across multiple connected realities.

"Potential connection to the entity manifestation warning from Timeline M-17," Alice noted to Maya as she prepared final equipment for the investigation. "The description suggests perception frameworks operating through principles fundamentally transcending current understanding capabilities—essentially entities existing beyond conventional dimensional limitations."

"Exactly why we established the Interdimensional Detective Network," Maya responded, already activating comprehensive coordination protocols across connected timelines. "Some threats potentially manifest across multiple reality configurations simultaneously, requiring distributed response strategies transcending individual timeline limitations."

The network they had established following their discovery of probability nexus designations represented an extraordinary evolution in approach to investigating phenomena fundamentally transcending conventional parameters. The distributed observation capability essentially coordinated multiple versions of Alice Chen across connected reality configurations, creating comprehensive monitoring framework that no individual timeline could achieve independently.

"Implementing full-spectrum documentation protocols," Alice confirmed, ensuring comprehensive recording capabilities beyond standard parameters. "This potentially represents our first direct interaction with entities operating through principles fundamentally exceeding breach network dynamics."

This approach reflected Alice's methodical investigation philosophy—establishing comprehensive documentation frameworks even when addressing phenomena potentially transcending conventional understanding capabilities. The methodology essentially created foundational knowledge development regardless of immediate comprehension limitations, ensuring future analysis capability as understanding frameworks progressively evolved.

As final preparation completed, Alice's secure communication device activated with incoming transmission from her probability nexus counterpart in Timeline R-34—the reality configuration where Maya had successfully implemented the resonance stabilization framework before their own timeline.

"Priority advisory regarding entity designation 'Observer,'" came the transmission through secure probability resonance channel. "Based on successful interaction parameters within our timeline configuration, recommend approach utilizing direct probability resonance rather than conventional communication methodologies. Entity perception operates through frameworks fundamentally transcending linear temporal processing—essentially experiencing multiple timeframes simultaneously rather than sequentially."

This advisory contained critical engagement protocols based on successful interaction within alternate timeline configuration—essentially leveraging cross-reality experience to enhance response effectiveness within their specific parameters. The approach represented exactly the coordinated knowledge development the Interdimensional Detective Network had been established to facilitate.

"Understood and appreciated," Alice responded through the secure channel. "Implementing recommended interaction protocols utilizing probability resonance methodology rather than conventional engagement parameters."

With final preparations complete, Alice departed for Meridian Park—the detective's investigation kit containing both conventional tools and specialized equipment designed specifically for addressing phenomena operating beyond standard parameters. The combination represented perfect integration of her evolved approach to paranormal investigation—maintaining practical methodology while incorporating advanced technological capabilities appropriate to phenomena fundamentally transcending conventional understanding.

The journey from Echo Alley to whatever awaited at Meridian Park represented continued evolution rather than distinct transition—essentially ongoing development within investigation framework fundamentally transformed through extraordinary experiences. Alice Chen—paranormal investigator, interdimensional researcher, probability nexus across connected realities—had established an appropriate relationship with phenomena inherently exceeding complete understanding.

Not case closed, but case continuous—ongoing engagement with extraordinary forces connecting multiple realities through principles humanity was only beginning to comprehend. The Interdimensional Detective Network represented the perfect embodiment of this evolved approach—distributed observation capability coordinating multiple versions of herself across connected reality configurations, essentially creating comprehensive response framework transcending individual timeline limitations.

As Alice navigated through early evening traffic toward Meridian Park, she reflected on the extraordinary journey that had transformed her understanding of reality itself. The Echo Alley investigation had progressively revealed existence framework fundamentally transcending conventional comprehension capabilities—essentially demonstrating that the multiverse wasn't merely a theoretical concept but a practical reality requiring appropriate engagement protocols.

Whatever awaited at Meridian Park—entities potentially existing beyond conventional dimensional limitations, operating through perception frameworks fundamentally exceeding current understanding capabilities—represented continued evolution rather than distinct transition. The investigation would proceed through methodical protocols established through extraordinary experience, leveraging cross-timeline coordination to address phenomena potentially manifesting across multiple connected realities simultaneously.

Alice Chen had become exactly what circumstances across multiple reality configurations required—interdimensional detective investigating phenomena fundamentally transcending conventional parameters, probability nexus maintaining pattern consistency across connected timelines, consciousness gradually evolving toward enhanced understanding of existence fundamentally exceeding current comprehension capabilities.

The detective's journal documented this extraordinary journey—from paranormal investigator seeking explanations for mysterious voices to interdimensional coordinator establishing ethical relationship with phenomena inherently transcending complete understanding. The narrative remained continuous rather than discrete, evolving rather than concluding, transforming rather than resolving.

Not case closed, but case continuous—exactly as it should be when investigating reality itself.

Copyright:

First Edition

Published by Live For Excellence Productions

ISBNs:

E-book: 978-1-997784-33-3

Paperback: 978-1-997784-34-0

Audiobook: 978-1-997784-35-7

About the Author

Rae Stonehouse turned to fiction writing after establishing himself as a prolific author of self-development and professional growth books.

With over fifty published works helping readers navigate personal and professional challenges, he embarked on a new creative path with the Ethan Reeves Werewolf Detective Series.

When not weaving tales of supernatural sleuthing, Stonehouse continues to share his expertise in personal development through workshops and speaking engagements from his home in British Columbia.

The Ethan Reeves series marks his debut in fiction writing, blending his understanding of human nature with a newfound passion for urban fantasy.

The story doesn't end here. Scan for more books in the Daybridge Chronicles, part of the Ethan Reeves Werewolf Detective Series: https://my.linkpod.site/daybridgechronicles